Ghouls Rush In

THE PEYTON CLARK SERIES

Also by H.P. Mallory

The *New York Times* and *USA Today* Bestselling
Jolie Wilkins Series:
Fire Burn and Cauldron Bubble
Toil and Trouble
Witchful Thinking
The Witch Is Back
Something Witchy This Way Comes

The Dulcie O'Neil Series:
To Kill a Warlock
A Tale of Two Goblins
Great Hexpectations
Wuthering Frights
Malice in Wonderland
For Whom the Spell Tolls

The Lily Harper Series:
Better Off Dead

Ghouls Rush In

THE PEYTON CLARK SERIES

H.P.
MALLORY

This is a work of fiction. Names, characters, organizations, places, events, and incidents are either products of the author's imagination or are used fictitiously.

Published by Montlake Romance, Seattle

www.apub.com

ISBN-13: 9781477818558
ISBN-10: 1477818553

Cover design by Eileen Carey

Library of Congress Control Number: 2013919810

Printed in the United States of America

To Finn

It was time for a fresh start.

All my bags had been packed and I'd been more than ready to go, to quote John Denver.

And now that I'd escaped Los Angeles, and found myself safely ensconced in New Orleans, I could breathe a little more easily. Yep, with the two thousand miles that now separated me from Jonathon Graves, my recently declared ex-husband, my future never seemed brighter, nor life sweeter.

It's funny (well, not in a ha-ha sort of way) but I always thought of divorce as the last resort, as the ultimate failure. Somehow it seemed better, more courageous, more *right* to continue bearing the tattered and bruised flag of a failing marriage (regardless of how unhappy said marriage was) than to throw in the towel and admit that sometimes you screw up. Sometimes you make decisions you have no business making. Sometimes you desperately yearn to make a wish on a falling star that might rewind your life and allow you to skip whatever drastic decision you made that led to the biggest mistake of your life.

In choosing to accept Jonathon's marriage proposal five years ago, I'm convinced I must've been possessed by the ghost of June Cleaver, much to the chagrin of my true self. That, or maybe Nurse Ratched had performed a lobotomy on me without my knowledge.

Otherwise, I just couldn't reconcile how I willingly threw my lot in with his. Why? Because our lots never should have been thrown in together. Nope, we were like oil and water, cats and dogs, Lindsay Lohan and a law-abiding existence. Jonathon and I existed at polar ends of the personality spectrum. And in our case, while opposites did attract, the result was impending doom.

Regardless, at some point, I must have thought I was in love with him even though I'd always been convinced he was never in love with me. But sometimes you get bitten by the lunacy bug. Then you wake up one day to find yourself living an "inauthentic life" (to quote the innumerable self-help books I'd lost myself in for the last five years). And all you can do is ask yourself, in silent, nauseous wonder, how in the hell did I get here? The answer isn't a fun one, by any stretch of the imagination.

For the old me, though, the whys and hows of my situation weren't the important parts. I bought into the whole "when you've made your bed, you lie in it" mentality and consequently I'd become a marriage martyr; I'd tried to convince myself that I was truly happy. And even after I could willingly face that my happiness was a sham, I still wasn't sold on divorce. Instead, I figured my marriage was the same as any other marriage—that holy matrimony was, by nature, crippling.

All I could feel was intense relief—intense, wonderful, magnificent relief. Whatever my past, whatever exhaustive anger and depression I harbored for so many years, I'd escaped it all now. And that was the beauty of life. No matter how bad things got, no matter how much you hated your predicament, there was always a way out. And luckily for me, I'd found it.

And now as I stood on Prytania Street, in the middle of the Garden District of New Orleans, I took a deep breath of the humid air, the cloying scent of stale blooms of Cecile Brunner roses wafting over my neighbor's fence. But all I could really smell was the divine scent of freedom, the scent of the beginning of the rest of my life.

This new beginning just happened to be a three-story Greek Revival mansion from the late 1800s that was situated on the middle of Prytania Street, between a rambling, yellow Queen Anne Victorian and a four-story Italianate wonder with black wrought iron railings on all four of its porches.

I was starting over, finding myself again and thus, in need of a diversion. No, I needed something bigger than a diversion. I needed something that would wholly occupy me, something that would require the full extent of my energy. Getting out of my marriage had been such an emotional drain, I knew that I'd have to throw myself into an overwhelming project, something that would require the full commitment of my brainpower and time. I needed something that would exhaust me so I wouldn't be left at night with nothing but my wounded, naked thoughts. I required a project that would completely wipe me out and, in so doing, allow me to sleep at night. Having no children to aid in the task was actually a huge blessing. Though I did someday want children, I could only thank my lucky stars that Jonathon's and my relationship never evolved into the territory of having babies. Nope, I had no ties to Jonathon at all, which was exactly the way I wanted it.

Given my need for a diversion, renovating a three-story, five-thousand-square-foot mansion was just what the doctor ordered.

"This one's gotta be in the worst repair of any I seen in, oh, ten years, maybe," Hank said, his caterpillar eyebrows reaching for his grimy baseball cap. He frowned at me before turning to study the monument that I called my new home. Hank was old and had one of those faces that had weathered time, but as to how much time, I wasn't so sure. He could've been in his early sixties or his late eighties, for all I knew. Shit, if he were one hundred, I wouldn't have been *too* surprised. He sighed and shook his head like he thought I was getting in way too deep. "It's gonna be one heck of a project," he continued, his bushy mustache obscuring his entire mouth until it looked like a hamster was clinging to his face while having a seizure. Hank was a mechanic who owned his own repair shop just out of town.

I nodded. "Yep, that it is," I answered, a smile seeping into my words. For as much of a "project" that the renovations on my new home would prove to be, I still wasn't in any way concerned. Nope, that's because I was far too overcome by the possibilities, which only filled me with unbridled excitement.

And, yes, I could honestly say I was completely cognizant that I was absolutely getting in over my head. But I didn't care. I welcomed the challenge because how deep I sunk into the project wasn't the point. Instead, the point was my freedom and this being the first chapter in the book known as the rest of my life.

I gazed up at my new home again, feeling the pride I imagined a new parent feels. Yep, my life was now dominated by a three-story study of peeling paint, broken balustrades, dusty windows, and sagging verandas. It was a sorry sight, but one that filled me with pure anticipation and excitement of a new journey. I was on my way to uncovering a lost pathway, previously obscured by the foliage of "self-doubt."

"So you related ta Myra?" Hank asked while eyeing me pointedly, one bushy white eyebrow arched up in curiosity.

I nodded but then sighed because even though Myra was my great-aunt, I'd never known of her existence. "She was from my mother's side but, unfortunately, I never got to meet her."

Hank nodded. "So how'd ya come ta end up here then?"

I smiled and then cocked my head to the side as I considered it. "It was pretty coincidental, actually," I started. "On the same day my divorce was finalized, I also learned that Myra had passed away and left this property to me."

"An' you ain't never even laid eyes on 'er?" Hank continued grilling me, his expression one that revealed he wasn't sure if he should believe me or not. Why? I had no clue.

I shook my head. "Nope." And the other unfortunate part about the whole Great-Aunt Myra situation was that I had no way of questioning my mother as to the existence of her because my mother had passed away when I was eighteen. I'd never known my father.

So I was basically left with a huge mystery as to how I'd ended up with this old mansion, but, if anything, our cloudy pasts only connected me to the property more. And now standing here, in front of the house, I just felt as if I belonged here—as if the blood that pumped through my veins was tied to this grand mansion.

As strange as it sounds, I almost felt as if the house and I were buddies, friends. In my own bizarre imagination, I needed this house as much as it needed me. Just as I would be saving this old, dilapidated home and bringing it back to its former glory, it would also be saving me—by keeping me from focusing on my failed marriage. It would save me from wondering, in my heart of hearts, if I'd made a mistake in leaving Jonathon. As much as I knew the decision to get divorced was the only one that could be made, it didn't silence that nagging voice in the back of my head that doubted most of my moves, as well as most every decision I made.

The behemoth undertaking that renovating this nineteenth-century mansion would prove to be wouldn't allow that frustrating voice to speak. I only hoped that this incredible adventure would allow me to reunite with myself, the person who'd been mute for the last five years. My plan was to center myself and truly discover just who I was, and more importantly, who I wanted to be. Peyton Graves, wife, was dead and gone; but rising from her ashes, complete with her newly reacquired maiden name, was Peyton Clark. And I couldn't help but think this house was the key to finding myself, since the house represented a past I knew nothing about but a past that was still very much a part of me.

"You'se divorced?" Hank asked, still spearing me with that beady-eyed expression. I simply nodded. "Ain't you gotta 'nother fella ta help you?" he continued, shaking his head in what I perceived to be disappointment combined with disapproval.

"Nope," I shook my head more fervently than he had. My entire being rebelled at the mere thought of a "fella" in my life. "And that's exactly the way I want it."

He laughed, making the sound of someone who'd smoked unfiltered cigarettes for far too long. "You ain't gonna be off the market for long, missy," he said with a wide smile that revealed missing teeth on both sides of his worn-down canines. "Attractive woman like yerself is gonna find herself pretty much in demand."

I could feel my cheeks blushing as I dropped my attention to my hands. I suddenly wished I were better at accepting compliments. 'Course, I wasn't exactly well acquainted with them. In the five years I was married to Jonathon, I could have counted the rare moments he complimented me on one hand.

"Yep, just gotta stand up straight an' give 'em a view of that dazzlin' smile, and them warm brown eyes an' I reckon any feller'll be yours."

I laughed, even as I realized Hank had a point about me standing up straight. 'Course, when you're five-foot-ten, and you tower over most people you come into contact with, it almost seems natural to want to hunch over. But Hank was right—I needed to be comfortable with myself even if I sometimes found it difficult. The truth was that I wasn't even really sure what I wanted the new "me" to look like. Aside from the obvious things that I couldn't change (well, without surgery anyway) like my bone structure, the color of my eyes, and the shape of my nose, I'd already subjected the easily changed aspects of myself to a complete makeover.

Yep, as soon as my divorce was legal and I'd received my settlement, I'd promptly attempted to erase everything that reminded me of the married me, the me who'd tried so hard to be everything Jonathon wanted me to be, even at the cost of self-betrayal. As soon as I'd received that glorious announcement that I was no longer connected to Jonathon, I'd thrown out my entire wardrobe. It had been an easy task to accomplish because it wasn't like my closet was full of fun, flirty pieces. Nope, instead it amounted to an array of blah slacks, knee-length skirts (yawn), blasé silk blouses, and blazers in earth tones, black, white, and the full spectrum of gray.

Well, not any longer.

In just the course of a week, I'd managed to replace my wardrobe with myriad miniskirts, hip-hugging jeans, spring dresses, plunging blouses, and bikinis. And Betsey Johnson would have been proud of the bouquet of colors that now bloomed in my closet.

But my wardrobe hadn't been the only area that was in need of an overhaul. I'd also hacked off my elbow-length, mousy-brown hair in favor of a chin-length bob. Then I'd bleached it the exact same shade of platinum blond it was in my twenties. Even better, I'd encouraged the makeup artist at the NARS counter to use my face as his own personal canvas. The result? A Peyton that felt much more like the old Peyton, the girl who loved to party like a rock star and looked the part. With my new wardrobe, haircut, and overall ensemble, it was almost like I'd rewound time and returned to the woman I'd been before Jonathon had crossed my path.

At thirty-one years old, I was finally learning how to be me.

"Thanks, Hank," I started, remembering the conversation. "But I'm definitely not looking to date anytime soon." I took a deep breath as he offered me a confused expression. "I just really need some me time," I finished.

"Just don't let yer life pass ya by," he answered with another shake of his head that told me he didn't understand independent women. He turned around and faced the barbarian that was my new (but very much pre-owned) vehicle behind him. It was a 1980 International Scout II with a burnt-orange paint job. It looked like it was right out of the seventies, complete with a rainbow stripe of brown, yellow, and white that ran the length of the entire truck. The Scout reminded me of a giant box on wheels, something between a Ford Explorer and a Hummer—and I do mean the authentic type of Hummer, the army-issue Hummer, not the one you see yuppies driving on the freeway.

The Scout was worlds away from the black Mercedes SLK Roadster I'd been driving only weeks earlier. But, strangely enough, I didn't miss the Mercedes for a minute, not even a split second.

"So she's all good to go?" I asked Hank, stealing another glance at my new ride while grinning like a teenager just receiving her first set of car keys.

"Yep, new tires, new brakes, and basically a new engine. She'll run you good for a long time, Miss Peyton."

"Thanks, Hank," I said, smiling because he refused to call me by just my first name. Instead, he insisted on adding "Miss" to it. "What do I owe you?"

"I ain't done the math yet, honey," he said with a chuckle, running his hand across the hood of the Scout as if he would miss it, or did already. Hank had not only sold me the Scout, but he'd fixed it up as well. And since the Scout was older than I was, and Hank was a mechanic, I figured he and I would be seeing a lot of each other . . .

"So . . ." I started.

"So I'll just call ya when I got it all figured out." He patted the top of the Scout as if it were a loyal dog, before wedging his hands into his oil-stained coveralls. Then he offered me another gap-toothed smile. "That is, if you gotta phone hooked up somewhere in that museum of yours?"

I laughed, ignoring the jab because truthfully, I didn't have a home phone. Not that the house wasn't set up for phone connectivity, I just figured since I had my cell phone, why bother with a house phone? "Believe it or not, that 'museum' even has electricity and running water."

"Well, consider me surprised," he said with another throaty smoker chuckle as he walked over to a Ford truck that was so covered in rust, it appeared brown. I glimpsed traces of white paint peeking through the coppery oxidation. He glanced back at me and shook his head. "Almost as surprised as I am ta find that ol' biddy Myra actually had her some family."

"How well did you know her?" I asked.

He shook his head and kicked at the ground with a boot that looked as if it had survived World War II, which it very well might have. "Not too good," he said and shook his head. "She kept ta herself mostly, holed up in that there house. I think I seen her . . ." He scratched his head. "Ah, maybe three times in the thirty years I been comin' ta these parts."

So Hank wasn't exactly a good source when it came to finding out more about my lineage. I couldn't say I was surprised. "Thanks, Hank," I called out as I waved to him. With a long exhale, I turned to face my new home.

Two nights later, it was pouring rain.

The skies erupted into a garish display of yellow lightning as thunderclaps interrupted the otherwise comforting sound of the rain pelting the roof and windows, warning everyone to keep inside. I, for one, dared not upset the god of thunder by even thinking of venturing outside and, instead, sat huddled beneath a heavy wool blanket in front of my electric heater, praying the portable appliance wouldn't blow another fuse. The sounds of raindrops leaking through the roof and plopping into two iron pots, four iron skillets, and five glasses made a symphony in their own right.

I glanced up at the door when I heard what sounded like a knock, but dismissed it, figuring the wind must be causing something to rap against the house. Besides, who would decide to visit in the middle of a storm? The only person I knew in New Orleans was Hank, and it was way past his bedtime, or so I assumed. Granted, it was only nine o'clock, but I had a feeling Hank was an early-to-bed, early-to-rise kind of guy.

The second strident knock on the front door convinced me that it didn't have anything to do with windblown drops of rain. I pushed on my slippers and padded over to the front door, wearing the blanket around my shoulders and probably resembling an old crone with the flu. After checking the peephole, which afforded me no more than a blurry view of someone in a white shirt, I pulled the door open as far as the chain would allow and poked my nose out.

"Hi," I started, my eyebrows furrowing in the middle as soon as my gaze settled on the impossibly tall man looming before me. "Can I help you?"

Now, I'm pretty sure that fate had nothing to do with this gigantic and, ahem, *very* handsome man randomly showing up on my doorstep, but I was at a complete loss as to who he was or why he was visiting me. Last time I'd checked, I wasn't in contact with any broad-chested, golden-haired Adonises with . . . dimples?

"The name's Ryan Kelly, ma'am," he said as he offered me a beefy hand along with the most charming smile I'd ever seen. His pronounced Southern accent was easily as appealing as his boyish grin.

"Oh," I answered, making no effort to shake his hand. It wasn't that I was trying to be rude, but I had no clue who this man was and I had a sneaking suspicion he was going to try to sell me something.

He laughed as if it was of no consequence to him whether I shook his hand or not and then plopped said hand into his jeans, shaking his head at his apparent mistake while his dimples continued to deepen. "You must be wonderin' what the heck I'm doin' on your doorstep?"

"Um, yeah, something like that."

He chuckled again and the sound was so inviting, I could feel my lips beginning to part in a reflection of his smile. Hmm, maybe fate did have something to do with Ryan Kelly? Maybe he was the god of thunder, who just happened to ride in on the storm, fleeing his kingdom up in the clouds.

"I'm your neighbor," he said finally as he motioned over his right shoulder. "I live up the street, maybe five houses." He brought his gaze back to mine and I felt myself flushing. "I just wanted to make sure you were doin' okay in this storm."

"Oh," I said, feeling incredibly relieved that he wasn't going to try to sell me a vacuum cleaner I didn't want or a set of stainless-steel knives. Taking a deep breath, I realized how completely unfriendly I appeared—especially to a neighbor. "I'm, uh, I'm fine, thanks."

Ryan had to be six-five, six-six if I had to guess, and his incredibly broad shoulders and overall giant frame made him look like he'd missed his calling as a football player or a wall. He didn't say anything for a few seconds, just appeared to be taking stock of me, as if trying to decide if I were being honest about my announcement that I was fine.

He extended his hand again. "Let's try this again. Ryan Kelly, ma'am, pleased to meet you."

I laughed nervously as I unlatched the chain and opened the door. Reaching my hand out from beneath my blanket, I allowed him to shake it. I tried to ignore the charismatic and charming drawl that decorated his words, but with little luck. I wasn't from the South—nope, I was born and bred in California, so I was definitely unaccustomed to Southern hospitality. I'd actually only ever been to New

Orleans once, when I was a junior at Cal State Northridge, working my way toward my bachelor's degree in history. It was summer break, and after spending a year and a half working part-time gigs, a girlfriend and I had saved up enough money to take a road trip across the country. Or so we'd thought. We'd actually ended up running out of money in New Orleans so we spent a few days here—a few days that had found a permanent place in my heart. Of course the Cajun food had been a good selling point, but the pull I felt to New Orleans was much more about the culture itself. The people were among the most open and friendly I'd ever come across, and the sense of history was both pervasive and awe-inspiring. All told, the Big Easy had existed in my memories as a place where I felt . . . home.

"Peyton Clark," I managed after a protracted silence. "Pleased to meet you."

Ryan laughed a deep, infectious sound. "I apologize for gettin' off on the wrong foot, so to speak. I hope I didn't frighten you?" he asked quickly, as if the thought just occurred to him. That was when I realized my hand was still in his. I pulled it free and smiled apologetically, as if it were an odd thing for me to pull my hand away from his, even though I knew it was much odder still that he'd held it so long. Thinking I could have been, and, therefore, probably should have been, frightened by some random dude showing up at my house at night, I realized I wasn't frightened at all. That thought actually scared me more than Ryan's unannounced visit. "Um, you didn't frighten me."

He nodded and offered me another winning smile. "I'm happy to hear it. Just wasn't quite sure what sort of impression I was makin' on you. I hope it's not a bad one."

"No, it's not a bad one," I answered quickly.

"You sure you're okay here?" he asked again, offering me a drawn eyebrow and a general expression of disbelief. He even looked past me, craning his head as if to take stock of my home's interior.

"I've got a few leaks," I admitted at last, then shrugged like the eleven canisters filling up with rainwater around the house weren't any big deal.

"I knew it," Ryan said with another boyish grin. "And I should also probably admit something . . ."

"What?" I asked, immediately overcome by a wave of suspicion as visions of Hoover vacuum cleaners started to dance before my eyes.

"My visit wasn't just to be neighborly," he started with a heartfelt sigh. "Hank asked me to come by and check on you." He smiled broadly. "Ol' coot was convinced this place was gonna fall apart on top of you." Then he glanced past me again, chuckling. "An' can't say I disagree with him!"

I laughed. "So you know Hank?"

"We go way back," Ryan said in explanation as he flashed his toothpaste-commercial smile. "Hank's been our family mechanic since I was in diapers."

"I see," I answered with a quick smile as neither of us said anything else for the space of four heartbeats. "I . . ."

"So," Ryan started at the same time I did and then chuckled as I shook my head and let it be known he could speak before me. "I guess you're plannin' on fixin' this place up?"

I nodded immediately, pleased to have a new topic of conversation. I wasn't one who dealt well with uncomfortable silences. "Yeah, that's my plan."

"By yourself?" he continued, his eyebrows raised as I nodded.

"Well, I'm obviously not going to do the work myself . . . I figured I'd hire it all out."

He nodded. "And you're livin' in it at the same time?" This time he shook his head. "Probably not the best idea, Ms. Clark."

"Just call me open-minded, I guess."

He frowned. "That's one way to look at it." He continued to look past me, into the living room, as if taking stock of myriad needed repairs already.

"Do you know anything about construction?" I hesitated.

I couldn't tell if he nodded or shook his head. It was a perfect mixture of both. "I dabble, Ms. Clark."

"Please, call me Peyton," I said quickly, suddenly realizing I hadn't yet invited him inside. The rain splattered him from behind and an errant leak above the door kept dripping onto his shoulder. I was also slightly afraid that the termite-infested floorboards of the porch might give way under his weight. And that wouldn't be a pretty picture.

"I dabble, Peyton." The way he said the words caused me to swallow down a large lump of what I imagined was nervousness. I didn't say anything but watched him glance around the foyer before bringing his dimpled smile back to me. "Big job."

Then I remembered I was planning on inviting him in. "Would you, uh, like to come in?"

"Thought you'd never ask!" he said with a chuckle and took a quick step inside, the floorboards creaking in time with his footfalls.

"So, you dabble," I started, suddenly nervous that this enormous man was inside my house. It wasn't so much because I was afraid he might hurt me—I believed his story about being my neighbor and figured a friend of Hank's was a friend of mine. My disquiet arose from the thought that here we were, alone, in my house. I shook the thoughts right out of my head, irritated with myself. I was acting like a total and complete moron—like I'd never seen a hot man before. And I had definitely seen lots of hot men . . . And once upon a time, the party girl Peyton had done a lot more than just look . . .

"I do," he answered matter-of-factly.

"Does your dabbling ever include renovations on very old homes?" I asked, sounding beyond hopeful. One of the first items on my to-do list was to find a general contractor to run the show on my remodel. And, while I didn't suppose Ryan, as a "dabbler," could fit the bill, maybe he knew of someone who could.

He stood in the foyer and appeared to be taking in the house as he gazed first to the left, then the right. Finally, he spun around and faced me. "In the past," he answered somewhat evasively and then eyed my house again, shaking his head. "But what I *can* tell you, Peyton, is that this place is not fit for you to be livin' in." Then he made a point of eyeing the pots and glasses already overflowing with rainwater. "Case in point."

"What's a little rainwater?" I asked with a smile and a shrug, completely not okay with the knowledge that I was definitely attracted to him. 'Course, what straight woman wouldn't be? With that height and build, and those warm eyes and that damned smile, I was more than sure that Ryan Kelly was quite popular with the ladies. Which was just as well because I wasn't interested in dating or men in general . . . or so I continued to remind myself.

But I couldn't ignore the stirring of butterflies in my stomach. Was this how it was going to be now that I was divorced? After being with only Jonathon for the last five-plus years (and it wasn't like he was very good in bed), was I now going to take note of every attractive man like a cat in heat? Because if that was what lay in store for me, I couldn't say I was exactly thrilled.

"Well, first off, I wouldn't describe this as a 'little rainwater,'" he said with a knowing smirk. "Your livin' room looks like the backdrop for Noah's Ark."

We both laughed but then I sighed as I glanced around the room and realized I'd been looking at it with rose-colored lenses. Realistically, the roof was leaking like a sieve; there was a perpetual musty, damp smell; and it wasn't exactly warm. But, hey, it was mine.

"You know this whole setup isn't exactly safe?" Ryan continued as he waved dismissively toward the heater in the center of the living room and all the pots and glasses surrounding it.

"How often does it rain?" I asked with a shrug, like whatever point he was making wasn't too important.

He chuckled. "Often enough that I'm gonna give you some free advice."

"Here we go," I muttered, unable to keep the smile from my lips even as I chastised myself again for flirting with him.

"My sister is the manager at the Omni Royal hotel in the French Quarter. I could hook you up with a very good rate."

"I want to live in my house during the remodel," I argued, even going so far as to cross my arms against my chest, which, when in context with the blanket draped around my shoulders, probably made me look like I was imitating Hiawatha.

"I meant you could stay at the Omni just until the rain ends," he answered quickly before offering me a cocked-brow expression. "I'm sure it's not exactly comfortable livin' here. It smells like a wet dog."

I laughed because that was the exact smell I'd been trying to put my finger on for the last few days. Then I sighed as I realized he had a point. But I also didn't like the idea of throwing in the towel and moving into a hotel for who knew how long? I glanced around the completely barren house, realizing maybe I had been a little too hasty in wanting to move in right away. I mean, there wasn't any furniture, not even a rug. I had a closet full of clothes, which were probably being rained on, a portable heater, a mattress, and linens upstairs in the only dry bedroom I could find. Oh, and I also had the blanket around my shoulders. I guess I hadn't exactly planned very well.

"Really, I'm fine," I started, completely aware of how empty my words sounded.

"The rain is supposed to last another four days at the least," Ryan said with a triumphant grin. Then he glanced over at the pots and glasses spread across my floor. "An' by that time, this place will be a flood zone."

"Okay, point taken," I grumbled.

"Is that a yes?" he continued, sporting that impossibly charismatic smile of his.

"A yes to what?"

"To my incredibly generous offer of housin'," he answered without a beat.

I smiled and in doing so, realized I'd just ceded him a victory.

The ringing of my cell phone woke me up. I rolled over, opened one eye, and glanced through the plantation shutters, which had once been white but now lay under a filmy cloud of gray. Seeing storm clouds still dominating the sky, I noticed the sound of raindrops pelting against the windowpanes. Shivering, I pulled the duvet cover all the way to my chin and wished my portable heater could ward away the chill in the air. With a humph, I rolled over and closed my eyes again. But my phone refused to be silenced. Grabbing it, I glanced at the caller ID and saw a number I didn't recognize, but a local one nonetheless. Maybe it was Hank with a final invoice for the Scout.

"Hello?" I asked in a sleep-laden, gravelly voice.

"Mornin', Sunshine," Ryan's Southern baritone pealed. "Just makin' sure you were gonna keep your word to go visit my sister."

I cleared my throat and felt a smile curling my lips on its own accord. But even though my initial response was to smile upon hearing the incredibly charming Southern accent on the other line, I didn't exactly want him to know that. "Yeah, yeah," I said, aiming for cool, calm, and collected.

"The weatherman said we're in for another five days of rain, Peyton, and that was as of, oh, two hours ago . . ."

"Blah—" I started, but he interrupted me.

"I, quite frankly, am convinced you won't survive another two days in that disaster which you call a house." He paused for a second or two after laughing at his own joke. "An' is that the fire hazard I hear in the background?"

I figured he was referring to my space heater. In response, I turned the heat up higher and smiled smugly. "Yep, you do."

He heaved a sigh as I felt a laugh tugging at my lips. "You do know that weather forecasters are usually . . . wrong?" I asked, just itching to spar with him. "Truth be told, it will probably rain for another five minutes, not days."

"In your case, I would say it's better to err on the side of assumin' they're right," he replied, wasting no time in responding. There was a slight pause before he added, "You have mornin' voice. What are you still doin' asleep?"

"Um, it's like the crack of dawn," I answered with a yawn for dramatic effect.

He chuckled again and it was such a charming sound, I felt another smile pulling my lips up. "Peyton, it's eight in the mornin'. I've already had two cups of coffee and I worked out. There's no reason for you to be lollygaggin' about."

"Okay, Dad," I answered with a heartfelt grin.

"Early to bed and early to rise makes a man, or in your case, a woman, healthy, wealthy, and wise," he pedantically quoted Ben Franklin, sounding completely self-satisfied.

"And boring," I added. I didn't intend to sound so put out, but it wasn't like I'd slept well. Not while enduring the Chinese water torture of numerous leaks throughout the house, or worrying that maybe my electric heater *would* short circuit and burn the place down. "I'm not a morning person."

"Regardless," he admonished, "you made me a promise, and therefore, you have a promise to keep. So get yourself up and try not ta trip over all the pools and puddles in your livin' room. My sister's waitin' for you at the Omni. Her name is Trina."

"You already talked to her?!" I asked, unable to conceal my shock because it seemed like no time had gone by at all. I sat upright and stretched the hand that wasn't holding my phone high above my head. My eyes were still puffy, a tacit testimony of my restless night, and my eyelashes pulled my lids down like burdensome weights.

"Like I said, I've been up since six a.m. and already accomplished most everythin' I set out to do today."

"Well, good for you," I muttered with irritation. So what if Ryan had basically conquered the world in two hours and I was still having a hell of a time just trying to keep my eyes open . . .

"Time's a wastin', Peyton," he rhymed back at me, with the hint of a chuckle in his tone.

"I should never have given you my phone number," I murmured even though I had to admit I enjoyed talking with him and even more, I liked him taking it upon himself to serve as my wake-up call. Even though I really didn't want to admit it, I liked Ryan Kelly. I couldn't help it.

"Givin' me your number was the neighborly thing to do." He paused. "I mean, what if I ever need to borrow a cup of sugar?"

"Isn't there a grocery store nearby?"

"Don't think you're gonna get out o' your promise with a little verbal sparrin', Peyton Clark," he reprimanded me. Honestly, it was the sexiest scolding I'd ever had the good fortune to deserve. The flirtatious tone to his voice combined with how he said my name made me catch my breath for a second. I nearly forgot what the hell we were talking about. Oh yeah . . . giving him my phone number the evening before.

"Well, let's just say that if I realized you were such a drill sergeant, I would've pretended not to have a phone," I finished, sounding haughty despite my amusement.

"No more excuses, Ms. Grumpy-Pants."

"Okay, okay," I said and attempted to stifle a yawn as I stretched my legs out before me. Standing up, I lumbered over to the electric heater, which began making a zapping sort of sound it hadn't been making yesterday. Maybe Ryan was right about it being a fire hazard. Surprisingly, I hadn't electrocuted myself or burned my house down yet, considering a portable heater and ancient electrical outlets weren't exactly ideal bedfellows when mixed with water.

"I'll meet you in the hotel lobby at noon with a list of some reliable general contractors in the area, should you need one." He said the last part without even trying to conceal the smile in his tone—making it more than obvious that Ryan thought I needed a general contractor or two. Or maybe even three.

"Thanks," I answered, feeling somehow deflated that our conversation switched from heated flirtation to mere business so quickly. I reminded myself that first and foremost I had a mission to see to fruition—remodeling my house. Flirting with Ryan Kelly didn't fit into my plans. That's all there was to it.

"And another thing, Peyton, I know the contractors on this list personally, so I'll make sure they give you a good deal," he added.

"The neighborly rate?" I asked with a laugh. Luckily for me, my divorce settlement was a decent one, which would allow me to rebuild my dream home. Granted, it wasn't going to see me through the rest of my life, but I figured the settlement would last me a good year. By that time, I'd very happily be ready to work again. Actually, the idea of getting a job didn't depress me at all. During the stint of my marriage, Jonathon forbade me from working. I was convinced he didn't want anything to detract from him being the center of my world.

Because I didn't work during my marriage, I never felt as if anything surrounding me was mine. I'd had zero say in the purchase of our home—Jonathon had just shown up one afternoon with the news that he'd bought a house. My car appeared one day just as mysteriously as the house; even the clothes in my closet bore Jonathon's stamp.

A successful Los Angeles attorney, my ex-husband had more money than he could spend. And despite the fun of never having to worry about anything financial, I would have traded the Bel Air mansion, sports cars, fair-weather friends, and all the rest of it for real love—for a husband who loved me for the true me, not the woman he wanted to me to be. And, even if I could've changed myself into that Stepford wife, I still doubted Jonathon would really have loved me. Nope, the only person Jonathon could love was Jonathon.

Thankfully, I wouldn't have to worry about finding a job for a little while but when the time came, I would welcome it because it would be another example of how I was now living for myself. And what was more, I was excited about the prospect of actually being able to put my flare for history to use. Maybe I'd take up a position as a museum docent or a librarian at the historical society. Whatever job I ended up with was really beside the point at this stage. What mattered to me most was that every decision I made would be just that—a decision *I* made.

"No," Ryan chuckled. "It's not the neighbor rate. It's the 'I better get someone to lowball the job so this girl will hire someone to renovate her deathtrap so I can sleep at night' rate."

The Omni Royal hotel was a nineteenth-century marvel of vastly high ceilings, ornate crown molding, vanilla-colored walls, expansive white marble floors, and elegant crystal-prismed chandeliers. True to his word, Ryan hooked me up with a room, and his sister, Trina, was kind enough to comp the entire thing. A free room at the Omni Royal was beyond generous in its own right, but I was more than shocked to find that my "room" was actually a suite, complete with a living room separated from the bedroom by double doors. With a wrought iron balcony overlooking the very fashionable Royal Street, I swallowed a large gulp and took in the plushness of a velvet gold sofa and mahogany table with two dark-brown velvet club chairs. All faced a flat-screen TV that was at least sixty inches wide. Rich coppery drapes trimmed the sides of the French doors, which opened to the wrought iron balcony. The room was stylish with the essence of ornate finery.

Just as awe-inspiring as the living room was the bedroom. A king-size bed first captured my attention, with its rich mahogany headboard and the taupe silk pillows piled high in front of it. A mahogany bench upholstered in gold velvet occupied the end of the bed, a nice contrast to the two chocolate boudoir chairs that faced the room.

"This is too much for me to accept," I started, turning to face Trina and shaking my head. Trina was tall, eye to eye with me. I had more of a curvaceous body—natural C-cup boobs and wide hips that would have made me look like a pear were it not for my bust—while she was rather slender and small-framed. She looked younger than Ryan . . . I would have pinned her around thirty, maybe. Ryan appeared to be in his late thirties. Trina's eyes were hazel with flecks of gold in them, making them look more amber. Full lips, oval face, high cheekbones, and golden hair, Trina was definitely a looker. And very definitely Ryan's sister. The family resemblance was uncanny.

"Don't be silly," she started in a voice reminiscent of Scarlett O'Hara. I was just waiting for her to bust out with "fiddle-dee-dee!"

"Please, I insist you let me pay for it," I continued. I was entirely uncomfortable with accepting Ryan and Trina's generosity, especially since it wasn't like I couldn't afford it.

The attractive blond shook her head with a duplicate expression of her brother the previous night. Apparently, obstinacy ran in the

Kelly family. "I'm goin' to give you a brief lesson on Southern hospitality," she interrupted. "You'll find people down here happily go out of their way to help you. That's because we like doin' it, honey. So please, just let us."

I laughed and nodded my consent, feeling immediately drawn to her easy yet direct manner. "Point taken and lesson learned. Thank you."

"Don't mention it," she finished, dismissing the conversation with a French-manicured hand. I noticed she wasn't wearing a ring on her graceful fingers, so I assumed she wasn't married. Not that I could swing both ways . . . Nope, I was very happy in my fully convinced heterosexuality. But I could also appreciate true beauty—be it male or female.

But while I could recognize Trina as a beautiful woman, it was her brother I couldn't seem to get out of my mind. Which in a word . . . sucked. My rational side kept insisting that my attraction to Ryan Kelly wasn't part of my plans. I was newly divorced and needed to focus on living by myself, for myself. In no way was I ready for any sort of romantic liaison, not that Ryan was looking for one . . .

While the rational side of me could see things plainly in black and white, the emotional side of me, also known as the idealistic, girly side, couldn't stop thinking about Ryan. His dimpled smile and the way his Southern accent sounded so lazily relaxed . . . as if he didn't have a care in the world.

"Besides, this hotel already owes my brother quite a few favors," Trina continued with a knowing smirk. "And he phoned in one of those favors for you, so you better accept it!"

I laughed and nodded, liking how immediately at ease I felt around her. So at ease, as a matter-of-fact, that I dared to do some digging where her brother was concerned. "The hotel owes your brother some favors?" I repeated. "Why is that?"

She shrugged like I should've already known the answer to my own question. "Ryan was the general contractor on the remodel."

My eyebrows raised up in surprise as I studied my surroundings again with renewed interest before bringing my confused expression back to Trina. "He was the general contractor?" I repeated dubiously. Something here didn't ring true . . . hadn't Ryan told me he only "dabbled" in construction? Looking around myself again, there was no way a "dabbler" could have achieved such a magnificent result.

"You better believe it, honey," Trina said, nodding all the while. "If my brother excels at anythin', it's his talent to accurately restore old mansions."

"Hmm," I said with a deep breath. I wasn't sure if I was setting myself up for an unpleasant outcome, but I wanted to get to the bottom of whether Trina or her brother was stretching the truth. "Ryan told me he only 'dabbled' in construction?"

Trina nodded without surprise. Then she sighed. "Yeah, that sounds about right."

"So there's a disconnect there somewhere?" I spoke before thinking I might be treading into personal territory where I had no right to intrude. "I'm sorry . . . it's none of my business."

Cocking her head to the side, Trina didn't argue with me. Instead, her attention was on the French doors, where she seemed to zone out on the view just beyond them. "Ryan used to own the largest construction company in N'awlins," she said with a wistful smile. "Kelly's Construction," she finished softly.

I glanced around myself again, taking in the lushness of the living room before recalling the immense foyer of the Omni Royal. If Ryan could manage a project this massive, Trina was right—he was well beyond talented. Even more, he was easily more than qualified for my remodel. Well, that is, if he was still in the construction business. Seeing the nostalgic expression on Trina's face, I got a feeling the answer to that question was a resounding no. "So, is Kelly's Construction still around?" I asked sheepishly.

Trina immediately shook her head as the wistful, sad smile returned to her lips. "Unfortunately it hasn't been around for the last—what?—four years now."

"What happened?" I asked even though I knew I was becoming nosy again. "Did business dry up or something?"

Trina shook her head. "Findin' jobs and keepin' clients have never been a problem for Ryan. He's always gotten more work than he could handle. He actually had waitin' lists."

"So why isn't he still doing it?"

Wrapping her fingers around the back of her neck, a general expression of worry came over her face, like she wasn't sure if she should tell me or not. Reluctant to corner her into a tough position, I interrupted. "Trina, you don't have to tell me, really. I've already asked you too many questions and stuck my nose where it doesn't belong. I have a tendency to do that," I continued apologetically. I sighed. "I really don't want to make you uncomfortable and I apologize."

"No," she said with authority. "It's better I tell you than for you to ask him, especially since you *are* lookin' for a contractor to remodel your home." She continued nodding vehemently, as if she were trying to convince herself as much as me. "It's probably just a matter of time before the conversation comes up anyway . . ." she said mostly to herself.

"Well, as for contractors, Ryan said he would meet me in the lobby at noon with a list of names."

She nodded, but didn't seem convinced. Then she sighed despondently. "I'm sure they are all good, Peyton, but not one of them is Ryan Kelly."

I shook my head, failing to grasp what she was trying to tell me. "But, by the sound of it, Ryan's no longer available?"

She nodded again with a deep breath, only to exhale it for a count of three. She cleared her throat and brought her eyes to mine. "Ryan was married for maybe six years," she started. I felt a spire of disappointment jet through me at the thought that he was off the market . . . or was. Irritated, I shoved the thought right out of my head. "Elizabeth was his whole life," Trina continued, smiling fondly as if she were looking at a picture of them together. Then her smile fell. "One day, she was visitin' one of his job sites. While she was waitin' for him to free up, she took a walk around the property and . . . just happened to be in the wrong place at the wrong time."

"What happened?" I asked quietly, dreading the answer but unable to hide my curiosity.

"One of the foremen was workin' on the balcony a few floors above her, and somehow or another, the balcony collapsed right on top of her. She was killed instantly."

"Oh my gosh," I whispered, suddenly understanding why Kelly's Construction was now silenced. "And the foreman?"

"He broke his back and remains paralyzed," Trina answered and sighed as she turned away. Even though the accident happened years ago, it was still very obvious she was haunted by it. She shook her head and dropped her eyes onto her fidgeting hands.

"I'm so sorry," I said, at a complete loss as to what I should say.

"It hit Ryan hard," she continued, glancing up at me. "He closed shop that day and never worked on another construction job again. Luckily for him, he'd made enough money that he didn't need to."

I was quiet, searching for something to say. But everything I thought of just seemed to fall flat, sounding inauthentic or flimsy. "I don't know what to say except I'm really sorry," I managed at last.

She nodded as if she understood my loss for words. I had nothing to offer that could in any way ease the pain her family had to have endured. "I have one favor to ask you," she started with a sweet smile.

My eyebrows rose up on their own accord. "Sure."

"I would really love it if Ryan were the general on your job."

My eyebrows rose even higher. "Trina," I started, shaking my head at the realization of the monumental task that would surely be.

"I know what you're goin' to say," she interrupted me. "And the chances of him takin' your job are next to nothin'; but I'm his sister and I want to see him get better, Peyton." She was quiet for another few seconds. "It's been a long time," she continued. "I expected him to be back in business one or two years ago."

"Maybe he just doesn't enjoy it anymore," I started.

She shook her head. "Ryan loves construction. He often said how restorin' historical places gave his life meanin'. I know he misses it." She chewed on her lower lip. "I really want him to put the past behind him, to move on."

"I definitely get that . . ."

"Will you please just ask him to take on your job?" she interrupted. "All I'm askin' is for you to ask him to be the general, and if he says no, we'll have to leave it at that."

I studied her for a second and saw the fight in her eyes, which I admired. She was a good sister. But, good sister or not, I didn't want to disappoint her. "You realize, of course, he's going to say no, right?"

She shrugged. "You never know until you ask, right?" Then she smiled knowingly. "Besides, I have a feelin' he might have a soft spot for you."

"For me?" I asked incredulously. I shook my head and took a few steps away from her, as if my whole body resisted the very idea. "I don't even know him!"

"I know, I know," she said, holding up her hands in mock surrender. "But he did tell me that he went to check on you in the middle of that nasty storm last night . . ."

"Hank was the one who suggested it," I interrupted, feeling as if I were trying to talk not only Trina out of this ridiculousness but myself also. There was no reason to get caught up in thinking that Ryan might be interested in me because there was also a good chance that he wasn't. Furthermore, I wasn't shopping for anything romantic . . .

She frowned at me. "Well, did Hank call me to say I'd better set you up with a free room for as long as you needed it or he'd disown me?"

I laughed. "I'm guessing the answer to that question is no?"

She nodded. "I'm just sayin' I think my brother has a soft spot for damsels in distress, and given the shoddy nature of your roof, I'd say you're in dire distress, honey."

"I guess I can't really argue that one."

"So just do us all a favor and tell him you want him as the general. And, trust me," she continued as she opened the doors to the balcony, and the transparent white curtains beneath the gold tapestry drapes fluttered in the breeze, "he'll do an amazin' job on your renovation. He's remodeled most of the renowned mansions in the Garden District and the French Quarter. He's sort of a household name around these parts . . . well, at least he was."

"I can tell he is very good at his job," I admitted before returning my attention to Trina, who was smiling back at me.

"Will you ask him, Peyton?"

I nodded but frowned all the while. "Of course I will."

"That's all I want," she said, suddenly excited again, almost like a child. "Who knows, the obstinate man might even say yes!"

Speaking of the obstinate man, I spotted a clock hanging above the dining table and saw it was already noon. Ryan would be waiting in the lobby for me. Trina followed my gaze and nodded, escorting me to the door.

"If you need any help retrievin' your belongings from your house, just let me know. I can send one of my bellmen."

I shook my head. "I think I can at least handle packing my own clothes," I laughed. "Thank you though."

I followed her down the hallway and into the elevator. In true elevator protocol, neither of us said anything for the entire ride down. When we reached the lobby, Trina held the door for me and I walked out, immediately noticing Ryan's imposing form on a chair beside a baby grand piano. As soon as he saw us, he stood up and, with a boyish smile, approached us. He immediately threw his bulky arms around his sister, enveloping her until she nearly disappeared.

"You're gonna suffocate me, you big brute!" she called out as she playfully swatted him away.

He shrugged. "I can always put you in a headlock instead?"

She laughed, taking a few steps away from him before facing me. "He would too."

I laughed even though I couldn't help feeling awkward, like I was a third wheel. Ryan cleared his throat and gave me a smile, his big brother antics apparently now behind him. "Did Trina set you up with a nice room?"

I nodded immediately. "It is beautiful, and way more than I could ask for." Then I faced Trina. "Thank you both so much. I can't tell you how much I appreciate it."

"She owed me a favor," Ryan said with a twinkle in his eye. He playfully elbowed Trina in the upper arm.

She rolled her eyes and faced her brother in mock exasperation. "I swear, Ryan, no one would believe you're thirty-six years old when you act like you're goin' on twelve."

"Key to longevity is stayin' young at heart, T."

She shook her head and started to walk away. "Have a good day, Peyton!" she called out behind her. "Let me know if you need anything at all!"

"Thanks, Trina!" I replied before returning my attention to the handsome man in front of me. "Your sister is really wonderful."

Ryan nodded and his smile told me exactly what he thought of her. "She's a gem."

"Yes, she is," I said softly and then suddenly blanked on anything more to say. Instead, we both just stood there for a few seconds staring at each other like both of our brains had gone on vacation.

"I'm hungry," Ryan finally announced. "You wanna get somethin' ta eat, Pey?" he asked, and I couldn't help but feel giddy that he'd taken it upon himself to shorten my full name into what I hoped might be a . . . pet name?

"Oh, you gotta take her to Croissant d'Or Patisserie!" Trina piped up from nowhere, suddenly appearing right beside me.

Ryan rolled his eyes. "What is it with you and that place?"

But Trina was ignoring him, her attention completely on me. "Peyton, it's *the* best place in N'awlins for pastries and croissants. Their napoleon is to die for!" she continued, her eyes wide and her head bobbing up and down as if she were subconsciously agreeing with herself. "I'm tellin' you, it's to die for!"

I glanced up at Ryan and shrugged. "Well, how can we turn that down?"

Ryan chuckled. "Guess we can't."

Croissant d'Or Patisserie was located on Ursalines Avenue in the French Quarter. It was a cute little place with high ceilings and white subway tiling on all the walls, offset with blue tiles around the perimeters of the doorways. The decorative accent that caught my attention immediately, though, was the incredibly intricate crown molding. In contrast with the baby-blue ceiling, the crown molding (which had to be at least a foot or two tall) featured a white background with inset white ribboning above cascading boughs of pink, yellow, and white roses.

"Ryan Kelly, long time no see," the girl behind the counter said with a half-smile aimed at the man in question. She leaned against the glass case covering myriad pastries, croissants, and sandwiches and raised a brow at Ryan who seemed a bit . . . uncomfortable. He cleared his throat and I could see the surprise registering in his eyes as soon as they focused on her.

"Hi, Jenny, how are you?" he asked, thrusting both of his hands inside his pockets while he displayed a sudden and thorough interest in a piece of carrot cake behind the glass.

"I'm fine," the girl answered. She was pretty with long, straight dark hair and large brown eyes . . . brown eyes that narrowed once she focused on me. "And who is this?" she asked, feigning interest but there was definitely something closer to jealous annoyance behind her eyes.

"Ah, excuse my poor manners," Ryan said with a put-on cough as he took the few steps that separated us and, reaching out for my forearm, pulled me in front of him before then deciding he wanted me standing beside him instead. "This is . . . Peyton," he finished.

"Nice to meet you," I said with a hurried smile as I wondered why in the world Ryan was acting so bizarre. He cleared his throat for the second time in the course of four minutes and then pulled me into him, wrapping his arm around me as he pointed at what looked like a ham and cheese croissant sitting on the top shelf behind the glass. I was so surprised by the sudden physical contact that I didn't even respond.

"Those are pretty damn good, Pey," he said, still pointing at the croissants. When I glanced up at him with a confused expression, he simply shrugged and smiled in such a manner that I realized he was begging me to play along . . . why, I had no clue, but figured I'd find out shortly.

"Ham and cheese croissant for you, Ryan?" Jenny asked impatiently and then frowned at me. "You know what you want to order?"

"Um, I'll have the same," I answered with a sheepish smile before I remembered Trina's comment about the napoleons. "Oh, and a napoleon."

Jenny nodded but didn't say anything more, simply ringing us both up. She then spouted out our total with stiff lips. Ryan was just as quiet as he paid and then led me through the bustling room to a small table in the corner, just beside a door that led to the bathroom, which appeared to be outside in a courtyard of sorts.

"So, lemme guess, bad date?" I asked as I realized neither of us had ordered anything to drink.

He glanced at me and smiled, shaking his head. "Never even had a date with her."

"So?"

He sighed. "She just has . . . this . . . thing for me," he finished finally and then threw his hands up in the air like he just didn't understand why any woman would have a "thing" for him. Apparently he hadn't looked in the mirror lately. "That's why I usually try to avoid this place." He took a breath and then offered me a smile of consolation. "I'm sorry I had to recruit you."

"Ah, you mean, into playing the part of the girlfriend?" I asked with a small grin.

"Yeah, thanks for playin' along."

I caught the whiff of freshly brewed coffee coming from the counter area and had a sudden thirst pang. Damn it all, but I was going to have to brave the scorned woman, otherwise known as Jenny, because I really, really wanted a cup of coffee. "Welcome," I answered absentmindedly. "That coffee is calling my name."

"That's right!" Ryan exclaimed with a slight chuckle as he shook his head. "We didn't order any beverages!"

"Yeah, you were too concerned with escaping the lovelorn looks of your admirer over there," I answered with an amused smile as I inclined my head in Jenny's direction.

"I'll get us some coffees," Ryan answered as he stood up and, eyeing Jenny, grumbled something unintelligible.

"Going back into the trenches?" I asked with a slight laugh.

He cocked his head to the side and sighed dramatically. "The things I do for you, Peyton Clark."

I laughed again and watched him meander to the front counter where he made small talk with Jenny, who still looked like she was pretty ticked off that he and I were here together. His shoulders were tight, giving him the overall look of someone completely uncomfortable. Moments later, he paid for the coffees, thanked her, and lumbered back toward our table.

"Was the mission successful?" I asked as he handed me a mug of steaming coffee, followed by a small carafe of cream. I dutifully accepted both, immediately pouring half of the cream into the coffee and following suit with two packets of Splenda.

"As successful as it could be, given the circumstances," he muttered.

I smiled at him innocently and even batted my eyelashes, deciding to play the fun game of prying. "So, what's wrong with Jenny? She's a pretty girl and she's obviously into you . . ."

He shrugged and feigned interest in his coffee, not even bothering to glance up at me when he answered. "She's not my type."

I took a sip of my coffee. "Why not? What's your type?"

"Not her," he answered evasively and then turned around in his seat, presumably to check and see if our food was on its way.

"Why not her?" I continued prodding, determined to get some juicy morsels out of him.

He chuckled, bringing his attention back to me. "You are relentless!"

I shrugged. "Hey, I figured you owed me one for forcing me into playing the part of your girlfriend and, consequently, suffering the wrath of Jenny, the harpy!"

"The harpy!" he repeated and exploded into a raucous laugh.

I smiled but wasn't quite finished. "That's right, the harpy! I can also tell that this whole subject makes you very uncomfortable so of course I want to stick my nose where it doesn't belong . . ."

He laughed again but didn't seem in the least bit offended or irritated that I was prying. "Okay, Peyton," he started, leaning toward me as he enunciated each syllable of my name. "She's very clingy, she's not interestin', and I'm not attracted to her. How's that for why she isn't my type?"

I shrugged and sipped my coffee, not sure why I was so incredibly happy to hear him say those words. "She's a pretty girl."

He nodded but then glanced around the room before his eyes settled back on me. "This room is full of pretty girls."

I took another sip and glanced around, realizing he was right—there were quite a few attractive women around us. Realizing my mug had given me a coffee mustache, I licked the top of my lip. "So what's the problem with them?"

He chuckled and shook his head, like I was trying his patience. But it was all very much put on because a smile lurked at the corners of his mouth. "I'm talkin' to the only pretty girl in this room who I care to talk to."

I plunked my coffee mug on the table and leaned back, realizing surprise was already echoing through my entire body. "Wow, Ryan, that was a good one!"

He chuckled and nodded. "Yeah, you liked it?"

"I did! So tell me, did you come up with that one yourself or was that borrowed from a Hallmark card?"

He shook his head and playfully swatted at me. "You, Peyton Clark, are a ballbuster."

I laughed and even though I knew I was headed into dangerous territory, I couldn't seem to stop myself. "Are yours feeling a little sensitive?"

Ryan's eyebrows reached for the ceiling in obvious surprise that I was referencing his man beans. But the surprise only lasted for a few seconds before a knowing smile captured his mouth, and I realized he could play as down and dirty as I could, which was a relief because the last thing I wanted to do was offend his genteel Southern manners. "Nah, I'm all man . . . these puppies are made of steel!"

I couldn't help my laugh but then struggled to hold back another quip, instead burying my face in my coffee mug as I emptied the last few drops into my mouth. When I put the mug back on the table, I watched Ryan reach inside his back jeans pocket and produce a folded-up piece of paper, which he handed to me. "Here are the names of three contractors I told you I'd recommend for your remodel."

"Oh," I said, surprised our conversation had taken this turn and disappointed all the while. Even though I'd thought Ryan was right there with me, enjoying our flirtation, it seemed like maybe he wasn't as comfortable with it as I'd thought. And, yes, I had to wonder if maybe it was because I wasn't his type either? Or it probably had to do with his deceased wife.

"Like I told you, I know these men personally," Ryan finished at the exact moment that Jenny appeared at our table with our food order. She said nothing as she unloaded both croissantwiches and my napoleon. She then spun on the ball of her foot, returning to the counter just as quietly as she'd come.

I swallowed hard as I unfolded the paper and glanced down at the scratchy handwriting that said, "Swan's Remodeling," "Tate Construction," and "Tandy and Sons." I cleared my throat and folded the paper in half again, feeling the color draining from my cheeks as I glanced up at Ryan, who was studying me intently.

"Don't tell me you've changed your mind?" he asked. I didn't answer, so he shook his head. "Peyton, that's too much work to take on yourself. Not only that, but if you bid out each and every job, you'll end up spendin' a fortune."

"Ryan, I want you to be the general." I wasn't sure I'd said the words until they were already out of my mouth, and Ryan looked back at me like I'd just sprouted another head.

"What?" he asked.

The color returned to my cheeks and I could feel myself blushing from my head to my toes. "I want you to be the general contractor on the job," I repeated, my heart in my throat. It wasn't lost on me that both of our ham and cheese croissants and my napoleon sat untouched.

Running his hands through his hair, he suddenly seemed distracted, his attention riveted on the view beyond the front windows. "I, uh, I can't," he said finally, his gaze settling on me. "I'm no longer in the construction business."

"I know."

He pointed to the folded paper clutched in my right hand. "So, choose someone from that list. I can show you lots of the homes they've worked on, if that's what you're worried about. If you don't want to take my word—"

"I trust your word," I interrupted. "I'm sure they're great."

"They are all highly qualified for your job, Pey—"

"But I want you to run my job," I interrupted him again.

"I don't know what that sister of mine put into your head," he started and shook his head.

"She didn't put anything into my head," I answered immediately. I definitely didn't want to get Trina into any sort of trouble. "She just told me you remodeled the Omni hotel, and that was enough for me." I took a breath and beamed at him. "And the Omni hotel was beyond impressive, Ryan. I mean, hot damn, you did a good job!"

He cleared his throat and frowned at me, but a smile burned at the ends of his eyes and lips. "Flattery won't get you anywhere."

But I had a feeling it would. "Going to play hardball, are you?" I asked with a quick laugh. "Okay, how about this—I know you and I don't know them."

"I could introduce you and then you would know them."

"Blah," I said and stuck my tongue out at him as I searched for another good reason why Ryan should run my job and not someone else. "You're my neighbor."

"So what?"

"Soooo, that bodes very well for me."

He crossed his arms against his chest and studied me with dancing eyes. "Why?"

"Because it means you have to do a good job!" I answered with a heartfelt smile. "Because if you don't, I know where you live and I *will* come after you!"

A smile cracked its way across his lips but vanished just seconds later as he shook his head and sighed. "I, uh, I'm sorry . . ."

"If you don't take on the job, I won't hire anyone at all," I said finally, huffing out my frustration as I tightened my arms against my chest to prove I was serious. "And even though you don't know me that well yet, I promise I'm stubborn when it comes to getting my way."

He laughed and then grew quiet, studying me while a smile still crested his lips. "Trust me, I believe you."

"And it wasn't *that* cold with the heater on . . ."

He sighed. "Goddamn, that bloody heater . . ."

"It's your choice."

We just sat there looking at one another, me with my arms crossed and a severe-looking expression on my face, while he wore a poker face. Neither of us had so much as touched our food. Finally he sighed and thrust both of his hands onto the tabletop, making it shake. "I don't have a work crew anymore. I don't even know what tools I still have," he protested, but I shook my head.

"You can figure all that stuff out." I took a deep breath, wondering if he would actually go for it. "I expect you to give me a fair price and I also want to know how long you think the project will take to complete."

He didn't reply for a while but looked at me as if he were seeing right through me. "I'm not agreein' to anything before I inspect it," he started with a determined look in his eyes. Probably the same expression I had in mine.

"That's fair enough," I answered, smiling up at him. "So when shall I schedule the inspection?"

He frowned, but it seemed insincere. "No time like the present, eh?"

Ryan frowned, then sighed, then frowned again. I'd just given him a tour of my house, and from the looks of it, he wasn't impressed.

"She's a beauty, don't you think?" I asked hopefully, nudging him in the arm like a used car salesman while beaming the widest smile I could manage. We'd worked our way through all five bedrooms, four bathrooms, the living room, family room, dining room, laundry room, and the kitchen. Now we stood on the curb outside, both of us gazing up at the monstrosity that I called my new home. While my face reflected hopeful optimism, Ryan's did not.

"It's saggin' on one side," he answered, straight-lipped.

"What? Where?" I demanded, moving my attention to the far west side of the house where Ryan pointed. Yep, it definitely looked as if the house was a tad shorter on one side. "That just gives it character."

He glanced down at me and raised both brows. "That, or it's got a shoddy foundation."

"I'm gonna go with it's got character."

Even though the rain had been nonstop for the better portion of the day, it had paused for the moment, although dark-gray clouds still occupied the skies and the wind hadn't let up. I wrapped my arms around myself and pulled my blue raincoat closer, adjusting the brim of my baseball cap so it didn't sit too low on my forehead.

That was one thing I loved about having shortish hair—it always looked good underneath a ball cap. It was like the two were made for one another.

Ryan glanced over at me again, this time only arching one brow, but a smile still pulled at the corner of his full lips. And, yes, his dimples were very much present and accounted for. In his dark-brown sweater and navy-blue jeans, he had a relaxed yet preppy look, like he'd just jumped out of a J.Crew catalog. But his calloused, large hands, along with the expanse of his incredibly broad shoulders, definitely were tacit testimony that he wasn't afraid of hard work. He probably welcomed it.

When he looked back at my house, his smile faded. "Peyton, this job is enormous," he announced before looking down at me and shaking his head. "I don't even know what would possess you to want to take on such a huge project."

I exhaled and felt my shoulders droop. "It's destiny."

"Destiny?" he asked with a crooked smile.

"This house was left to me by a great-aunt I've never met, and I received the deeds to the house the same day that my divorce was finalized. Now if that isn't an example of the hands of fate, I don't know what is."

"You were related to Myra?" Ryan asked with interest.

"She was my great-aunt," I repeated, suddenly becoming increasingly interested in whether Ryan might be able to shed some light on this family connection of mine. "Did you know her?"

He chuckled. "No one 'knew' her," he started and then sighed like the news he was about to impart might not be welcomed. "Pey, your aunt . . ."

"Great-aunt."

"Great-aunt wasn't exactly what I would consider a . . . friendly woman," he finished with a slight smile. "By any stretch of the imagination."

"Hmm, Hank said she tended to keep to herself."

Ryan nodded. "I tried to be a good neighbor and checked in on her a dozen or so times but my visits were always very unwelcome."

I sighed and then shrugged. "Well, good thing I'm not following in her footsteps."

He chuckled. "Damn good thing!" Then the laugh died on his lips and he just smiled down at me, a wistful expression in his eyes. "Even though I think this house is way too much for you to take on yourself, I must admit I'm glad you're here." He swallowed. "I like you, Peyton."

"I like you too, Ryan," I answered with a genuine grin. "And want to know something else?"

He chuckled. "Of course."

"I'd like you even better if you agreed to be the general on my job!" I finished with a huge grin and wide, happy eyes.

Ryan shook his head and laughed as he eyed the ground before returning his gaze to mine. "You should know that your house is in terrible shape and it's completely unsafe for you to even consider livin' in it."

"I refuse to move," I said in a tone that brooked no argument, dropping my playfulness from earlier. "I came here with a dream and I intend to see my dream to fruition."

"Well, can't you still have your dream, but also get a rental somewhere in the interim?"

I frowned up at him. "No."

"How did I know you were gonna to say that?" he grumbled, although the smile on his face gave him away.

"Regardless of whether the house is unsafe or a huge job, that isn't to say it can't be fixed up?" I continued optimistically. I kept grinning up at him in such a way that I hoped it would be difficult to trample my hopes.

"Of course it can, but as far as me doin' it . . ."

"No job is too big, no remodel too challenging," I started, doing my best Superman narrator imitation as I held my arm up like Rosie the Riveter.

Ryan immediately started chuckling, then shook his head again and gave me an expression that said it would be tough, if not impossible, to change his mind. Damn, but this guy was stubborn! "Your job will require a huge crew, an enormous amount of time, machinery that I no longer have . . ."

"Blah," I said, waving him away with an unconcerned hand. "You can find a crew, and I'm happy to rent any equipment you might need. Don't you Southerners have Home Depots down here?"

He narrowed his eyes on me but didn't look angry. Rather, he seemed more amused—like he was trying to talk a determined kid out of a trip to the toy store. "You have got to be the most stubborn woman I've ever met . . . well, aside from my sister."

He was going to have one hell of a time on his hands because this kid was going to give him a run for his money when it came to stubbornness. "And proudly so," I answered with a big grin.

Speaking of his stubborn sister, I was determined to get Ryan to acquiesce to my demands, for my own selfish reasons, yes, but also for Trina. There had been such an expression of desperation mixed with hope in Trina's eyes when she'd asked me to try to win Ryan over to the idea of remodeling my house that I really wanted to persuade him. If construction truly was in Ryan's blood, I wondered if I'd be doing him a favor, as Trina seemed to think. Maybe getting back into renovating old houses would be cathartic for him? Maybe it would be healing in some way. Or maybe it would only remind him of his deceased wife . . . That was a thought I didn't want to ponder for long. But, in the end, I decided that Trina probably did know what was best for her brother. She *was* his blood, after all.

"I'm stubborn when I want the best, Ryan," I said in a soft but serious tone, deciding to try my hand at flattering his ego.

He chuckled again and shook his head. "And how would you, Peyton, who just happened to move here—what?—a month ago? How would you even know I'm the best?"

I shrugged, thinking he made a good point. Including Hank and Trina, Ryan was one of only a handful of people I'd met so far in New Orleans. "Because I saw the amazing job you did on the Omni hotel and more importantly, Trina told me you *were* the best. She said Kelly's Construction was a household name around New Orleans. " Then I smiled broadly again, pleased with my quick response. "And I never settle for anything less than a household name."

"You do realize I haven't even lifted a hammer in years?" he asked, rolling his fingers through his thick hair. His cheeks, jaw, and chin were shadowed by stubble, which meant he hadn't shaved in a day or so. It gave him a certain mountain man look, or maybe it was something more roguish—like the hero you'd see on a romance novel cover. Either way, I found it hard to resist reaching out to run my fingers along his square jaw.

Realizing he was still trying to talk me out of hiring him, I offered him the expression of someone unimpressed. "You haven't lifted a hammer in years?" I repeated, shaking my head like I wasn't buying it even for a second. "I'm sure that's stretching the truth."

But he immediately nodded. "I'm rusty, Peyton. It's been a long time."

"So what?" I started.

"So I'm not available," he interrupted, eyeing me pointedly. There wasn't anything in his gaze that said I was annoying or taking the conversation too far. "I stopped the construction business for personal reasons and I'm not in a rush to start up again. I'm enjoyin' my retirement."

"Your retirement?" I reiterated, frowning up at him as I decided to avoid the "personal reasons" discussion at all costs. If he brought up his late wife, I'd be done. There was nothing I could argue that would in any way compensate for his loss. It was much better avoided or, if unavoidable, left alone.

"Yes, I'm retired."

"At thirty-six?" I asked, crossing my arms against my chest. I tried to hide the smile that was already developing on my lips.

"I'll be thirty-seven in a month or so," he answered, also attempting to hide a grin. We ended up looking at one another with puckered lips.

"You have no business being retired at thirty-six or thirty-seven," I muttered.

"Why?" he asked with a shrug, like my point wasn't a good one. "I have plenty to fill up my time—golfin', the gym, spendin' time with friends, with my dogs, and interferin' in my sister's life."

"What sort of dogs do you have?" I asked, suddenly enjoying the image of this man's man interacting with his dogs. Somehow, it made him even more boyish than his dimpled grin. "Wait, let me guess," I interrupted myself. "Something small," I started. "And yippy."

"Small and yippy?" he spat back, going for offended but not quite getting there.

"Yeah, like a miniature pinscher or a Chihuahua or something." Then I smiled even more broadly. "You totally dress them up in little outfits, don't you?"

"Good Lord!" he exhaled loudly as his entire body shook with a baritone laugh. "No, I'm not fond of small dogs." Then he took a breath, still smiling down at me. "I have two Saint Bernards, Peyton," he answered, shaking his head. "A brother and sister—Ralphie and Stella."

"Ralphie as in *A Christmas Story*?" I asked with a smirk. He simply nodded. "And Stella as in . . . Steeellllaaa!" I finished, imitating Marlon Brando in *A Streetcar Named Desire* and not doing too bad a job, if I did say so myself.

"Yep, nicely done there, neighbor," he replied flirtatiously. I felt my heart race at seeing his sly smile and the way his dimples seemed to light up his entire face.

Suddenly feeling uncomfortable, I cleared my throat. "Thanks," I said, emitting a strange sound that halfway resembled a laugh cut short by a croak. "But, um, getting back to my remodel . . ."

"Will you please call one of the contractors on that list I gave you?" he continued as I shook my head. "For the love of God, woman!" He fake bellowed as I continued to shake my head. "Hell, I'll call them for you, if you want."

"No," I answered with finality. "If I can't have you, I'm happy being my own general. I can simply hire people as I need to," I finished, remembering how he'd already advised me against it. I tipped my chin up into the air to make it known that I wouldn't be silenced so easily.

"Good God, woman, you are exasperatin'," Ryan said with a deep, sonorous chuckle. Then he glanced at the house again before running his hand through his wheat-colored, wavy hair. "What you see in this place is beyond me . . ."

"That is *such* a lie!" I ground out. He glanced over at me, surprise ricocheting through his eyes, but I didn't allow him to defend himself. "Ryan Kelly, both you and I are more than aware that you love preserving old things. That's why you got into the construction business to begin with, isn't it? Nope, don't answer," I said, holding my hand up to silence him when it seemed like he was about to. "Just as you have a passion for the historical, so do I."

Ryan smirked down at me but exhaled a breath and leaned against the wall like he knew this soliloquy was going to be a long one. "This should be interestin'."

"I'll have you know I was a history major in college," I started.

"You've got a history degree?" he asked, sounding genuinely interested.

"No, I never finished," I answered with a sigh. "I got married instead to an asshole who thought a history degree was a waste of time."

Ryan's mouth became tight and his eyes took on an angry glow. "I'm sorry to hear that, Peyton."

I shook my head and waved away his concern. "It was a mistake that is now in the past and I don't think about it at all so neither should you."

He smiled and nodded. "You're a smart, strong woman. I like that."

I cocked a self-impressed eyebrow in his direction and continued my monologue. "Going back to my love for history, which echoes yours . . ."

"Ah, yes," Ryan said with a quick nod. "I apologize for interruptin'."

"Where was I?" I asked in mock irritation.

Ryan glanced up at the sky as if he were remembering. "Um, somethin' about me havin' a passion for the historical and you havin' that same passion."

"Right!" I answered with a melodramatic nod. "Just as you found your niche in restoring old, dilapidated, unloved, and unsightly hovels into the mansions they once were, I want to find my niche. I want to experience the satisfaction of seeing this," I glanced around me and sighed. "This . . ."

"Dump?" Ryan asked with a spark in his eyes.

I frowned at him. "This ghost of its former self—"

"Wow, nice one, Pey," he interrupted me.

I shot him a cross look but continued. "I want to breathe life back into this old house not only for myself but for my family too, Ryan. Like I said, I never met my Great-Aunt Myra, and unfortunately, I can't ask my mom about her because she died a long time ago."

I watched Ryan swallow, and with the sadness that suddenly descended into his eyes, I realized he was coming my way. And while part of me felt like maybe I was manipulating him with my sad but true story, I figured it was for his own good anyway—well, at least that's what Trina seemed to think, and I had decided to throw my lot in with hers.

"I'm sorry," he said genuinely.

"Ryan, this house is all I have left of my family. I never knew my father and now that I'm divorced, I have no more connections in the world. It's just me." Yes, it was a bit melodramatic, but it seemed to be working so I was going to go for it. "That's why this house means so much to me and why I can't and won't sell it." I swallowed hard as I realized the truth in my words. "I think of the renovations on this house as the project that's going to get me through the difficulty of my divorce. I know it seems like a huge undertaking to you and the truth is that, yes, it is a huge undertaking, but it's exactly what I need right now."

Ryan was quiet for a few seconds before he finally nodded and exhaled. "I'll make you a deal . . ."

"I'm all ears," I answered with a genuine smile, wondering if he was finally coming around.

"Because I can tell you aren't gonna to stop until I give you an inch," he started and then laughed, "and because you did get me with your sob story, I'm willin' to give you an inch."

"And what exactly would this inch entail?" I asked with an expression of absolute interest, because I was beginning to feel like there might just be a light at the end of the tunnel.

"I'll renovate one bedroom and one bathroom so you can comfortably live in your house while the rest of it is bein' remodeled . . . by someone else."

I frowned and propped my hands on my hips. I thought we'd come so far, but apparently we hadn't. "What, do you think I'm only going to use a bedroom and a bathroom?" I demanded, not meaning to sound so put out, but I *was* disappointed. "I have to eat, man!" I finished with a laugh. It suddenly dawned on me that I was very comfortable around Ryan. I felt like I could be myself and, even better, he seemed to enjoy me being me. Well, judging from the smile on his face anyway, and the way he laughed so much during the course of our conversation. "I thought you said my story meant something to you!"

"It did!" he exclaimed, holding his hands up in mock surrender before dropping them and shaking his head as he exhaled a pent-up breath. "I swear you will drive me to the nuthouse, Peyton Clark!" he finished with a hefty chuckle and a dramatic sigh. "The kitchen is the most work of any room!"

"Oh, please," I said, crunching my lips up like I wasn't impressed. "Cry me a river—to quote Justin Timberlake." Then an idea occurred to me and I beamed up at him, even going so far as to bat my eyelashes. "Ryan, I will see your inch and raise you one more."

"Here we go," he grumbled, but his attention was riveted on me, his eyes buoyant with excitement and undisguised curiosity. "What's your inch?"

I didn't drop my eyes from his. "You remodel the entire bottom floor and make it livable, so I can at least be comfortable while the top two floors are being renovated." I paused for a breath. "I mean, there is that sagging concern, right? You wouldn't want to just renovate two rooms if the house sinks into the ground, now would you?"

"That's not an inch, that's a mile," he muttered, shaking his head in mock exasperation. Well, for all I knew, maybe it was real exasperation at this point.

"Is that a yes?" I asked confidently.

"No."

I narrowed my eyes at him. "Hmm, it sounded like a yes."

"It wasn't."

"I'll take your dogs for a walk every day," I started, searching for any other ideas that might sweeten the pot.

"I already take them for a walk every day, and what's more, I enjoy it."

"I'll do your gardening."

"The gardener does that."

"I'll clean your house."

"Already have a cleanin' lady."

"I'll cook you dinner," I blurted without even really realizing I'd just basically asked him out on a date. Or had I? Was cooking him dinner actually a date? Or was it just being friendly? Neighborly? I wasn't sure how he would take it. Crap, I wasn't even sure how I was taking it! He just stared at me for the next three seconds, saying nothing, so they felt like hours.

"Deal," he finished, and the look in his eyes was suddenly smoldering. It was so primal, I felt my entire body flush in response. Somehow we'd gone from mere flirtatious repartee to something much more passionate—something that felt sensual, magnetic. Well, something that caused goose bumps to travel up and down my arms, anyway.

"Um, good," I started, giggling a horrible sound that I then muffled with my hand. It was more than obvious that I'd lost my cool and sheer nervousness had already set in.

"But we'll have to take a rain check on dinner," Ryan said, seeming completely nonplussed by what just passed between us. He didn't look embarrassed, awkward, nervous . . . nothing. He seemed like he was totally in control of himself, just like he had been a few seconds ago.

"Rain check?" I asked, still feeling like a rock was lodged in my throat.

He chuckled. "Your kitchen isn't exactly in workin' order, is it?"

"Oh!" I said loudly before laughing uncomfortably again. "Yeah, that's right."

He flashed me his pearly whites and shook his head, dropping his gaze to the ground as he chuckled. "You should consider goin' into sales, Peyton, if you aren't already."

"Sales?"

He glanced at me again and nodded vigorously. "Yes, you've got a gift, I reckon. Hell, you convinced me into doin' somethin' I had no intention of doin'."

I laughed, taking it as a compliment. "Well, if it ever comes down to it, I hope I can use you as a reference."

Later that evening, I relaxed in the gold velvet comfort of the two-person sofa in my suite at the Omni Royal hotel. Kicking my feet up on the coffee table, I let out a sigh, which was quickly followed by a self-impressed smile. It had been a long day, but I'd gotten a lot accomplished. Most importantly, I'd somehow worked the miracle of getting Ryan Kelly to agree to participate in my remodel.

Even though I was a bit disappointed that he wouldn't agree to take on the whole project, I wasn't *that* disappointed. On the contrary. I thought I'd actually made leaps and bounds just by getting him to have anything to do with it. Yep, it was definitely better to hope for the best but expect the worst, leaving no room for disappointment—only surprised elation.

After my taxing day, I retired into my makeshift accommodations with a smile on my face and a Dos Equis in my hand. Relaxing on the upholstered couch, I turned the TV on but couldn't say my mind was in any way focused on the images blurring before me, or the nondescript sounds of commercials and sitcoms. Instead, my mind hummed with the possibilities regarding my new home. Ryan suggested I spend the next few rainy days hunting for images of home interiors that I liked—something to give him an idea of my taste. I figured I could pay a visit to the bookstore tomorrow where I could look through as many *Better Homes and Gardens*–type magazines as I could find. For now, though, I just wanted to relax and bathe in the glow of my successful day.

It was maybe a few hours ago that I'd unloaded my entire wardrobe into the closet, which hadn't been an easy feat. As part of my "deal" with Ryan, I'd agreed to live in the Omni hotel just until Ryan finished fixing up the guest room and bathroom on the first floor. After they were done, I'd move back into my house. He imagined it wouldn't take much longer than a week or two to renovate the small bathroom and bedroom. I figured I could handle living at the hotel until then.

Completely relaxed, I was startled by the sound of a shrill ring. Realizing it was the hotel phone, I reached for it, my heart still hammering away in my ears. "Hello?" I answered.

"See? I knew you'd be able to pull it off," Trina laughed into the receiver. "I just spoke with Ryan and forced him to give me all the details. I had all the faith in the world in you, girl!"

"Well, I wouldn't say it was easy," I replied with a smile. Downing the last gulp of my beer, I thought about getting another one. "I had to pull out all the stops!"

"I have to admit, I'm impressed, honey," Trina continued. "You did good, Peyton, and he wasn't exactly happy that I put you up to it! Believe me, I got read the riot act!"

"Well, hopefully he doesn't think you're the only reason I pressured him!" I said, concerned that Ryan might think I was just acting on his sister's behalf. I mean, I valued him too!

"Nah, he knows he's good at what he does," Trina said in a tone that said she was brushing off my worry. "Anyhow, I can't tell you how thrilled I am. This is exactly what that boy needs, Peyton." She paused for a second or two. "So, I just wanted to call to say thank you."

"There's really no need, Trina," I started.

"No need!" she scoffed. "You've managed to do the unthinkable! Gettin' that stubborn man to agree to anything is a feat in and of itself."

"Well, he could always back out . . ."

"His word is his bond," Trina answered flatly, as I wondered if I'd offended her. A few seconds later, though, her original enthusiasm was back. "Ryan will come through for you, best believe it!"

"I hope so!" I laughed, deciding to go for the next beer. "I never did get around to discussing a price with him . . ."

"Don't you worry, my brother is a good man. He'll give you a fair price."

I nodded, then realized she couldn't see me. Collapsing into the sofa, I pried the top off the beer bottle and propped one foot over the other on top of the coffee table. "I'm not worried about it. I just wish this rain would let up so he could get started!"

"Amen to that!" She laughed, then sighed like she was in a hurry. "I gotta run, doll, but you just holler if you need anything at all, you hear me?"

I laughed. "Loud and clear."

"And, thanks again, Peyton. I . . . I can't tell you how much this means to me. I owe you one!"

"Since you're giving me a free ride here at the hotel, let's call it even," I said, finally feeling comfortable that I could somehow repay my debt. I definitely didn't like feeling indebted to anyone. I never had.

"Agreed," Trina said with a small laugh, hanging up as I did the same.

I sat up with a start, my breath caught in my throat as my heartbeat echoed in my ears. I blinked a few times; the darkness in the room cast everything in navy blue. Glancing around, I vaguely recognized my surroundings—a massive television ahead of me and a four-person dining table to my right. I was still in the hotel suite, and more specifically, the living room of the hotel suite.

I rubbed my eyes and tried to remember what caused me to wake up in a cold sweat. There was an overall feeling of dread settling in my stomach, as if I'd just witnessed something far beyond frightening, something horrible. The strange thing, though, was that I couldn't put my finger on just what "it" was. Normally, I could easily recall my dreams, or nightmares, as soon as I woke up; but in this case, there was just a blank void in my head, an empty slate.

I took a deep breath and tried to allay my fears, to calm the feeling of unease that was still upsetting my stomach.

It was just a nightmare, Peyton! I reprimanded myself. *Stop acting like a child!*

My gaze fell on the two empty beer bottles still sitting on the coffee table, and I wondered if they were the source of my less than refreshing catnap on the sofa. Checking the clock on the wall, I realized it was midnight. Way past my bedtime. I stood up and, using the light of the moon as it streamed in through the French doors, I wandered over to the bedroom, where I tore off my clothes and unceremoniously tossed them on the floor. Heading into the bathroom, I nearly blinded myself when I flipped on the switch. After blinking a few times against the garish light, the first object to catch my attention was a scale lazily leaning against the wall.

Overwhelming feelings of revulsion and anger welled up inside me and I immediately grabbed the offensive thing, shoving it under the sink cabinet. It certainly didn't belong to me, which meant it must have been supplied by the hotel. Not that I blamed them. I mean, how could anyone here know how much I detested scales? They couldn't.

I shook my head as memories started to plague me, pouring through my head even though I tried my best to ignore them. I sat down on the toilet and cradled my head in my hands, forcing my eyes shut so I could erase the stream of images already unleashing themselves before my eyelids . . .

Every week Jonathon subjected me to the same thing . . . every week he insisted I step on the scale in front of him to ensure I wasn't even a half pound over one hundred and thirty. And if I was heavier, the ensuing conversation was arduous—was I comfort-eating? And if so, what was wrong with me? Wasn't I aware of how fortunate I was? Was I pushing myself hard enough at the gym? Didn't I care about my marriage enough to maintain my figure? Didn't I understand that there were countless women who would jump at the opportunity to be in my place? Didn't I realize how lucky I was to be Mrs. Jonathon Graves?

As soon as we separated and I moved out, I left the scale with Jonathon, telling him all those women who were dying to be weighed in my place could have it! I hadn't weighed myself in over a month and I never planned to weigh myself again. I could tell I'd put on weight, but I didn't care. If anything, the five or ten pounds suited me—I had curves again—a butt and boobs that actually made my waist look smaller. And my face was softer, not so angular. I looked younger, or so I thought. . . . I definitely looked happier.

I felt tears start in my eyes and blinked them back. I wouldn't cry. The past was the past and I was firmly rooted in the future, in my own present. That didn't include Jonathon or any of his head trips. I was my own person now, free to live my life the way I chose to.

I arrived at my house at eight a.m. sharp on Monday morning. The rain had finally let up, so today would mark the first day of my remodel. To say I was excited was an understatement. In fact, I'd endured a restless night of sleep in my suite at the Omni, my brain too busy with thoughts of crown molding, colors of paint, stains of hardwood floors, and light fixtures.

When I pulled up, I noticed there were already two enormous white trucks parked just outside my sprawling home. One of the Ford F350s was actually parked on the roots of an ancient oak tree that spread into the street, causing the concrete sidewalk and the asphalt to crumble away. With the two trucks hogging the street in front of my house, I was forced to park at the top of Prytania Street, where it intersected Eighth Street. Unluckily for me, my house didn't come with a garage.

Men strolled in and out of my double front doors, carrying all sorts of tools while they attempted to balance their coffee cups in their free hands. From the looks of it, Ryan was able to find six or so men to make up his crew. Not bad for someone who complained about the task being a difficult one . . .

Once I killed the Scout's engine, I hopped down from the driver's seat and jogged around to the other side of the truck, opening the passenger door and reaching for my safety helmet and tool belt (already supplied with an impressive array of tools) and then buried my purse behind the passenger seat, underneath my rain jacket.

Plopping the safety helmet on, I hurriedly fastened the work belt around my waist and smiled at my reflection in the window. The plastic helmet and the leather tool belt were exactly the same shade of bubblegum pink as my lip gloss. The hammer, pliers, utility knife, chalk line, and even the carpenter's pencil were all a corresponding pink. To break the cloying sweetness of the ensemble, though, was a repeating pattern of black skulls and crossbones on the handles of each tool, and the belt had a checkerboard pattern. The safety helmet also echoed the skull-and-crossbones theme but had a large bow on top of the skull, imbuing it with a girly sort of macabre touch.

Gripping my cup of coffee, I started up the front walkway, making sure I smiled and said "good morning" to each of the guys who passed me. Granted, most of them looked confused—I wasn't sure if it was due to my outfit or my being there.

"I like it!" one of them called out as he eyed me up and down while nodding appreciatively on his way out the front door.

"Thanks!" I called back as I made my way into the foyer and immediately recognized Ryan standing at the end of it, in conversation with a shorter, older, and chubbier man. Ryan's back was to me, but the breadth of his shoulders and his golden hair gave him away. At the sound of my voice, he turned around but didn't say or do anything for the space of three or four seconds as he apparently took stock of me. Feeling slightly squeamish beneath his scrutiny, I smiled sheepishly.

That was when a scowl took hold of his lips. "Oh, hell no!" he exclaimed, shaking his head as he took a few steps toward me, his eyebrows still arched in surprise.

"Well, good morning to you too, neighbor!" I answered with a mirror of the puzzled frown he continued to give me.

"Please tell me it's Halloween an' you decided to go as some sort of"—he seemed at a loss for words as he first studied my helmet and then my tool belt—"pirate-themed construction worker?"

I laughed, taking a swig of my coffee before swallowing and clearing my throat. No, we hadn't talked about whether or not I could be one of his crew members; and yes, I'd already figured he wouldn't be exactly pleased when I revealed my intentions. "No, Ryan, it's not Halloween."

"Then why are you wearin' that ridiculous getup?"

I pouted, feeling slightly offended that he didn't find my whole "getup" charming. And, really, "ridiculous" was an exaggeration. "I'm wearing this because I figured no one would appreciate it if I borrowed *their* tools," I started, motioning to my belt before fingering the brim of my safety helmet. "And as for this, well, safety first, right?" I smiled wistfully.

Ryan crossed his arms against his chest, and his lips were tight. "Peyton, we never discussed, and furthermore, I never agreed to havin' you . . . here . . . workin'."

"Well, then this is your lucky day because you've got one extra crew member and you don't even have to pay me!" I held my arms out wide and did a funny jig sort of thing with my feet, like I was practicing for vaudeville before finishing the routine with a flash of jazz hands.

Ryan couldn't help his smirk, try though he did. It took him a good few seconds to banish the grin from his mouth. "No way," he said, shaking his head, although it wasn't lost on me that he was fighting against another smile—I mean, I *had* used jazz hands on him. . . . Moments later, apparently when he realized exactly what I was proposing, there was no hint of amusement in his eyes or on his lips at all. "It's way too dangerous."

"I won't get in the way, I promise," I started, instantly dropping my previous song and dance. "I really want to be a part of the remodel, though, Ryan."

"Bloody hell," he grumbled as he glanced down at the floor and shook his head again, running a hand through the unruly waves of golden hair. Of course, it did occur to me that he might take extreme exception to having me on the job, after what happened to his wife, but I wasn't going to let that stand in my way. What happened in the past was the past, and the chances of something similar happening again were next to nil. Besides, I wanted to be involved in my remodel.

"Looks like you've got your hands full," the man Ryan was in conversation with announced before offering me a quick smile.

"Hi, I'm Peyton," I said, extending my hand, which he heartily accepted with his own sweaty one.

"I'm George Tate," he responded, and his round face, laughing eyes, and red cheeks made him look like he could have been a good Santa Claus.

"George is the owner of Tate Construction," Ryan added. "I invited George over to give me his opinion on your remodel. He's incredibly well known around these parts and very talented."

"Said by a true artist," George answered, patting Ryan on the back before bringing his attention to the room around him and sighing. "You've got quite the job here, Kelly, quite the job."

Ryan's eyes met mine when he responded and they didn't stray. "Unfortunately, sometimes you can't talk your way out of such things."

I frowned, arching one eyebrow to indicate I wasn't feeling sorry for him. George apparently caught my expression because he laughed. "I can't recall you ever agreein' to anything you didn't want to do," he said, nudging Ryan in the arm with his plump elbow.

"I knew it!" I said, grasping the life raft George threw me as I elbowed Ryan's other side.

"Ouch! Will both of you stop attackin' me?" Ryan demanded.

George and I laughed at the same time while I shook my head and crossed my arms over my chest, eyeing George with a frown.

"Do you know that he gave me a huge guilt trip over agreeing to take on this job?"

"It appears like it was a war of wills," George answered matter-of-factly.

"Some advice, George; never go up against her because you *will* lose!" Ryan said with the hint of a laugh.

George just shook his head and smirked at the both of us, like he knew something we didn't. "Well, I've got places to go an' people to see," he said as he turned on his heel and started for the front door. Apparently remembering himself, he called over his shoulder, "Nice to meet you, Miss Peyton!"

"You too!" I sang to his retreating figure before bringing my attention back to Ryan, only to find his gaze still on me.

"You can give me all the crappy jobs," I continued, pursuing my argument to convince him to hire me, for lack of a better word. "I'll do coffee runs for the guys, lunch, you name it," I persisted, starting to sound desperate. I glanced down at my tool belt. "I can hammer stuff, screw stuff in . . ." I pulled out the measuring tape. "I can even measure!"

Ryan sighed long and hard while continuing to shake his head, but I could see a twinkle of amusement lighting up his eyes. Before long, a recalcitrant smirk captured the ends of his lips, forcing them upward into something that resembled a smile. "You are gonna be the death of me, Peyton Clark," he grumbled. I didn't say anything but allowed him to study my helmet before his eyes fell to my waist again, and he seemed to be taking mental stock of my tools.

"Come on, you like it," I prodded. He glanced up at me but said nothing, so I continued, "You think I actually look incredibly cute with my matching pink toolwear."

"Toolwear?" he asked with a shake of his head.

I nodded. "Yeah, that's what I call it. Fashionable tools, you know?"

He chuckled, his warm eyes settling on mine. "If you must know, Peyton, yes, I do like it. I think you look incredibly"—he looked me up and down—"cute."

"I'll take it."

He continued to inspect me, looking as if he were at a loss for words. "Where did you find all that ridiculous stuff, anyhow?"

I beamed, pleased I'd apparently won the argument over whether or not my ridiculous stuff and I could stay on. Then I glanced down at my fingernails before buffing them against my white button-down shirt and gave him my best smug expression. "Oh, just at the hardware store."

He shook his head again and started forward, glancing quickly behind him when I didn't take his lead. "Are you comin' or what?"

"Yessir, boss, sir!" I said in the best serviceman impersonation I could muster as I hopped forward before saluting him.

"Wrong hand," he said with the expression of someone unimpressed. "Always salute with your right hand."

"Whatever!" I responded with an indifferent wave of my hand as I followed him down the hallway into the guest room, located at the easternmost corner of the house. I could already hear the sounds of demolition, and the air was thick with dust from what, I imagined, was the drywall being torn down.

"Gotta pair of gloves in that silly getup?" Ryan asked, glancing over his shoulder at me.

"Shoot," I said with real disappointment as I shook my head.

"What? They didn't have any pink ones?" he asked with a laugh.

I shrugged. "Maybe, I just forgot to look."

"Well, I'm sure we can find an extra pair for you somewhere around here, but put them on your shoppin' list."

"Sir, yessir!" This time, I saluted him the proper way.

"Good Lord!" he grumbled. "If you weren't so damn cute, I would've fired you a long time ago!"

As soon as we entered the guest room, I noticed two men working demolition—each on opposite sides of the room. Ryan approached the man closer to us, who was covered in fine white dust. The man pulled down his breathing mask and smiled at both of us.

"How's it goin'?" Ryan asked as he leaned onto his knees and inspected the nearly bare wall. The man had half of one wall completely stripped down to the studs. Ryan ran his fingers across the rough surface of one of the studs, dipping his fingernail into what looked like honeycomb in the wood. "Termites?" Ryan asked his worker.

The man pointed at a few of the studs. "Yeah, but looks like it's old damage. Ain't come across nothin' new . . . yet."

Ryan nodded as I stepped over the pile of debris on the floor. Glancing down, I recognized large pieces of drywall; the remains of aged flowery blue wallpaper; and what looked like whitewashed wooden boards. I reached down and picked up one of the boards, which was maybe a foot long by a foot wide. I wasn't sure why it caught my attention, but I flipped it over all the same, only to find a very aged and yellow newspaper clipping attached to the back of it. The heading of the newspaper was torn, presumably from when it was ripped off the wall, but I could make out that the rest of it was an advertisement of some sort. There was a torn image of a horse and beneath that, the words: "Use Jona's Salve to Keep Your Horse in Good Health!"

Realizing its significance, and that I was uncovering a historic time capsule, I couldn't help thinking there was probably a whole lot more of it behind the façade of the wall. I felt my anticipation growing. "Wait!" I called out to Ryan as he started for the other side of the room, to talk to the other man on demolition duty. When he turned to face me, I excitedly held up the newspaper clipping. "Look!"

"Ah, this one used newspaper too?" Ryan asked, wearing an expression of mild interest as he faced both the men in the room.

The one nearest me nodded. "Found quite a few glued to the wall beneath these stubborn-ass boards!" The man held his crowbar up like he was ready to dig back into the wall again when I stopped him short by stepping in front of him. My attention, however, was on Ryan.

"You can't just go in and demolish this room if there are ancient newspapers on the walls!" I protested. "That's sacrilege!"

Ryan shook his head. "Peyton, it was a common practice hundreds of years ago to use newspapers as insulation. I've come across this situation countless times."

"And you just trash them?" I asked, my mouth agape in horror.

"The newspapers are usually so torn up by the time we're finished, we have no choice," Ryan answered, not particularly bothered by the fact. "And homeowners rarely want to take the time to salvage somethin' that usually is already illegible, owin' to its age."

"Oh my gosh," I continued, shaking my head as I turned back to the pile of debris. "I can't even fathom that," I continued as I bent down and started rifling through it, separating out the pieces of antique newspaper as I came across them. Ryan wasn't exaggerating—most of the newspaper was reduced to mere scraps, thanks to the demolition. I glanced up at him and frowned. "These newspapers represent moments in time that will never exist again," I said in a hollow voice as I looked at the fragments of a bygone era surrounding me. "And time is so fleeting." I glanced up at Ryan again and shrugged. "Maybe that's why I always found history so fascinating and why I decided to major in it."

Ryan nodded and then offered me a hearty smile. "You believe in preservin' the past."

"I do," I agreed as I continued rummaging through the pile. At the bottom of the mound, I recovered a full page that was safeguarded by the wooden board it was attached to. Pulling it free from the wood fibers, I smoothed it out against the floor and found myself gazing at the portrait of what appeared to be a policeman.

If I had to guess, I would have deemed the article as dating from around the early twentieth century—the image just didn't appear older than that. There wasn't a title or a date accompanying the picture that might have given me an indication of the year it was printed, but judging by the officer's somewhat contemporary uniform, I figured the article couldn't have been *that* old.

As far as I could tell, the man was sitting (the article was ripped just above his hips) and his hands might have been clasped in his lap. He was facing the camera, and even though the clipping was incredibly old and faded, it was still very obvious that whoever this officer was, he was exceedingly handsome. He wasn't smiling, but there was an echo of something flirtatious in his eyes. The longer I studied him, the more I wondered whether it was a "come hither" expression in his gaze, or a cold, calculating one. It completely depended on whether I imagined the person taking the picture to be a woman or a man. Regardless, he looked like he was in his early thirties maybe, and his clean-shaven face revealed a square jaw, high cheekbones, a pronounced but symmetrical nose, masculine eyebrows, and penetrating, large eyes. I couldn't make out whether his hair was dark or light as it was eclipsed by the modern-looking officer's cap. His shoulders were broad and his neck thick. His officer's jacket was dark, maybe navy, black, or charcoal gray. Three metal buttons appeared on either side of his collar, and his badge shone on his left side, along with a nameplate above it. I strained my eyes to make out his name, but failed.

"What did you find?" Ryan asked as he approached me. I glanced up at him and offered him the newspaper. After studying it for a few seconds, he handed it back to me. "Hmm, cops back then looked pretty similar to today."

I nodded and, gazing at the image again, felt myself zoning out on the officer's eyes. That was when I remembered there was probably a whole minefield of undiscovered history still behind what remained of the walls. I darted over to the wall and shoved my hand behind the drywall that was still intact.

"Bloody hell, Peyton, you're gonna snag yourself on a nail!" Ryan objected.

"I'm fine," I answered absentmindedly, fingering the edge of a piece of paper attached to another board. I glanced at Ryan and beamed. "There's more here!"

"Peyton," he started and shook his head. "If we lollygag around with this, it's goin' to push your job out even longer!"

As soon as I recalled the officer's eyes, I shook my head emphatically. It was a bizarre reaction I had to him—but I knew I couldn't allow whatever existed beyond the walls to be further damaged. There was a calm certainty that took over me—an absolute assurance that I needed to make sure nothing else beyond the walls was damaged. It almost felt as if a foreign being was somehow in control of me. But of course, that was ridiculous.

"I don't care," I said with finality as I turned to face the men in the room. "I want these boards removed carefully." I was quiet as I continued fingering the brittle pieces of newspaper when something dawned on me. "Ryan, these weren't used as insulation."

"Why do you say that?"

"Because they're single sheets of paper, not entire newspapers."

Ryan approached the wall and inspected it before taking a step back and nodding at me. "I think you're right. Ordinarily, we find whole newspapers wadded up and shoved into the recesses of the wall."

"But these are stuck to the boards, which tells me that someone posted them on the wall and then boarded them up later," I finished.

Ryan cocked his head to the side before nodding. "Could be." Then he sighed as he apparently realized what a behemoth undertaking he now faced. "Peyton, are you sure you want to bother with this?"

"Yes," I answered immediately before offering him a big smile. "I can help."

He shook his head, but his eyes settled on what was remaining of the wall. He was quiet for a few seconds before he faced the man nearer him. "The best way to do this is to remove the drywall first. Just be careful that you don't go very deep. When you're down to the whitewashed boards, lemme know."

The man nodded as Ryan faced me again and expelled a pent-up breath. "Lunch is on you," he said with a slight smirk, while poking me in the upper arm with his index finger.

"So what do you know about my house?" I asked Ryan, reaching for a French fry on his plate, before smiling apologetically for mooching it.

He cocked a single brow at me but smiled all the same. I thought lunch being on me meant that I'd buy all the guys lunch, but I'd come to find that Ryan had only meant him. It was just as well because I enjoyed any alone time I could get with him. I felt like there was definitely something between Ryan and me, but I wasn't sure exactly what "it" was—just casual, innocent flirtation or something more?

On Ryan's suggestion, we piled into the Scout and I drove us to the French Quarter, where we tucked into a tiny, deli-like restaurant called Johnny's on St. Louis Street.

"Like I told you before when we were talkin' about your Great-Aunt Myra, I don't know much about her or your house," Ryan answered as he took an enormous bite of his catfish po'boy, chomping it for a few seconds before wiping his mouth with a napkin and taking a few sips of his Coke. He smiled and asked, "Are you gonna dive into that or what?" before motioning to the alligator sausage triple-decker po'boy I'd ordered.

"I'm still deciding," I answered honestly. I'd never had alligator before, but Ryan convinced me it was the be all and end all. As for a triple-decker on Texas Toast? Yep, that was his idea too—promising he'd finish whatever I didn't.

"Dive in, girl!" he said with a laugh, hiding his fries behind his gigantic hand. "Or else you're cut off from my fries."

I eyed my side salad forlornly before frowning at him. Then, taking a deep breath, I picked up my alligator sandwich. "Here goes!" I took a bite and after a few chews, realized it was actually pretty tasty. Heavier than chicken and more like the consistency of steak, it wasn't scummy or moldy at all, as one might expect of a swamp-dwelling creature.

"So?" Ryan asked, leaning toward me.

I finished my mouthful and sipped on my iced tea. "It's actually not bad."

"Not bad as in . . . good?"

"I don't know. Let me take another bite." I held the sandwich up to my lips, but before I took a bite, I added, "While I'm chewing, you can tell me what you *do* know about my house."

"So demandin'!" he teased me with a laugh before taking a deep breath. "I've lived on Prytania Street for, oh, ten years now."

"You bought your house when you were twenty-six?" I asked, surprised.

"Peyton, your mouth is still full," he pointed out with a shake of his head and a put-on wince.

"Sorry," I managed with a sheepish smile, my mouth no less full.

He chuckled before remembering my question. "I've been doin' construction since I was twenty, an' luckily for me, I was good at it. So, yes, to answer your question, I bought my house when I was twenty-six."

I sipped the last of my iced tea through the straw until it snored when it encountered the ice cubes. Ryan raised his brows at me, but I just smiled and mooched another of his fries. "I'd love to see it sometime." I was suddenly struck with the notion of how completely refreshing it was to be able to be as candid as I was right now, to be able to be silly and flirty. They were feelings that had been foreign to me for years. And now, as I laughed and played with Ryan, I felt like I was coming into my own again, relearning what it felt like to be Peyton Clark.

"You always have an open invitation. You should know that."

"Why should I? It's not like you ever invited me . . .," I said with a shrug as I stole another fry and used the last of his ketchup. He smiled and, grabbing the bottle, squeezed out another red mound on the corner of his plate. I plopped the fry in my mouth and moaned with pleasure. "These fries are so good!"

"Mouth full!" Ryan chided me.

"Blah," I waved him away.

"Well, I apologize for not invitin' you," he started, while intercepting my attempt to steal a long and especially doughy-looking fry, plopping it into his own mouth with a smug smile.

"Hey!" I swatted his upper arm, feigning offense as he finished his mouthful.

"It never actually crossed my mind that I hadn't invited you over," he continued. "But I would like it known that you, Peyton Clark, the most stubborn woman I've ever met, with the worst table manners I've ever seen, are always welcome at my home."

I laughed and couldn't stop the blush across my cheeks. Sometimes he just said things that made me melt. "Thanks, Ryan."

"And as to what I do know about your house," he started, reaching over to grab my alligator sandwich with both hands. "I'm guessin' you're finished with this since you haven't touched it in the last five minutes?"

I just nodded. "Let's switch. I'll eat the rest of your fries."

"Deal," he answered, taking such a huge bite of my alligator triple-decker sandwich that only two-thirds of it remained.

"Jeez, careful you don't swallow your hand!"

He waved me away in the same way I had earlier. Then, once his mouth was empty, he continued. "For the entire time I've lived on Prytania Street, Myra owned your house."

"And you said you stopped in to check on her a handful of times?"

He shook his head. "Well, truthfully, it was more often than that. I would visit her about once a month to make sure the house was in order and she wasn't in want of anythin'."

"Nice work you did for her on the leaky roof, by the way," I taunted him.

He held his hands up in mock defense. "Hey, she died five or six years ago and the house just sat there, empty, before it fell into disrepair. I had nothin' to do with that leaky roof!"

"She died five or six years ago?" I asked, finding the news surprising. "I wonder why it only came to me recently?"

Ryan shook his head as if to say he didn't know. "Maybe the courts had a hard time locatin' you?"

I nodded, thinking that made sense given the fact that I never even knew I had a Great-Aunt Myra and my mom had been deceased for quite some time. Whatever the reason, all that mattered now was that the house was mine. "So you didn't know much about Myra?" I continued. "Do you have any idea who that policeman pictured in the newspaper was?"

He shook his head. "No clue. I do remember Myra saying she'd lived in the house with her mother, who'd owned it since the thirties. I reckon those newspapers are about that old?"

"Maybe thereabouts or the twenties would be my guess."

Ryan nodded. "As to the identity of your mystery cop, I have no idea. I guess we'll have to wait and find out once we get the rest of those boards down."

It was a mystery I couldn't wait to solve.

I was so anxious to uncover the riddle regarding the newspaper clippings that I spent the majority of the evening pulling nails from the whitewashed boards in order to free up the pages behind them. Both of Ryan's men who had been working demolition on the guest room were able to remove the remaining drywall on all four walls without upsetting the boards underneath.

As I busily pulled nail after nail from the splitting, aged planks of wood, my thoughts were mostly centered on Ryan Kelly. Despite my attempts to hide the obvious from myself—my undeniable attraction to him—doing so was pointless. There was no way I could fool myself into thinking that I was some sort of detached ice queen who could control my wayward emotions as easily as flicking off a switch. I couldn't. And even though I was convinced as a new divorcee, I shouldn't have any interest in the opposite sex for at least a year, it was now obvious to me that I was simply deluding myself.

Try as I might, I couldn't get Ryan off my mind. I genuinely cared for him and what was more, I hoped he cared for me . . . as something more than a friend. I mean, of course I valued his friendship enough that if he chose to see me in a purely platonic way, I could definitely deal with it. But that wasn't to say I didn't hope there might be something more.

I faced the wall again and realized I was finally pulling the nails from the last wooden board. Once I freed both nails, I pulled the board off the wall and discarded it into a pile in the middle of the floor, which was now nearly as tall as I.

Before Ryan's men started removing the remaining drywall, I ransacked the two piles of debris on the floor to salvage whatever newspaper clippings I could find. My attempts didn't amount to much—just a few tattered articles that were so ripped, they weren't legible and probably would end up being thrown away. I couldn't say I was *that* concerned, though, because as soon as I was able to remove the whitewashed boards on the wall facing me, I found my holy grail.

From floor to ceiling, and spanning the entire width of the wall, which had to be twenty feet, were yellowed newspaper pages still clinging to the boards beneath them. As I stared at the articles and images that had been meticulously excised a long time ago and were now displayed before me, my mind raced with the need to read and inspect each one. I took a few steps closer, suddenly irritated with the sun for setting. Now all I had to rely on was the overhead fluorescent lighting of a two-foot-long shop light. It threw garish shadows against the walls in some areas and was so exceptionally bright in others, it was like trying to read a blob of gray print in a blazing spotlight.

"What do we have here?" I whispered aloud, taking another step closer. My gaze was affixed to another picture of the young police officer. This one depicted him in a three-piece black suit and a tie. He was offering a smile and handshake to a beefy woman who resembled a large hen with her pointy nose, billowy cheeks, miniature chin, and beady eyes. The enormous plumes exploding from a comical hat perched precariously on her head completed the fowlish comparison. She was smiling coyly at the handsome officer, but I couldn't make out the expression on his face as he was depicted only in profile. Above the image, the headline read: "Corporal Drake Montague Greets Guests at Gala Benefitting Charity Hospital."

So I now had an identity for the devastatingly handsome young man whose police portrait I'd uncovered in the rubble earlier. I wasn't sure why, but my discovery made me inordinately pleased. In learning his name, maybe I'd somehow opened a door to the past—a door that was, for all intents and purposes, buried in time and hidden by myriad whitewashed boards.

With renewed fervor, I shifted my gaze to another article, just below the one regarding the Charity Hospital Gala. The *Times-Picayune* was displayed across the top of the page in bold Edwardian script. Beneath it were the words: "New Orleans, Friday, May 24, 1918."

"1918! Aha!" I said out loud, not exactly sure why I felt the need to speak, considering the only ears listening were my own. "Scene of the Latest New Orleans Murder," I read as my eyes skimmed the image of a rustic one-story house. The words "Grocery and Bar. Joe Maggio" were painted on the fascia board along the top of one wall. Just beneath the image of the store and bar was a picture of Mr. and Mrs. Maggio. Mr. Maggio's suit was complete with a vest, and he had a handlebar moustache. Mrs. Maggio's updo and high-necked black dress made the picture look as if it dated from the late nineteenth century.

"Joseph Maggio and his wife, from a photograph taken on their wedding day fifteen years ago, and the house in which they were killed while asleep in their bed." I read the caption appearing just below the image of the Maggios. Above the caption was a picture of the layout of the Maggios' home, showing how the killer entered the home by way of the back door, apparently, chiseling out a panel of it. A dotted line revealed the trajectory the killer took, showing how he traveled through the kitchen and the hall before executing his grisly task in the Maggios' bedroom.

I couldn't help but wonder if the handsome policeman were involved in the crime, so I read the lengthy article, only to discover that the unfortunate Maggios were hacked to death by their own ax before having their throats slit with a razor. Apparently, the brother of Joseph Maggio was charged with the murder, but nowhere was there mention of Drake Montague. I took a deep breath and realized my heart was racing. I could definitely recognize the fact that I was intrigued by the story but there was something else lurking just below my fascination and that felt very much like fear.

I quickly turned my attention to the article at the left of this one and read the title: "Another Hatchet Mystery; Man and Wife Near Death." This article also managed to make the front page of the *Times-Picayune*, and judging by the date, occurred roughly a month after the Maggio murder. I scanned the next newspaper clipping, which appeared just below that one, and noticed it, too, dealt with what appeared to be a spree of ax-related crimes. The title of this article was: "Police Believe Axeman May Be Active in City," the byline reading, "One Explanation of Murderous Assault on Mrs. Edward Schneider." This article was dated August 6, 1918, just three months after the Maggios' murders.

Now faced with a mystery, I was only too excited to uncover why these articles had been pasted all over the room. I immediately turned my attention to the clippings appearing at the bottom of the wall. All three had ties to the ax murders, the third referring to the killer as the "Axeman." My heart strumming in my chest, I hurried past the pile of debris beside me and skimmed the subject lines of the various articles still remaining on the wall.

"Victim of Axeman Is Near Death After Operation," I read out loud. I skimmed through five more articles, which all named additional victims of the Axeman's wrath. When I reached the headline farthest from me, at the bottom of the wall, I stopped short. The date read March 10, 1919, and, beneath the title "Three Gretna

Victims of Ax Murderer," there was an image of a child dressed in a long white nightgown. Although her hair was cut short, it was obvious she was a little girl by her outfit, as well as her large, innocent eyes. I imagined she must have been about two or three years old at the time the photograph was taken. Below her picture was the portrait of a couple I supposed were her parents—a man and woman on their wedding day—and beside them, an image of their home, which also happened to serve as a store. Above that image was another map detailing the dotted-line route the Axeman took from his point of entry at the back door to their bedroom. The depiction of three bodies sprawled atop the bed made my heart sink. I read the caption: "These photographs show the Cortimiglia family, victims of the latest axeman mystery, and their Gretna home. The child, Mary, aged two years, was slain outright. Charles Cortimiglia is dying in Charity Hospital. His wife's condition is serious."

I took a step back and felt my shoulders droop. Any excitement I previously felt with the discovery of Drake Montague and my curiosity regarding why these articles were glued to the walls dissipated instantly. Instead, I was left with an overwhelming sense of grief. Even though the death of this child occurred nearly one hundred years ago, I couldn't suppress the overwhelming tide of heartache that surged through me.

I couldn't focus on my sorrow long, however, because I was suddenly covered in goose bumps from head to toe. I rubbed my arms to ward off the sudden arctic chill in the air and glanced around myself, searching for an open window that might explain the sudden plunge in temperature. Finding both of the windows latched and secure, I turned around and started for the door, wondering if maybe there was an open window in the hallway? Fear was already burrowing its way into my gut, and I took a deep breath, all the while asking myself why I felt so afraid of a simple chill in the air? I exhaled and saw the cloud of my hot breath directly in front of me. That was, in one word . . . strange.

I stopped short as the thud of heavy footsteps filled my ears. It sounded as if they were directly above me, as the ceiling creaked just above my head. My heart pounding in my ears, I didn't realize I was holding my breath until I felt light-headed. I exhaled, only to inhale once more as I stayed stock-still and listened for more footsteps. I couldn't help wondering if I'd simply imagined the first set. But I knew better. I hadn't imagined them. I'd heard them as clearly as if someone walked up right beside me.

If someone was in the room directly above me, that meant he or she was in the master bedroom, the bedroom I'd been sleeping in up until I moved to the Omni hotel. I exhaled again, still able to see my breath on the air in a frosty display dissipating into the ether. The heavy footfalls started up again. This time, it sounded as if someone was walking to the far side of the room, as if to look out the window.

Now convinced it wasn't my imagination and that someone was in my house, I seemed to go into autopilot, reaching into my jeans pocket and producing my cell phone. I immediately turned to Ryan's contact info and clicked the "Text" icon.

At my house. I think someone broke in. I hear footsteps above me, I typed. I hit "Send" and then gulped while straining to hear more footsteps that might give some sort of indication as to where the intruder was. Nothing but the still Southern air responded.

How could there be someone upstairs, Peyton? I asked myself. *You never heard anyone go upstairs in the first place! What's more, wouldn't you have heard them breaking in?*

I couldn't answer my questions because I hadn't heard the front door open, nor any windows breaking; and it was true, I never heard any footsteps going up the stairs in the first place. The guest bedroom I was currently standing in was located down the short hallway from the foyer, which meant I would definitely have heard something if someone came through the front door. So how was it possible for someone to be upstairs? Maybe they broke in earlier and just waited around for everyone to leave? That seemed to be the most plausible explanation.

It doesn't matter how he got in, Peyton! I chided myself. *All that matters is there's someone in your house now!*

When my phone vibrated in my hand, I nearly dropped it. My next thought was that my heart was pounding so hard, I could be experiencing cardiac arrest. But realizing the buzz was a simple text notification, I unlocked the screen and read: *Try to get out. Either front door or window. If you can't get out, hide and be quiet. I'm on my way.*

I glanced down the hallway to the front door, glimpsing the staircase off to the left side. Could I make it to the front door without the intruder seeing me? And if the front door was locked, how long would it take me to unlock it before the guy was on me? More importantly, did he have a gun? Would he just shoot me if he saw me? And, really, who could say he was even still upstairs? I hadn't heard anything in a while so maybe he'd sneaked downstairs and in my attempt to flee, maybe I would run right into him?

I turned around and spied the only two windows in the room, which were maybe three feet wide by three feet tall. Figuring they were a better option than the front door, I started tiptoeing forward. Even though I was already halfway across the room when I started back toward the wall, it seemed like it took an eternity to reach the other side. And in the mere seconds it truly took to reach the wall, I didn't hear so much as a peep from upstairs. Nervous that the intruder was either listening for me or on his way downstairs, I attempted to push the windowpane up and open. But it wouldn't budge. I tried again, this time throwing my entire body into it, but the thing just sat there, defying me. Cursing beneath my breath, I didn't waste any time and moved to the other window. But just like its neighbor, this one was also painted shut.

Okay, so getting out is not an option, I said to myself. *Plan B . . . Hide.*

I released a pent-up breath and turned to the task of finding somewhere to hide. The closet would have been a good choice, but Ryan's guys already pulled off the doors and stripped off the drywall. My only alternative was to hide behind the bedroom door. My heart in my throat, I began to tiptoe toward the door. As soon as my toes touched the hardwood floors, however, I heard heavy footsteps again. This time, it sounded as if the person was running toward the door upstairs, in pursuit of or running from someone. I froze. Then, remembering Ryan's instructions, I hurried the remaining ten feet and edged the door wider so I could fit behind it.

That was when I realized the footsteps didn't continue beyond the periphery of the doorway upstairs. It was as if the person stopped short before entering the hallway—as if he were listening for something or waiting for it. I grabbed my phone and texted Ryan again: *I'm in the guest bedroom where we found the newspaper articles. I'm behind the door. Please hurry.*

Then I clutched the phone in my hand while I tried to figure out what the person was doing upstairs. But he didn't make a peep. I bit my lower lip to keep it from trembling as I realized whoever had broken in had to know I was in this bedroom because it was the only room with a light on! That meant whoever was inside my house knew I was down here. So why wasn't he coming for me? I shook my head against the thought, a new wave of fear spiraling through me. Maybe he didn't want a run-in. Maybe he just wanted to scope out the house and grab whatever he could and run. But there wasn't anything in the house to take. It was empty . . .

The footsteps sounded again. This time, they were softer, and from what I could hear, the intruder was now walking back toward the window again. He seemed to pause once he reached the wall;

and then I heard the very obvious sounds of him walking back toward the hallway again. Then he turned around and started for the window again. I shook my head, trying to understand why he was pacing back and forth. It just didn't make any sense. Usually, break-and-enterers were quick—get in and get out.

Then there was complete silence. I held my breath, trying to peek through the tiny gap in the hinge side of the door. I couldn't make out much—just the corner of the hallway leading into the foyer. Pulling my attention back from the gap in the door, I heard footsteps again, only this time, they were much closer. They sounded as if they were coming down the hallway, toward me. I held stock-still, my heart pounding in my chest as I tried to figure out how I was going to protect myself if the intruder walked into my room. Figuring one of the discarded wooden boards was my only option, I carefully reached down and grabbed the one closest to me. Then I stood up and held the board above my head, baseball bat–style, waiting for the trespasser to make his move.

Another few heavy footfalls and I could tell he was right beside the doorway. He paused as if hesitating before entering the room. I looked through the gap in the door, but could only make out a white T-shirt. He was so close to me now, just on the other side of the door! I gripped the board as tightly as I could and promised myself that as soon as he walked into the room, I would bash him over the head with it.

"Peyton!" Ryan whispered. "Are you in here?"

Relief suffused my entire being and I dropped my arms, allowing the board to rest against the floor.

"Yes, I'm behind here," I said, pushing the door away and stepping into the room. Ryan spun on his toes so quickly that, moments later, I was up close and personal with the end of his gun.

"Jesus, Peyton!" he breathed out at the same time that he dropped the gun. "You should have warned me it was you! I could have blown your head off!"

I was still in so much shock at nearly meeting my maker, I didn't even know how to respond and managed to say nothing.

"Are you all right?" he asked in a much softer tone as he tipped my chin up and appeared to inspect me.

"I'm fine," I said at last, accepting his outstretched hand when he offered it. "Thank you."

He immediately tucked me in beside him, wrapping his arm around me. He held his gun arm straight out before him as we started down the hallway, toward the foyer. "I already called the cops so they can deal with whoever is in your house," he continued, moving as quickly as he could in the direction of the front door. "We just need to get outside."

I didn't say anything, brooking no argument with him. When we reached the front door, I felt relief already washing over me. He pulled me closer beside him, opened the door, and we were suddenly blinded by headlights. I shielded my eyes with my arms against the garish attack as I heard a man yell.

"Drop the gun!"

Completely confused and still unable to see clearly, I heard the sound of Ryan dropping his gun as he yelled, "I'm the one who called you!"

"Get down on the ground!" the officer responded, apparently not hearing him or not caring.

"What's going on?" I asked Ryan, turning to face him as I tried to understand why they seemed to think he was the intruder. But Ryan's attention was completely on the three patrol cars, each of which had two officers, all of whom were aiming their guns at Ryan. He held his hands up behind his head and stepped away from me, dropping down to his knees.

"Get down on the ground completely!" the officer yelled.

"He isn't the one you're looking for!" I called out to the man, but no one seemed to care what I said. I don't even think they bothered to glance in my direction.

"Spread your legs and put your hands out to your sides," the officer continued barking at Ryan. I turned my attention back to Ryan and watched as he obeyed the officer, spread-eagling his body, face down against the grass.

When I felt a strong hand wrapping around my upper arm, my first instinct was to try to free myself.

"Easy," I heard the officer say in a deep voice as he glanced down at me and smiled warmly. "I'm not going to hurt you."

He was clean-shaven and handsome with dark-green eyes and black hair. He looked like he was in his mid-thirties and was nearly as tall as Ryan, maybe six-four, if I had to guess. He escorted me to the far side of my house, away from the lights of the squad cars and the other officers. I glanced over my shoulder to watch an officer cuffing Ryan while another one searched him, presumably for more weapons.

"He isn't the one you're looking for," I said again, my voice sounding more desperate. "He's my friend from down the street. I asked him to help me."

"It's okay, ma'am," the officer answered, his green eyes as warm as his smile. "This is just protocol—he's not under arrest."

"But," I started, shaking my head. "Why are they . . . ?"

"We're just detaining him for questions. Once we check out the house and he answers all our questions, we will let him go." I studied his honest expression for a few seconds until I felt convinced he was telling me the truth. Then I simply nodded. "Now would you mind answering some questions for me?" he asked, his voice much softer. His smile lent him a boyish, charming quality. I was more than sure he was playing the part of "good cop," but I couldn't say it bothered me.

I glanced over to make sure Ryan was okay and noticed he'd been placed in the back of the car. "Are you sure they aren't arresting him?" I asked the handsome officer, seeing "Officer Gunner" on his nameplate.

"No, like I told you, they just want to ask him some questions," Officer Gunner responded, offering me another heartfelt smile. "Now, can you tell me if anyone else is still in your house?"

I shook my head, and then nodded. "I mean, I don't know. I heard footsteps on the second floor, just above me, and I texted Ryan and now here we are."

"So you never saw anyone enter or leave your house?" he asked, his eyes piercing beneath their deep green. I shook my head as he continued, "Are there any garages or sheds, anything like that on the property where someone might be hiding?" I shook my head again as he smiled down at me. "And you're sure you heard footsteps?"

I frowned at him, even going so far as to raise one brow. "Yes, I'm sure."

We were interrupted by the appearance of another officer. Officer Gunner smiled down at me and excused himself. The two of them spoke for a few seconds before he returned and announced they were going to check the house to make sure it was clear. He led me to the patrol car where Ryan was still handcuffed, seated in the back, and looking decidedly annoyed. "When are you goin' to release me?" he demanded.

Officer Gunner smiled lazily at him. "When the time is right." Then he offered me a bemused smirk before stalking off to join the other officers who were getting ready to check the house.

"I said you were innocent," I told Ryan, shrugging all the while.

"We'll let him go soon," a female officer announced, appearing on the opposite side of the squad car. She gave me a quick smile before watching the officers approach the house, their guns drawn but pointed down at the lawn. She glanced over at me again. "They just have to make sure everything's okay inside, and that your stories match up."

"That our stories match up?" I repeated, at a loss as to why they wouldn't.

She shrugged and glanced back at Ryan with distrust. "Sure, he could have threatened to hurt you if you didn't do as he said. . . . We never know what's going on in these sorts of situations, so it's best to assume everyone is guilty and go from there."

I nodded, figuring it made sense, but whatever happened to being innocent until *proven* guilty? Especially since the neighbors were now gathering along the street, wearing a wide array of colorful robes, pajamas, and furry slippers. They looked like a pack of zombies who just raided the sleep section of J. C. Penney.

Fifteen minutes later, the officers emerged from my house empty-handed. They didn't find anything or anyone, and from the expression on most of their faces, I wondered if they thought I'd just imagined the whole situation.

"We'll complete a report, and if anything happens again, give us a call," Officer Gunner announced, mostly to me, even though he was standing between Ryan and me. Another officer was busy releasing Ryan from his handcuffs.

"Okay," I said as I exhaled deeply and tried to figure out what it meant if no one was in my house.

"Just be sure to lock all the windows and doors," Officer Gunner continued. "And if you're still uncomfortable, consider getting a dog, maybe motion lights or a security system."

"Thanks, Officer, but I can take it from here," Ryan interrupted with a definite frown, apparently ill at ease with the way the officers had treated him; or maybe it was the flirtatious smile the handsome policeman was still in the process of giving me.

"Thanks, Officer Gunner," I said with a sincere grin, although I couldn't get my mind off what in the hell I heard if it hadn't been footsteps.

You heard footsteps, Peyton! I shouted at myself. *You know you heard them!*

"If you're still too shaken up, you might consider staying with a friend tonight," Officer Gunner continued, his smile going beyond suggestive.

"She can stay with me," Ryan interrupted.

I didn't say anything because I really didn't know what to say. I was tired—no, I was beyond exhausted. In the course of the last hour, I'd uncovered a mystery that took place nearly one hundred years ago; my house had been broken into, even though no one seemed to believe me; and now Ryan was inviting me to stay the night at his house?

I first glanced at Ryan—he was scowling at Officer Gunner, who was still smiling at me—before I took in the throng of my neighbors, who were all whispering to each other. I needed nothing more than a few shots of Patrón.

"If you're nervous about bein' alone tonight, Peyton . . ." Ryan started, and actually seemed somewhat tense himself as he led me back into my house. He dropped his eyes to the floor before bringing them back to mine again. This was after he cracked his knuckles on both hands twice. "I meant what I said—you can stay at my place." He cleared his throat and quickly added, "I have quite a few guest rooms."

I would've been nervous about everything that had just unfolded if I were living in my house. But, really, what was there to be scared about when I was headed back to the Omni hotel shortly? It was now maybe ten minutes since the police had left and it was also nearly midnight. The officers had spent another twenty minutes or so ensuring that Ryan's gun was registered and he possessed the proper permits to carry it. Once they were content that he was completely legal, they went on their merry way. Well, all except for Officer Gunner. The handsome man (who, I imagined, was also quite the Don Juan) asked me twice if I felt comfortable being left with Ryan, to which I, of course, responded affirmatively. Then, as if sensing his window was closing, Officer Gunner immediately announced he would be getting off work soon and would happily return to keep me company. After seeing Ryan's expression of disbelief mixed with extreme irritation, I politely declined.

And as to Ryan? Although the idea of spending the night at his house was akin to eating Toblerone when you're PMSing, I knew I had to decline. Why? Because I wasn't sure Ryan truly meant to invite me. Instead, it seemed more likely that he simply asked in order to keep Officer Gunner from getting any ideas about seeing more of me.

Despite Ryan's reiteration that I was free to stay the night at his place, I still wasn't sure he wanted me to. And worse, I didn't want him to feel like I'd backed him into a corner. The more I considered it, the more it occurred to me that Ryan seemed hesitant about the whole thing, like he was uncomfortable with the idea. That was enough for me to begrudgingly decline. Truthfully, however, I could think of nothing more wonderful than driving away my fears and concerns in Ryan's arms. With an inward sigh, I promised myself that if and when Ryan ever invited me over to spend the night again, it would be for the right reasons—not because he felt roped into it.

"I'm fine, Ryan, but thanks, I really appreciate it," I said with a quick smile that I hoped seemed genuine. The smile deepened as I realized how grateful I was to have him in my life. I couldn't imagine going through everything I just had without him. "I mean it, I really do appreciate everything," I repeated for emphasis.

"You're sure you're okay?" he continued, eyeing me skeptically. "I can give you a lift to the hotel if you're too frazzled to drive?"

I shook my head. "Really, I'm fine. I can drive." I laughed as if to prove I was just as okay as I pretended to be. Although I was still a bit shaken up, I didn't see how staying at Ryan's or asking him to drive me to my hotel would help. Besides, he'd already gone above and beyond for me. I winced as I recalled everything he'd had to endure in the last hour, and all on my account. "I'm so sorry you had to go through . . . all that."

"It was to be expected," he answered noncommittally with a shrug before glancing out the front window again, checking to see if all the neighbors had gone back to bed. Looking back at me, he smiled, holding up three fingers. "Three left." Then his gaze returned to the street and he shook his head, seemingly annoyed. "Nosy bastards!"

A laugh died on my lips as I eyed the foyer of my house again, trying to figure out just what the hell had happened over the last two hours. Despite my repeated attempts to make sense over the police not finding anything or anyone, none of it added up.

"What's on your mind?" Ryan asked, reacting to my silence.

I shook my head as I faced him, the worry gnawing at my lips and eyebrows. "If no one was in my house, I just don't understand what those sounds could have been. I mean . . . I heard footsteps. I *know* I heard them!"

Sighing, Ryan cocked his head to the side before staring out the window again, this time holding up two fingers. He faced me with a boyish grin. "You heard Officer Dreamy . . ."

I laughed, recalling Officer Gunner's handsome face and pretty green eyes. Officer Dreamy was a good nickname for him, I had to admit. But of course, I wasn't going to admit that to Ryan, who was clearly not one of the policeman's fans. "Officer Dreamy? Really?"

Nodding, he chuckled a deep, hearty, and infectious sound. "I saw the way he was lookin' at you, an' my Lord, how many times was he goin' to ask if you were okay stayin' with me?" He shook his head as he threw his hands up in the air in mock frustration. There was something that made me incredibly happy at Ryan's response—it appeared that Officer Gunner really ruffled Ryan's tail feathers. And I could only wonder if that meant Ryan was—dare I say it?—jealous?

"You have a point," I conceded with a small smile. I figured there was no reason to try and figure out if Ryan was jealous, because ultimately, what did it really matter? Yep, that was a good line of thinking, I firmly decided. Whatever was meant to happen with Ryan or wasn't meant to happen would reveal itself. I intended to remain an innocent bystander.

"At any rate," Ryan continued, apparently returning to our previous conversation and eyeing the window again. "Still two," he said softly, as if to himself. He turned from the window and faced me fully. "Officer Gunner was right—your intruder could have high-tailed it out the back door and none of us would have noticed."

"The back door was still locked from the inside, Ryan," I argued, trying to ignore the rock taking shape in my stomach. Pondering the facts over the last two hours was making me nauseous.

"Or maybe he opened a window an' crawled out?"

I shook my head. "The police said they checked every window on the first floor, and they were all either painted shut or still locked from the inside."

Ryan nodded but didn't look convinced. "The upstairs windows?"

I frowned. "If he chose that route, he'd either be dead or, at the very least, wounded somewhere in the bushes around the house." I took a deep breath. "That's a long fall." I took another breath. "Besides, the police checked the perimeter of the house, remember?"

Ryan nodded and became quiet for a few seconds as he ran his hand through his wavy hair and expelled a breath, looking like a frustrated god. Good Lord, did the man have no idea how incredibly attractive he was? He finally faced me with an expression that suggested I probably wouldn't like what was going to come out of his mouth next. "Well, honey, maybe you've got yourself a genuine—how should I say this?—ghost?"

I immediately scoffed at him, my eyebrows rising on their own accord. "A ghost? Really, Ryan? Next, are you going to tell me Scooby and Shaggy are coming to solve the mystery?" I crossed my arms against my chest and frowned. "And wouldn't you know it? I'm fresh out of Scooby Snacks."

He held his hands up in mock surrender, a smile forming on his mouth. "Hey, back down, Ms. Uptighty-Whities." I laughed as he shook his head, the smile vanishing from his lips. His expression conveyed more gravity, or more than before. "This isn't Los Angeles, Peyton. N'awlins is much more open-minded when it comes to that sort of stuff."

I tried to decide if he was still trying to pull one over on me. I mean, we were talking about ghosts, things that went bump in the night, things that I was afraid of as a kid. But that sort of stuff was exactly that—kids' stuff. None of it was real. "So you're telling me you believe in ghosts?"

He shrugged again but seemed a bit ill at ease with the conversation, almost like he wasn't sure what he believed, or maybe he felt uncomfortable admitting it. "Let's just say I don't disbelieve."

For a few moments, I quietly started to consider whether or not I'd simply been visited by someone from the beyond. In lots of ways, having a ghost made sense—well, if ghosts actually existed. I faced Ryan again and sighed, not liking where the conversation was headed or that I was about to recite some facts that might support his observation, but I couldn't help it. "I'm not saying I agree or believe in anything we're talking about right now, but just in support of your argument, even though I am definitely, one hundred percent, not convinced . . ."

"I get it, Peyton," Ryan said with the hint of a smile.

"Right before I heard the footsteps, the temperature in the room became arctic." I shivered, remembering how cold it was. "It got so cold in that room, I could see my breath."

Ryan nodded but didn't seem the least bit surprised. "Sounds pretty haunted to me."

I was quiet for a few seconds as I reconsidered it. Wasn't that what all those ghost encounter shows touted? That spiritual manifestations caused the temperature in the room to freeze? I threw my hands in the air and shook my head, immediately forcing the ridiculous notion right out. "Oh my God, this is completely crazy! We're trying to convince ourselves that my house is haunted!"

Ryan didn't seem fazed though. He simply continued studying me before he shrugged. "Well, last I heard, burglars can't magically control the indoor climate and drop the temperature until you see your own breath."

I frowned and then sighed. "Maybe it was just a cold wind. This is an old house and, no doubt, drafty . . ."

"A cold wind?" Ryan repeated, with a raised brow expression that said he wasn't buying whatever I was hawking.

"Yes, it could have been a breeze."

"That blew into the guest room, when no windows or doors were open in your entire house, and the place doesn't have air conditionin'?" Ryan interrupted, this time raising his other brow.

I frowned because I didn't have any rebuttal. He was right. There was no reason for the temperature to plunge so low, much less so quickly.

"If it looks like a ghost, smells like a ghost, sounds like a ghost," Ryan started. He had that dimpled, winning smile on his mouth, making him look like a thirteen-year-old boy after stealing a kiss.

"One other point that I did find interesting . . . " I interrupted, consciously ignoring his dimples, as well as the idea of kissing him.

"Yes?"

I cleared my throat, momentarily forgetting what I was about to say. "Um," I started, shaking my head as I ordered my mind to get back into gear. Luckily, my previous thought reentered my head, sparing me from looking even more stupid than I already did. "I never heard footsteps going up the stairs in the first place. It was like they just materialized in the master bedroom, directly above me."

"Maybe that's where your haunt spent his last moments of life?" Ryan asked in a level tone, like he wasn't surprised in the least that my house might be haunted, but rather, like he was already convinced it was.

I stared at him with a vacuous expression for the span of a few seconds before shaking my head. "This is absurd, Ryan! We're talking about a haunted house! We're actually considering that everything that just happened was because of a ghost?"

"Haven't we already established that?"

"No!" I shook my head, still trying to wrap it around the idea that the footsteps belonged to someone deceased, someone ethereal, someone ectoplasmic. "But . . . but you called the cops, Ryan! You don't call the cops on a ghost!"

He shrugged, seemingly nonplussed by the conversation. His expression revealed so little surprise, we might as well have been talking about the weather. "I didn't realize it was as simple as a hauntin' when I called the police," he replied. "But, now, I'd say your problem isn't an intruder, but rather a specter."

"I'm not there yet," I admitted. "I don't believe in ghosts."

Ryan grinned. "Then, honey, it's probably about time you started!"

Sitting in my bed at the Omni hotel, I tried to persuade myself to sleep. It was now one a.m. and despite my exhaustion, my mind continued racing. Thoughts about my house beleaguered me—specifically, whether or not it was haunted. Had I encountered something not of this earth? And if so, how could I tell said ghost to leave? Should I host a séance? Get a priest to bless or cleanse the place? And more importantly, how in the world did one go about doing either of those things? It wasn't as though they taught Séances 101 in school, or like you could buy an exorcism kit from Target. Lastly, I didn't know the first thing about contacting, let alone evicting, the dead!

My mind wasn't only centered on the idea that I was now roomies with the dead. My thoughts alternated back and forth between ghosts and Ryan. I kept wondering if I should have taken him up on his offer to stay in his house. Passionate, erotic sex was probably the best antidote to getting one's mind off the idea that her house could very well be haunted. Of course, who was I really kidding? It's not as though sex was sitting on the table between Ryan and me.

That, my dear, is called wishful thinking, I said to myself.

Whatever it's called, go to sleep! I barked back angrily.

Feeling slightly offended, I closed my eyes and tried to count sheep; but once I got to fifty, I figured it wasn't working. Allowing my mind to travel where it would actually ended up being a good thing because, before I knew it, I woke up only momentarily to roll over and change position before I fell asleep again.

I was in the master bedroom of my house. Even though there wasn't a doubt in my mind where I was, the room looked completely different. My attention was first drawn to the dark walnut floors, which I instantly recognized, only now they were less faded and worn. The richness of the wood grain seemed restored somehow—newer, fresher. My eyes followed the length of the floor to where it met the wall. Then my gaze shifted up to three floor-to-ceiling windows. I knew the view outside these windows well—a sprawling green and white mansion on Eighth Street. Except when I glanced outside the window now, my neighbor's house was blue and white, and the oak trees surrounding the house were much smaller.

I shook my head, finding it hard to figure out how or why everything appeared so different. Then my attention fell on the heavy, navy-blue curtains beside the row of windows. They corresponded nicely with the charcoal-gray walls. But the walls in this room were covered in old ivy wallpaper. And where did the navy-blue curtains come from?

"*We meet at last,* ma minette."

I twirled around so quickly, I felt dizzy. Or perhaps the faintness was caused by the increased blood flow to my heart, which suddenly pounded apace.

"Y-you!" I said, hardly recognizing my own voice as extreme shock grasped my brain and wouldn't let go. I didn't know why or how, but I recognized the man instantly. It was his intense eyes, which I now realized were dark chocolate. A slight smile made his sculpted cheekbones more pronounced. His nose was just as chiseled as his square jaw, and his tanned olive complexion revealed an affinity for the sun. Staring at the physical embodiment of the policeman I'd seen in the newspaper clippings lining the guest bedroom downstairs, it suddenly occurred to me that his hair was just as dark as the walnut floors.

The man chuckled and took a sip of what looked like brandy. He was sitting in a brown leather club chair, looking comfortably content, his long legs stretched out before him resting on top of a leather ottoman. He wasn't in uniform; rather, he was wearing a crisp, white dress shirt, the first three buttons undone, and his tie hung in a large loop. It looked as if he had been in the process of removing it but got interrupted.

"I trust you remember my name?" he asked in an accent not quite French, although it wasn't quite English either. 'Course, after hearing the French term he'd used earlier, I assumed he was at least familiar with the language.

There wasn't a doubt in my mind as to who this man was. "Drake Montague," I said automatically.

He finished whatever he was drinking and leaned forward, dropping his feet from the ottoman onto the ground before pouring himself another glass. He finished, put the glass stopper on the decanter, and raised the glass to his nose, closing his eyes as he inhaled. He opened his eyes again and focused them wholly on me. His gaze was so piercing, so riveting, I felt like he could see right through me.

"Bien fait. *Well done," he said, tipping his glass in my direction as if he were toasting me. "I am quite pleased to make your acquaintance, Ms. Clark."*

I felt my eyebrows drawing together. "How do you know my name?"

He chuckled and took another sip of his beverage, running his tongue across his upper lip when he pulled the glass away. "You live in my home, ma minette. How could I not know your name?"

"Your home?" I repeated, finally coming out of my wooziness. Up until then, I'd felt as if I were in a dream—everything was foggy and nothing made sense.

"Bien sûr, *of course. Once upon a time, this home and this land belonged to me," he continued as he propped both of his feet back up on the ottoman and stared at me for a few seconds. I had no idea what was going through his mind—his face was a blank canvas.*

I shook my head, suddenly afraid of the direction this conversation might be headed. Still unable to comprehend the thoughts going through my head, I rubbed my forehead as if to rub away the realization that Drake Montague was alive nearly one hundred years ago. "You were a policeman," I started, but stopped short. I wasn't sure why.

"Oui," he laughed, a single eyebrow arching in what I imagined was an expression of amusement. "An officer of the law," he said in a put-on, highfalutin tone that seemed like he was ridiculing the very notion. Then he held his glass up, saying "cheers" to the air.

"But that was in 1918," I continued, remembering the date on the newspaper article that referenced Drake and the Charity Hospital function.

"Oui, c'etait ma minette, yes, it was." He grew silent, seemingly preoccupied at swirling the libation in his glass.

"So how is it that you're sitting here, talking to me now?" I continued, sincerely hoping for a plausible answer. At this point, it wouldn't have come as any surprise if someone told me I was now in The Twilight Zone.

He glanced up at me and smirked. His smile was honest, while also alluring—sexy even. The more I thought about it, the more I realized that this man had an aura about him, an indescribable air of sophistication, but there was something else lurking in his eyes—something wild and very dangerous. "Quite simple: You're asleep."

"This is a dream?" I blurted out, amazed by the idea, while at the same time realizing it made complete sense. Of course, it was a dream!

"Qu'il est, *that it is," he said softly, swirling his drink in his glass absentmindedly.*

"Then you aren't real?" I asked as I walked from the window toward his chair, wondering why everything seemed so real. I could hear the soft sounds of my feet shuffling through the thick rug that covered the walnut floors beneath his immense bed. And the smell of his spicy cologne hung in the air. It was a scent I immediately liked—something entirely masculine, but clean and captivating. I reached out and ran the pads of my fingers across the top of the leather club chair closest to me, one adjacent to his. I could feel the pliable, soft leather just as if I were awake and really touching it.

He chuckled and shook his head, his expression suggesting he thought my question silly. "Of course I'm real."

"But you just said I was dreaming?" I retorted instantly, throwing my hands on my hips as frustration coursed through me. I didn't know any of the rules in this dream world, which was exasperating to say the least.

He glanced over at me and took a long sip of his drink before licking his lower lip again. "Your dreaming has no consequence to my existence, ma minette."

"Well you can't be—what?—thirty-something and also have lived in 1918," I argued. "I might be dreaming, but I also understand basic math!"

He chuckled again, but this time, it was deeper. He stood up and placed his glass on a side table. When he turned back toward me, I realized how tall he was. Even barefoot, he was easily a head and a half taller than I. He took a few steps toward me until I could smell the alcohol on his breath, something I found oddly appealing, especially when combined with the heady scent of his cologne. He didn't say anything for at least three seconds, but continued to stare at me, his eyes alive and dancing as a smile began playing at the ends of his lips. He reached out and touched the bare skin of my upper arm, running his fingers from my shoulder down to my elbow. I could feel the rising of goose bumps as my skin responded to his warm touch. My heart started pounding, and even though I struggled for something to say, I was speechless. I felt as though I were suddenly standing in tar, my feet immobilized.

"Oui, you are quite right," he said in a low, deep voice. His breath tickled my cheek and I couldn't help inhaling. He pulled his fingers from the skin of my arm and ran them down my cheek. I closed my eyes, unaware of what I was doing. "I have so anticipated this moment, ma minette."

A cloud of confusion hovered over me and I opened my eyes again. "I don't understand . . . any of this. How do you know who I am? And how can you be real if you lived so long ago?"

He smirked and I felt a bolt of trepidation shoot through me. "I shall attempt to answer your question regarding how I know who you are first." He took a deep breath and then studied me with piercing eyes. "Although you believe this to be our first meeting, for me it is not. As you have taken up residence in my home, I have been afforded the luxury of watching you. Hence I am much more familiar with you than you are with me. Comprenez-vous? *Do you understand?"*

"Watching me?" I repeated as my eyes narrowed, and I decided to dismiss his question for the time being. "What does that mean?"

He shrugged as if the answer were obvious. "I liken it to sitting and observing a play. I watch your comings and goings, observe you in your day-to-day life, listen to your conversations, and in so doing, I feel as if I have come to know you quite well, ma minette." He took a breath. "And in coming to know you, I have also come to care for you." He took another breath. "Oui, beaucoup. Quite a lot."

I shook my head, not able to completely comprehend what he was saying. He'd watched me? Watched my comings and goings? Did that mean he'd seen me naked? Probably so—it was a question I didn't want to ask. Either way, it now made sense as to why he was acting as if he knew me—because in a strange manner of speaking, he sort of did. "Okay, so we've gotten that question cleared up but what about my other one? How can you be real if you were alive in 1918?"

Drake smiled and arched a brow as he studied me, his gaze traveling from my head to my toes and then back up to my eyes again. "I did live long ago, but now my existence, though in the same space as yours, is different."

I shook my head. "What does that mean?" Then it dawned on me, and my eyes grew wide. "You're dead, aren't you?"

He cocked his head to the side, never losing his devilish grin. "In a manner of speaking, I suppose so. Though I feel very much alive." He focused on my cheek as he said the last words, stroking my skin as if to prove that not only could he feel me, but I could very definitely feel him also. "La mort ou la vie, *death or life . . . to me they are one and the same."*

"Was it you?" I continued, starting to understand the situation, or at least hoping I was headed in the right direction. "The footsteps?"

He simply nodded. "I needed to make you aware of my presence."

I exhaled and he immediately inhaled through his nose, deeply. He closed his eyes and opened them again, his pupils dilating as he focused on my eyes. "Your smell is intoxicating, ma minette."

"Why do you keep calling me that? What does that mean?" I demanded, feeling suddenly rushed to press him for answers. I mean, who knew when I would wake up?

"My pussycat," he answered slyly.

I chose not to respond. His unapologetic sensuality was nerve-racking. It made it difficult to focus on anything besides the unconcealed lust in his eyes.

"Then you've been . . . here since I moved in?" I continued, trying to understand how he existed, in what reality. Could he see and hear just as I did?

"I've been here quite a bit longer than that," he answered with a small laugh. "And, yes, from the moment you first walked through the front door,

you captivated my interest. I have watched you ever since . . . tout à fait captivé, *quite captivated."*

"But you only made yourself known today," I continued, shaking my head to let him know that it didn't make sense.

"Making contact with your world can be a tricky thing, ma minette," he said. He stepped back, turning away from me as he exhaled and started for the window. Even though I couldn't hide the disappointment welling up inside me, I was nonetheless relieved to have my own personal space again. Drake Montague was, in a word . . . overwhelming.

"Why can it be tricky?"

Bracing both of his hands on the windowpanes, he dropped his forehead to the glass, as if he were looking down at the street. I could see his deltoids straining against the light cotton of his dress shirt. His sleeves were rolled up to his elbows, revealing dark, wiry hair that covered his tanned forearms. He pushed off the glass and faced me. From this distance, I could easily enjoy the sight of his broad shoulders and the way they tapered into narrow hips. I felt the breath catch in my throat and gulped down the thought that this man, this spirit, this whatever you wanted to call him, was painfully beautiful.

"Just because I am aware of you does not mean that you are aware of me," he answered simply with a shrug.

"So how could I hear your footsteps then?"

"You uncovered the newspaper clippings and you learned who I was. That understanding bonded us, ma minette, allowing your subconscious to open itself to me. Before, your psyche was closed off. There was no way I could have reached you."

I couldn't say I fully comprehended what he was saying, but there was so much more I needed to ask him, so many questions I wanted answered, that I decided to focus on other subjects. "So what happened to you?" I started, remembering the articles about the legendary Axeman. "And why are all those newspaper articles covering the walls downstairs?"

He held his hand up to gesture for me to stop talking. "Tout à l'heure, *ma minette, all in good time." Then he smiled a captivating grin and took the four steps that separated us. When he was directly in front of me, he brought his fingers to my cheek again, before securing a stray tendril of hair behind my ear. "I need you to do something for me," he started.*

"What?" I asked, at a complete loss. What could this spirit possibly need from me?

"Find every newspaper article you can about the Axeman. Devour them. Learn the story. Know the history as well as you know yourself."

"Why?" I started as he shook his head.

"Learn as much as you can. I will visit you again when I am able." He took a deep breath and pulled away from me, suddenly appearing exhausted. "I'm afraid this session has taxed me. It will take a while to build up my reserves again."

"I don't understand."

"You don't need to," he interrupted. "Please remember all I've said, Peyton."

The way he said my name suddenly made it feel as if we'd known each other all our lives. The air caught in my throat. "I will remember it."

"Very well, je vous dis au revoir, *I bid you farewell,* mon chaton, *my kitten." Then he reached for my hand, closing it in his very large, warm one, and brought his lips to my skin. A shiver started in my spine and worked its way clear up to the nape of my neck.*

I woke up with a start. Looking around, I realized it was still night and I was in my hotel suite at the Omni. I took a deep breath and rubbed the back of my neck, glancing at the clock to see it was ten past three a.m.

I took deep, cleansing breaths while I tried to make sense of the dream I'd just had. It was beyond bizarre. I'd never been aware in a dream that I was dreaming before and I'd also never dreamed in such incredible detail. I could smell and feel as if I were awake. It just seemed so real! Of course, my first instinct insisted that it was nothing more than my subconscious mind launching into overdrive. But somehow, I couldn't shake the sensation that it was more than that, much, much more than that.

The main reason I thought it couldn't have been a dream, and maybe Drake Montague really was trying to reach out to me was simple: I can't speak French.

Chapter 7

Over the course of the next week, I didn't have any more strange dreams, nor did I notice any other "ghostly" phenomenon in my house. As time went by, I was less and less convinced that my dream about Drake Montague had legitimately been him reaching out to me from beyond the grave. Yes, there was that little hiccup known as the French pet name he'd called me but I just dismissed it as something my subconscious mind had picked up somewhere. And as to the footsteps I'd heard upstairs? I was beginning to doubt whether I'd even heard them in the first place. My house was old and everyone knows that old houses creak and groan. All in all, I was very happy abandoning the idea that my house was haunted because the very idea went counter to everything I believed. What was more, it seemed the more time passed, the less convinced I was that anything otherworldly had happened at all.

The construction on my house was moving along rapidly—Ryan's sizable crew had already finished the guest bedroom and they were now putting the finishing touches on the bathroom. Ryan's guess was that I'd probably be able to take up residency in another few days. Even though Ryan continued to give me grief about it, I was on the job site every day, complete with my pink safety hat and my coordinating tool belt. In the course of a week, I'd learned more than I ever wanted to know about construction. What was more, I actually enjoyed it. It was fun to work with my hands and see the result of my labor every day. Even though Ryan acted like he was less than thrilled with my being there, I knew it was mostly for show because we continued to laugh and joke like old friends. We also ate our lunch together every day, and he seemed as happy to teach me as I was to learn.

As to the newspaper articles in the guest bedroom, I managed to recover all of them once Ryan and I finished removing the remaining whitewashed boards in the room. Even though I was pretty convinced that my Drake dream had been nothing more than a figment of my imagination, I was still eager to uncover the mystery of the ax murders that had occurred so long ago. By the time I'd removed each newspaper clipping, I was left with a stack of maybe thirty articles. I tried to organize the articles by date and was mostly successful, although there were a few pages where the dates were missing—either they'd been cut out way back when or the corners of the paper had crumbled away with age.

The articles I was able to recover painted a pretty complete picture of the terror the so-called "Axeman" had put on New Orleans. And with the added information and background provided by the Internet, I felt I had a very complete picture of the past . . .

From 1918 to 1919, this killer, who was later dubbed the "Axeman" by the New Orleans *Times-Picayune* newspaper, attacked twelve people. Some of his victims died, while others were merely injured (I couldn't seem to shake the visual of one woman who survived but also lost some teeth in the process of being bludgeoned in the face). Because seven of the victims were Italians and eight owned grocery stores, there was a belief that the murders were somehow linked to the Mafia. Then there were arguments posed against this line of thinking, the proof being that not all of the victims were Italian and, furthermore, many of the victims were women and one was a child (apparently the Mafia was against killing women and children). I also learned that all of the victims were attacked in the early morning hours and ten were struck with their own axes, which were then left behind for the police to find. In the majority of cases, the Axeman entered the homes of his victims by chiseling out a panel in the back door.

While these were the known facts, as far as I could gather, there were also quite a few lingering questions that no one then or now seemed to have the answers to. First, no one understood how the Axeman was able to chip away a door panel and enter a home without any of the residents ever hearing him. Furthermore, the Axeman appeared to be familiar with the layouts of each home, as he easily located the ax with which he attacked his victims and seemed to have no trouble navigating their homes, even in the dead of night. The biggest question posed, though, was how a grown man could fit through the impossibly small openings chiseled into the doors. Some people posed the theory that the openings were simply a way for the Axeman to reach in and unlock the door but this notion was quickly put to rest when it was reported that those first on the scene always found the doors locked—from the inside.

Quite a few of the articles referenced the idea that maybe the Axeman was some sort of "malign supernatural spirit." The more I read, the more I realized that people at the time were really beginning to believe that they were dealing with something or someone otherworldly. One eyewitness account described the Axeman as disappearing "as if he had wings." Apparently this belief that the Axeman wasn't mortal was even more pronounced once the editor of the *Times-Picayune* received a letter purported to be from the Axeman himself. In it, the Axeman (if, in fact, the letter was written by him) announced himself to be a demon sent from "the hottest hell."

Interestingly enough, when comparing the articles I'd uncovered from my house with the archives of the *Times-Picayune*, I realized my collection was complete, minus the article that included the Axeman's letter. I couldn't help but shake my head at this apparent oversight because it seemed to be one of the most important aspects of the case. Yet, whoever had gone to the trouble of cutting out and attaching each article to the wall had clearly forgotten this one. I just wasn't sure if the oversight was by design or by accident.

When I found the Axeman's letter online, it didn't really strike me as that interesting aside from the parts about him supposedly being a spirit or a demon. The only other section that caught my interest, though, was the Axeman's warning whereby he planned to visit New Orleans on the night of March 19, 1919. He went on to "swear by all the devils in the nether regions that every person shall be spared in whose home a jazz band is in full swing." The more research I did, the more I learned that the night of March 19 saw people "jazzing it up" all around the city and the Axeman apparently held true to his word, as no murders occurred that night. What was perhaps the most interesting sticking point to the whole case of the Axeman was that the killer was never caught. The murders just simply stopped as mysteriously as they'd started.

At the sound of a knock on my hotel door, I glanced up from my laptop, where I'd been devouring the Axeman's letter. I stood up and, glancing at the clock, realized it was seven p.m. I wasn't expecting any guests. Glancing through the peephole, I recognized Trina on the other side. I pulled the door open and wore my surprise as I took into account the bottle of wine she held in one hand and the Ouija board she had nestled beneath her other arm.

"Oh no," I started, shaking my head immediately as it dawned on me that we were about to go ghost hunting.

Trina offered a huge grin before immediately rushing past me, leaving behind a breath of floral perfume. She went straight for the bar, where she grabbed two glasses. "Come on, girl, we got us a date with your ghost."

"My ghost?" I repeated as I held my arms out helplessly. "I don't have a ghost."

She shook her head and pinched her lips together in the same way Ryan did whenever he was bent on getting his way. "That's not what my brother said."

I'd never told Ryan about my dream so I figured he must have told Trina about the footsteps I'd heard and how the temperature had dropped so unexpectedly. I had to wonder if he'd also filled her in on how he'd called the police, only to have them think he was the perpetrator. "Well, I've since decided my house isn't haunted," I replied flatly.

She threw her hands on her hips (which was a feat in and of itself considering she was still carrying the Ouija board underneath her arm and holding a bottle of wine along with two wine glasses) and frowned at me. "Well, Peyton, I don't mean you any disrespect but I think the Ouija board will know better than you."

I sighed as I realized the obstinate Kelly will was about to win out. "I'm not talking myself out of this, am I?"

Trina beamed at me and clinked the glasses together in a clear display of her happiness at having won the argument. "Nope." Then she started for the door again before glancing over her shoulder at me. "And grab your keys 'cause you're drivin'."

When I unlocked my front door and we stepped inside my dark house, I was immediately on edge even though I didn't know why. I'd done a damn good job of convincing myself my house wasn't haunted but I still had the heebie-jeebies. Maybe it was the mere chance that I could have been wrong, that maybe spirits did exist and one was busily existing in my upstairs bedroom. One that also happened to be incredibly attractive and charming, even if he was long dead. The more I thought about it, the more ridiculous it sounded . . . sexy, attractive, and flirtatious ghosts? Give me a break.

Not wanting to focus on the ridiculousness that was believing Drake Montague was haunting my house, I instead focused on the Ouija board still wedged beneath Trina's arm. Weren't Ouija boards considered dangerous? Wasn't that the general consensus among all those ghost hunters and people with psychic abilities? But I figured whatever reputation the innocent-looking board had, it didn't matter to me because I didn't believe in things that went bump in the night.

"Do you know how to use that thing?" I asked Trina, who was already starting for the staircase. I'd barely even removed my key from the lock.

She glanced back at me and nodded, looking like an overexcited little girl about to open a birthday present. "Yep, everyone does." I shut the door behind me and slipped the key into my pants pocket before facing her again. She was perched in the middle of the staircase, her hands on her hips. "Stop lollygaggin' and hurry it up, Peyton!"

"Why are we going upstairs?"

She took the last two steps and then turned around to take stock of me again, tapping her foot impatiently, apparently because I wasn't right behind her. "We need to attempt to contact your spirit at the location where you first noticed activity," she recited as if she'd memorized the sentence.

"Okay, I guess that makes sense," I responded as I reached the top step, and she smiled encouragingly.

"The footsteps you heard were in the master bedroom, isn't that right?"

"Yep, they were," I grumbled as I followed her into the master bedroom and watched her place the Ouija box on the ground, followed by the bottle of wine. Then she placed her glass directly in front of her and mine across from it, before patting the ground in an attempt to get me to sit down.

"Aren't these things supposed to be dangerous?" I asked cautiously as I watched her open the box and place the board on the floor, then the heart-shaped wooden indicator directly on top of it. Then she produced something spherical that was wrapped in what looked like muslin.

"What's that?" I asked.

"That's my candle," she answered and unwrapped the muslin cloth, which looked as if it was thick with Vaseline or something equally off-putting.

"What's all over it?" I asked, frowning.

"Abramelin oil," she answered.

"What oil?"

"It's a special oil that amplifies the cleansin' and purity powers of the white candle."

"Why is that important?" I asked, dumbfounded as I watched her place the discarded muslin to the right of the candle while she propped the candle up on a small pedestal and then lit it.

"Whenever you attempt to contact the dead, you must do so with the utmost care because, to quote Mr. Gump's mama, 'you never know what you're gonna get.'" Then she smiled at me knowingly, as if impressed with her borrowed quote.

"Great, that's reassuring to know," I grumbled, reminding myself that I was more than relieved that I didn't buy a bit of this mumbo jumbo nonsense . . . not even for a minute. Trina didn't say anything more but reached for the bottle of wine, pulled a wine opener from her jeans pocket, and popped the cork. She filled my glass to the brim and then hers.

"What's that for?" I asked, pointing at the wine.

"That's for us to develop a little liquid courage," she answered with a smile.

"Oh," I answered as I lifted my glass. "I figured it was an offering to the ghosts or maybe another way to protect us from that thing," I finished, glancing at the Ouija board.

"But you don't believe in ghosts?" she asked casually as she lifted her glass and tilted it toward me in a silent toast.

"You're right. I don't."

"Then why would you be concerned that this thing could be dangerous?" She had that same blasted look of self-assurance that her brother always did.

I frowned, not entirely sure I was as comfortable with this mumbo jumbo as I was trying to convince myself. "Just making conversation."

She giggled then held her glass up, apparently for a more formal toast. "To Peyton's ghost!"

I didn't say anything but couldn't hide my smile as I downed a sip of the cabernet and relished the burn in the back of my throat. Yep, nothing quite like getting one's intoxication on in order to ignore the current events of the evening.

"Now we have to cleanse the room," Trina announced.

"What does that mean?" I asked, frowning as I imagined us cleaning the windows and sweeping the floors. Needless to say, after a long day of construction, I wasn't exactly in the mood to become Holly Homemaker.

"It means that you need to close your eyes and imagine a bright white light startin' from within you." She closed her eyes and smiled as she continued. "The light is so bright and beautiful, it's difficult to contain, so imagine it spillin' from inside you and envelopin' the whole room." She opened one eye and frowned at me. "Close your eyes and imagine the light, Peyton."

"Oh, sorry," I responded, immediately doing as she instructed.

"The light is ensurin' that we are safe, that anythin' that would hurt us is forced from the room." Then she fell silent for a few seconds so I opened one eye to find her staring at me. "Are you imaginin' the white light?" she demanded.

I immediately slammed my eyes shut and nodded. "Yes."

"Is it cascadin' out of you, into the room?"

"I'm not sure I'd categorize it as cascadin'," I started as I tried to decipher exactly what that meant. "Maybe more filling the room?"

Trina exhaled what sounded like frustration. "Is it bright?"

"It's so bright, I'm imagining myself wearing sunglasses."

"Peyton!" she chided as I opened my eyes and found her frowning at me. "This isn't funny. We're dealin' with the unknown; it's not somethin' you should take lightly."

"Sorry," I muttered.

She offered me a quick smile, which I figured was to let me know that I was forgiven. Then she grasped each of my hands in hers. "Spirit, I light this candle to bless this sacred place. Let the light of the flame radiate protection to all four corners of this room. Please release any negative energies from this space. With a ray of white light, I ask that this area be cleansed and neutralized." She took a deep breath. "Now rest your fingers on the planchette but make sure you don't push it. We just want the energy from our fingertips, not anything else."

"The plant what?" I asked, at a clear loss.

She pointed at the small wooden piece sitting motionless on the board. "The wooden marker."

I simply nodded and rested my fingers on the wooden pointer thing, er, the planchette. Then I glanced over at her to make sure I'd done it correctly. She simply nodded. "Now what?" I asked.

"Now we summon the spirit or spirits who dwell here." She cleared her throat. "I summon the spirit or spirits of this house. Speak with me through this medium. If you are here, please respond by movin' the planchette to 'Yes.'"

I glanced down at the little heart-shaped wooden thingy and noticed it wasn't budging. I looked up at her and shrugged. "Looks like no one's home."

"Shush, Peyton, this takes a while," she scolded me. "Is anyone there?" she called out, but only the silence in the room responded. "If you are here with us, please let us know!"

I watched the planchette as it sat there, completely immobile. I looked over at Trina again as she spoke loudly. "If any spirits are present, please send us a sign that you are here with us!"

If there were crickets in the room, they would've been chirping.

"Spirits, please announce your presence!"

I waited another few seconds before I decided to stop wasting the rest of my evening trying to contact something that didn't exist. "Um, I don't think it's working, Trina. How much longer do we wait?"

"Hush, Peyton," she whispered and then speared me with her wide eyes as she glanced down at our fingertips. "Look!"

I followed her gaze and watched the planchette as it skidded across the board to the upper corner and settled itself on the word "Yes." "Did you just do that?" I whispered.

She shook her head immediately. "No, neither one of us did." Then she gulped and I got the distinct feeling that she wasn't as practiced with this ghost conversation business as she'd let on. "There's a spirit here with us." Then she sucked in a big breath. "Welcome, spirit!"

I wasn't sure if I was supposed to welcome it too so I added a quick, "Hello."

Trina didn't seem to notice and instead asked, "When were you born, spirit?"

I didn't move; I don't even think I breathed for a few seconds as the planchette began to point to numbers until it spelled out "1895." "Are you moving it?" I demanded.

Trina frowned at me. "No! I'm barely restin' my fingers on it!"

And I was barely resting my fingers on it as well, which had to mean one thing—that Milton Bradley knew their stuff. As soon as

I registered the fact that we *could be* conversing with the dead, I couldn't help but wonder if somehow we'd contacted Drake's spirit. But then I realized that if Drake had been born in 1895, that would have made him twenty-four years old when he died and he definitely looked older than that. Well, if he'd died in 1919, anyway. As to why I thought he'd died in 1919 I wasn't sure—I figured it was because all the articles covering the guest room were from 1918 to 1919, and I had a sneaking suspicion his death had something to do with them.

"What is your name?" Trina continued.

The board spelled out "Joseph."

Hmm, so maybe this wasn't Drake's spirit after all. I couldn't help the keen sense of disappointment that snaked through me.

"When were you born, spirit?" Trina asked as if she'd forgotten she'd just asked the exact same question. Afraid our ghostly visitor was going to get annoyed at being asked the same questions, I glanced up at her.

"You already asked that."

She frowned at me. "I know. I'm makin' sure this spirit isn't tryin' to trick us!" Then we watched as the planchette spelled out "Now."

I glanced up at Trina in confusion. She gave me the exact same expression. "It's playin' with us," she whispered before clearing her throat and saying in a louder voice. "Is this still the spirit of Joseph?"

The planchette slowly moved to the upper right hand corner and settled on the word "No." As soon as it did so, the candle's flame began growing very large, only to drop down again—almost as if someone were blowing it. And I hadn't noticed until now that the temperature in the room was freezing. I could see Trina's breath.

"Then who is this?" I said, not able to control myself. My voice was shaky, and in my head, I desperately wished that the response would be "Drake." Somehow, I thought I'd feel safer if I knew his spirit was with us. That and I had to know if Drake was really real—if he'd really visited me in my slumber.

The planchette moved quickly, but it didn't spell out Drake's name. Instead, it revealed the name "Charles."

"Charles?" Trina repeated and seemed confused. Her breath continued to billow out in front of her like white smoke. "Is this Joseph or is this Charles?"

The planchette didn't stop moving and it didn't appear to be responding to Trina's questions either. Instead, it continued to move from letter to letter. "B-E-S-U-M-E-R," Trina spelled out before glancing at me with a question in her wide eyes. "Besumer?"

I felt my stomach drop as I watched the planchette continue to spell out names—names that I recognized.

"Anna," Trina repeated as I stared at her, feeling the heavy weight of shock as it descended in the pit of my stomach. I had the ominous feeling that whatever we'd gotten ourselves into, we were in over our heads. The candle was now flickering as if it were in a heavy wind.

Trina faced the board again, her eyes settling on the candle as worry began to gnaw at her mouth. "We wish to speak . . . to speak with only one . . . one spirit, please," she stammered.

"We have to stop," I whispered, shaking my head as a bolt of icy cold air ricocheted up my spine. My heart pounded in my ears as every fiber in my being yelled at me to release the planchette.

"Why?"

"All the names," I started, hating the fact that I could see my breath. "They were all the victims."

"Who were what victims?" Trina continued, shaking her head as we both felt the planchette buck underneath our fingertips as it begin to race across the board. It began landing on letters so incredibly quickly, I had a tough time following it. "J-U-S-T," Trina called out, her attention riveted on the board. "L-I-K-E-M-R-S-T-O . . ."

"Toney," I finished for her and felt a blast of fiercely cold air explode right in my face. I blinked at the same time that Trina's candle went out, the acrid smell of smoke stinging my nostrils. I yanked my fingers from the planchette as if it had burned me.

"Peyton!" Trina yelled. "Quickly, put your fingers back on it!"

"No," I said, feeling true fear coursing through my body. I even scooted a few inches away as if to prove there was no way in hell that I would ever touch the thing again. Not after what it had just revealed, something that was seemingly impossible.

"We have to end the session properly!" Trina demanded. "We have to say good-bye!"

But before I could even consider putting my fingers back on the planchette, the thing pointed to number one, followed by two, then three, and so on. Trina immediately flipped the board upside down; the planchette flew across the room. We both jumped at the sound of the wood hitting the wall, but once it fell on the floor and lay still, neither of us said anything. We just sat there, staring at each other, shock registering in our eyes.

"What just happened?" I asked finally, looking around myself as I realized the temperature was now slowly warming. It was almost as if the board had been generating the chill in the air. Now that it was turned upside down, there was no chill to speak of.

Trina swallowed hard and glanced down at the board, flipping it faceup again. "Whenever the marker starts to move in alphabetical or numerical order, you have to flip the board over before it finishes."

"Why?" I asked even though I was deathly afraid for her answer.

"It means we've encountered somethin' that is tryin' to gain access to us through the board."

"Oh my God," I started as I shook my head. "Did you flip it before the thing finished counting?"

She nodded. “I think so.” Then she took another deep breath and closed her eyes. “Spirits, as I blow out this candle,” she paused and then glanced at the candle, apparently realizing it had already blown itself out. “As the candle is blown out, I close this sacred space and ask that protection surround Peyton and myself as well as this sacred space.”

She opened her eyes and exhaled deeply. “Did that work, you think?” I asked sheepishly. “I mean, do you think you got rid of whatever that . . . was?”

She nodded. “The closin’ prayer always shuts out whatever crossed over. The candle also protected us.”

“Even though it went out?” I asked, sounding unconvinced. I looked around the room but didn’t notice anything unusual, although I wasn’t really sure what I was expecting to see: Blood dripping down the walls, thousands of flies in the corners of the windows, an upside-down cross on the wall? Linda Blair sitting in the middle of a bed with her head spinning all the way around?

She just nodded but somehow I wasn’t sure if she was wholly convinced herself. She stood up and immediately started putting the board and the planchette away, as if she wanted nothing more than to leave the house. I couldn’t say I blamed her. I grabbed the bottle of wine and the two glasses and was right on her tail when she started for the door. Neither of us said anything as we hurried down the staircase and out the front door.

“Aren’t you goin’ to lock it?” she reminded me when I forgot. I just nodded and pulled the key from my pocket, my hand shaking as I fitted it in the lock and turned it. Then we both hightailed it for the Scout and only once we’d pulled away from my house and were well on our way to the French Quarter did Trina interrupt the silence.

“How did you know what the board was sayin’ before it finished?” she asked, her voice sounding strained.

I exhaled and remembered the line I'd read in one of my newspaper articles. "Mrs. Maggio is going to sit up tonight just like Mrs. Toney," I repeated from memory, the words feeling like molasses dripping out of my mouth.

"What does that mean?"

I shrugged because I didn't really understand what it meant. "It was scribbled in chalk on the sidewalk back in 1919," I started. "The police thought it was a message left by the Axeman."

"The who?" Trina began, leaning forward. I could see the fear in her eyes but I was sure there was more in mine. I couldn't even begin to understand what had just happened to me, to us.

I took a deep breath and wondered if my heartbeat would ever regulate itself. "Joseph Maggio, Charles Cortimiglia, Louis Besumer, Anna Lowe . . . they were all victims of the Axeman."

"Who was the Axeman?" Trina repeated, sounding exasperated and scared.

So I told her. I told her everything I'd discovered about the Axeman from my articles as well as the research I'd done on the Internet. The only thing I didn't mention was my dream about Drake Montague because I still wasn't convinced it was legitimate. A simple dream was a far cry from what had just occurred with the Ouija board. Furthermore, the Ouija board hadn't mentioned Drake the entire time so maybe he was simply a figment of my imagination.

I didn't know why but I sincerely hoped that was not the case.

Chapter 8

I couldn't sleep all night. My mind wouldn't stop thinking about everything that happened with the Ouija board. Last night, in the span of ten or so minutes, everything I thought I knew and believed in had simply crumbled away in front of me, until I had no certainty anymore, just questions. And the more I racked my brain, trying to understand what had happened, the more I couldn't comprehend how the board knew what it did. I was left with only one conclusion—that there was much more to this world than I'd previously imagined.

Once I decided I was okay with the idea that spirits, haunts, shades, ghosts, specters, whatever you wanted to call them, were real, my next line of thinking was, who in the hell contacted Trina and me? Did we somehow communicate with the spirits of all the Axeman's victims? Or was it more sinister than that? Was it possible that we actually made contact with the Axeman himself? I shuddered at the thought and forced it out of my mind, choosing to focus on the insulation I was supposed to be cramming between the two-by-fours of my bathroom wall.

"Someone's mind isn't on the job today," Ryan scolded me as he paused from stapling the insulation to the framework and arched a brow in my direction, giving me a knowing look.

Glancing over at him, I frowned and removed my breathing mask, deciding to come clean and admit he was right, my mind wasn't on the job. "Sorry."

"Don't be," he responded as he turned his enormous shoulders in my direction. I shook my head, in awe that mortal men could possibly be so large.

"If they ever make a movie about Thor or Hercules, you should try out for the part," I suggested, sounding less than thrilled about it.

"I think they already did," Ryan chuckled. "On both accounts. But, thanks . . . I think?"

"Welcome," I grumbled with a yawn, remembering at the last minute to cover my mouth. I was loath to get another lecture from Ryan about my manners or lack thereof.

"Peyton, you look beyond tired. Did you manage to get any sleep last night?"

"Um, no," I answered matter-of-factly, stifling another yawn.

He nodded as if he understood my pain. "Still thinkin' about what happened?"

I cleared my throat and nodded, zoning out on the dull metal sheen of the pipes, which stuck out of the bathroom wall across from me.

After I'd dropped Trina off at her apartment in the French Quarter and returned to my room at the Omni hotel, Ryan had called me. Apparently, Trina had told him all about our Ouija board experience, and to say he was concerned was an understatement. He read me the riot act about using Ouija boards in general, apparently the same lecture he'd given Trina. Once his sermon was over, he returned to the caring, consoling Ryan I liked so much.

"I can't stop thinking about it," I admitted. I took a deep breath as I stared at my open palms and flexed my fingers until my hands looked like starfish.

He shrugged and placed his massive hand on my shoulder, squeezing it tightly as if to let me know he was there for me. His touch felt so good, I wanted to close my eyes and melt. It felt like it had been so long since a man had held me, since I'd felt the warmth and safety of a man's chest. And as to my ex, Jonathon? He didn't count, seeing as how we very rarely, if ever, cuddled. Yep, as far as Jonathon was concerned, I considered him the Antichrist.

"Gotta be careful about messin' with things you don't understand, Peyton," Ryan said as he pulled his hand away.

"I know, I know," I replied grumpily before facing him with a snide expression. "I already got an earful on that exact subject last night!"

Ryan chuckled and, with a big smile, resumed his job of filling the walls with the pink fibrous insulation. Even though I hadn't done much in the way of work so far this morning, I decided to take a breather. I sat down in the corner of the bathroom, pulling my knees into my chest as I huffed out my exhaustion. I watched Ryan pause in his routine to study me.

"You wanna talk about it?" he asked.

I bit my lip and shook my head, but the words were already on their way out. "I just don't understand who we could have contacted with that board. I mean, how could some inanimate piece of wood know the names and other details of all those murdered victims, especially when it happened such a long time ago?"

Ryan shrugged. "Who's to say? That sort of stuff remains beyond our ability to understand, which is why any talk about the afterlife is better left unsaid." He stopped stuffing the walls and faced me, his expression serious. "Just promise me you won't get yourself into any more trouble?"

"I promise," I answered automatically, having already vowed the same to myself—well about not using Ouija boards, anyway. I narrowed my eyes as I scrutinized him, surprised such an undeniably macho sort of guy didn't laugh at things that defied explanation.

"Why are you lookin' at me like that?" he asked.

My eyebrows immediately shot toward the ceiling once I realized I'd been caught staring at him. I shrugged. "I'm just surprised you believe in all this stuff—I wouldn't think a guy like you would believe in ghosts."

He frowned. "What's 'a guy like me' mean?"

I laughed, amused to see he was on the verge of getting his tail feathers ruffled. "Don't get your panties in a wad," I started.

"My whats in a wad?"

I laughed again at his baffled expression. "I didn't mean what I said as a put-down. I just meant that you're a man's man, you know?"

He continued eyeing me suspiciously.

"Oh my gosh," I continued, rolling my eyes at the thought I'd have to spell it out for him. Maybe he was just fishing for compliments. "In other words, you're not some geeky, skinny, unattractive dude who spends all his time playing Dungeons and Dragons."

Ryan chuckled. "Okay, I'll take that as a compliment?"

"Yes, Ryan, it's a compliment," I assured him. "No more fishing."

"Fishin'?" he asked while innocently pointing to himself, like I had to be talking about someone else.

I continued to watch him as I wondered if there would ever be a time when looking at him wouldn't stir the butterflies in my stomach. "I just think it's funny to find a side to you I never imagined actually existed."

Shoving more insulation into the wall, he reached for the staple gun and attached the insulation in place before looking down at me with his eyebrows raised. "There's a lot more to me than you probably ever imagined existed."

I wasn't sure how to take the comment. His tone was clearly playful, even flirty, but his eyes were smoldering and very sexy. I gulped down a tide of anxiety that suddenly flowed through me. "I'm sure there is, Ryan."

He didn't break his gaze but continued to stare at me with a slight smile on his full lips. "Just like I'm sure there's lots about you that I don't know." He paused for a few seconds. "Lots about you that I would very much *like* to know," he added, his voice deepening.

Swallowing hard, I emitted a strange giggle-choke sort of sound. The few moments when my bizarre relationship with Ryan leaned toward the more passionate than platonic side always made me uncomfortable . . . in a good way, if that were even possible. I immediately ceased whatever odd noise I was in the process of making and cleared my throat. "I think I'm an open book."

"I think not," he answered immediately, and if looks could kill, I would have died right there on the spot. There was something so feral in his eyes, my heart sped up. I broke eye contact first. He suddenly made me feel like I was stark naked, standing in front of an audience with no place to hide. When I chanced to look up at him again, his eyes were still on me.

"Remember how you promised me dinner?" he asked in a low, rough voice.

I nodded. I was completely floored that we were even having this conversation—especially with me wearing coveralls, watching him stuff insulation in the wall, errant pieces of which kept falling out all over his hair. It wasn't the most romantic setting for what I was beginning to think might become a romantic conversation. At least, I hoped it would. "Yes, I remember."

"What do you think about me takin' you up on your offer now?" He asked, like there wasn't a frayed nerve in his body—like he possessed absolutely no trepidation or anxiety at all. Instead, it was like his fair share of apprehension had been most unfairly assigned to me.

I cleared my throat again, trying to buy some time because I wasn't exactly sure what he meant. "Um, last I checked, my kitchen wasn't even gutted yet?"

"I didn't mean you cookin' . . ."

"Okay," I started, sounding completely confused and awkward.

Ryan chuckled heartily while shaking his head as he secured the last of the insulation in the wall, stapling it in place. Then he turned to face me, still wearing a beaming grin. "Nothin' with you comes easy, does it?"

"Um, no?" I started, my eyebrows already rising in obvious puzzlement. "Er, I mean yes?"

Ryan's unconcealed amusement remained on his face. He crossed his burly arms against his chest and continued smirking at me. "I'm tryin' to ask you out on a date, Peyton."

"Oh," I answered immediately before chastising myself for acting so completely idiotic. I offered him a quick smile and lost the staring contest. Now I was paying way too much attention to the tops of my shoes.

"Not exactly the response I hoped for."

I immediately looked up at him, realizing how bad my utter silence must seem. Well, blast it, but where in the hell was my cool, calm, and collected side? Where was that part of me that could handle my own with Ryan? The part that could banter with him and keep him on *his* toes? "Well, you didn't exactly ask me right," I answered, hoping that part of me had returned.

"Oh?" he asked in feigned shock. "How's that?"

I stood up, suddenly wanting some space between us. I wasn't exactly comfortable with him staring down at me. It made me feel like I was as tall as a Smurf. "Well, you basically just told me you want me to cook you dinner, or, failing that, to take *you* to dinner!"

"What? No, I didn't." He shook his head and narrowed his amber eyes at me, but there was a challenge in their depths. Seeing the smile already cresting his lips, it was pretty obvious he was enjoying my bewilderment.

With a nod, I crossed my arms against my chest, attempting to mimic his body language. I figured since I'd already laid down the gauntlet, I'd have to pursue my argument, although I was sure my smile was already giving me away. "Yes, you did."

"How so?"

"If you recall," I started, my voice sounding lofty, "my offer was to cook you dinner and you agreed, with the single stipulation that my kitchen had to be finished first."

Ryan nodded, his grin widening. "Okay, that was true, but if *you'll* recall, just now, I said I didn't want you to cook at all."

"Right!" I agreed although my voice came out a bit harsh. "But all that means is that you expect me to take you out to dinner, since that *was* my original offer," I countered, desperate not to lose the silly argument. "Not that I mind taking you out to dinner . . ." I didn't want him to think I was cheap or anything. But I also knew no Southern gentleman would like having it pointed out that I thought he expected dinner to be my treat.

He shook his head immediately, just as I supposed. "That doesn't mean I wanted you to pay, silly woman."

"I don't mind paying . . ."

"Peyton, why is everything so difficult with you?" he asked while shaking his head again.

"Nothing's difficult with me," I argued. "You just don't have a good grasp of the English language."

He sighed. "Okay, let me do this again and make sure I *word* it correctly." Then he took a deep, showy breath. "Would you, Peyton Clark, care to dine with me, Ryan Kelly, on the evening of your choosin' this week? And I will happily pick up the tab."

I laughed. "Um, sure, I'd love to."

He clapped his hands together. "Finally! Something that could have taken all of two seconds ended up wastin' a good ten minutes of our lives."

"Blah!" I said with a laugh as I waved him away.

"Good Lord, remind me never to ask you out again!"

With my hands on my hips, I pretended to glare at him. "Stop lollygaggin' around," I said in a terrible rendition of his Southern accent. "I didn't hire you to gab, Mr. Kelly, an' this old house ain't gonna renovate itself!"

"Que pensiez-vous? *What were you thinking?" Drake demanded as he paced back and forth, pushing a hand through his unruly dark hair.*

"What?" was all I could think to say. Only seconds ago, I'd been in bed with Ryan. He was kissing me all over my face, while attempting to remove my jeans and whispering in my ear all the fantasies that awaited me. One thing I could say about Drake was, he had bad timing. Really bad timing.

"Peyton!" Drake persisted, even snapping his fingers to get me to focus on him.

I shook my head and took a deep breath, looking around as I sort of recognized my surroundings. The walls were cream, which threw me, but the large, black marble fireplace in the middle of one wall and the five floor-to-ceiling picture windows at the far side of the room told me I was standing in my own living room. The windows were trimmed in cornflower-blue silk drapes and the furniture in the room was decidedly less masculine than the furniture I'd seen in Drake's bedroom, er, my bedroom. There were two whitewashed, French bergère oak chairs in front of the fireplace, both upholstered in a light-blue fabric. The sofa, loveseat, and ottoman all matched the whitewashed, French country theme inspired by the bergère chairs, complete with the same light-blue upholstery. If I'd had a camera, I would have taken a picture because I quite liked the style.

“Ma minette, comment vous me vexez! *Ugh, how you vex me! Are you listening?” Drake continued, this time striding up to me until he was maybe four steps away. He was dressed in his police uniform, his black pants clinging to his shapely butt and long legs. I was surprised at how similar his uniform was to those of the present. His jacket looked a bit outdated, maybe, with numerous buttons going down the front and an overall amorphous shape. But, outdated or not, a man in uniform was a man in uniform, and it didn't matter if said uniform was from the early 1900s. Yep, any way I looked at it, Drake Montague was so handsome, my breath caught in my throat.*

I glanced up at him and nodded dumbly. “Sorry, I just thought I was . . . somewhere else.”

“Oui, yes, you were,” he answered, with a haughty expression and one arched eyebrow. He sounded somewhat displeased, maybe even irritated. He straightened his posture and rested his icy chocolate eyes on mine. His lips were tight. “Toutes mes excuses. *I apologize for interrupting your dreams of the large barbarian.”*

I laughed; I couldn't help it. Hearing Ryan described as a “large barbarian” was funny. That was my first thought. My second one was how did Drake somehow tune himself into my head? How did he know I'd been dreaming about sex with Ryan? That thought both unnerved and embarrassed me, a lot. But despite my discomfiture, it was more important to remember Drake was an eavesdropper. “So, can you just force your way into my thoughts and dreams whenever you choose?” I asked, sounding less than thrilled at the notion.

“Non,” *he said, shaking his head, his eyes still narrowed and his expression less than amused. “Only when my power is at its greatest and you . . .* ouvrez vos pensées, *open your thoughts to receive me.” Once he said those last six words, he smirked knowingly and allowed his eyes to travel my body from bust to legs and back up again.*

"Hey!" I started.

The corner of his mouth lifted into something not quite a smile but hinted at his amusement all the same. "I do approve," he said. I imagined he was referring to my figure. I just shook my head—one thing I was learning about Drake was that he appreciated women. If I'd known him better, I might have even gone so far as to say he was a womanizer . . . or had been.

A moment later, though, any residual sexual innuendo vanished. Instead, he started pacing back and forth again, his heavy footfalls pounding against the walnut floors. Apparently, he was back to being pissed off. And I had to admit I much preferred the lascivious Drake to the perturbed one.

"Okay, and why am I being reprimanded again?" I asked, opting to take a seat on the sofa because I had a feeling I'd be here for a while.

Drake faced me, throwing his hands in the air. Obviously, this spirit tended toward the dramatic. "You should not dabble in things you know nothing about!"

"Um, I'm not following you, Inspector Clouseau," I answered with a slight smile. Then I realized The Pink Panther *came way after Drake's time, so my quip was most definitely lost on him. What a shame.*

He looked slightly confused before jumping right back into his diatribe again. "The board!" he answered, his tone clearly conveying I should have known what he was talking about. Then I remembered our first conversation where he'd willingly admitted to "watching" me and I realized he'd probably watched Trina and my whole botched attempt to reach out to the other side, his side. He paced toward the bank of windows, turned on his heels, and strode back to me.

"Here we go," I grumbled. "Yes, I already got an earful about playing with Ouija boards, and already promised everyone who will listen that I won't have anything else to do with them."

"Un savon? *An earful?" he demanded, eyeing me carefully.*

"The large barbarian," I answered with a shrug while concealing a smile.

He frowned. "We shall discuss him another day," he answered indifferently. "For now, I am mostly concerned with undoing whatever damage you've enabled with your trifling."

"Damage?" I repeated, feeling slightly irritated with his pedantic air. How many lectures would I get on this subject? Then an idea popped into my head. "Well, I was trying to contact you, if you really want to know the truth, but you never responded, which makes me wonder now if you're nothing more than an illusion created by my dream imagination . . ."

He shook his head immediately. "Non, je ne suis pas une illusion!" he spouted out angrily before composing himself and translating, "I am no illusion."

"Then why didn't you reply when we tried to reach you through the board?"

He frowned at me. "When you open a gate, such as the one you did, there is no way to determine which spirits come through."

"What does that mean?"

He started pacing again and didn't answer until he reached the fireplace. "There was a surge of energy when you opened the portal, which I was unable to get through." He frowned at me. "Believe me, I tried."

"So who got through?" I demanded, suddenly unnerved, remembering how the board rattled off the names of the Axeman's victims.

"Je ne sais pas! I don't know for certain." Drake shrugged as he made his way toward me again. He was moving around so much, I was getting dizzy. "I tried to reach out to you, but the power was too great."

"What power?" I asked, shaking my head. "Whose power?"

"I cannot answer your questions," he said matter-of-factly. "But whatever it was, it is cause for concern, which is why you and I are having this conversation now."

I gulped. "Oh."

"You must fix the portal breach, ma minette," Drake continued, now directly in front of me. He kneeled down and took both of my hands in his. His eyes implored me at the same time they showed his concern.

"What does that mean? What breach?"

"Whatever breach you might have opened. You must cleanse the house." Seeing my expression of confusion and doubt, he continued. "I do not know what, if anything, will come of your dabbling, but il est préférable de préparer que d'être pris par surprise. *It is better to prepare than be taken by surprise."*

"I don't know how to cleanse the house!" I cried, my heart plummeting as the weight of the situation began to bear down on me. "I don't even know what that means!"

Drake's response was straightforward and succinct. "Then you must find someone who does."

I quietly pondered his reply for a few seconds. I was in New Orleans, a spiritual mecca, basically the seedbed of voodoo. If I had to cleanse the house of spiritual energy, where better to find someone than here? That was when something occurred to me. I glanced up at Drake, finding his eyes already riveted on me. "But, but if I do find someone to cleanse the house . . . what does that mean for you? Wouldn't you be cleansed from it as well?" I didn't know why, but I was suddenly afraid of losing him. It was strange because I wasn't wholly convinced that he really even existed beyond the confines of my mind; but truthfully, I wanted him to be real.

With a chuckle, he shook his head, running his fingers down the side of my cheek. "Cleansing will only eradicate entities that intend you harm, ma minette." He bent down and brought his mouth to my ear, whispering, "Je ne te ferais jamais de mal. *I would never harm you."*

I started to close my eyes at his touch. Incredibly, in this dream world, he felt whole, tangible, and nothing at all like a spirit, or what I imagined a spirit would feel like—air. His touch was as real as my own. His breath against my ear sent shivers up my spine. God, how I wanted him to be real, to exist outside the boundaries of my imagination.

Then, like a slap in the face, I suddenly jolted back to reality and remembered the information from the Ouija board. I swallowed hard and pulled away from him, savoring the feel of his fingers still grazing my cheek.

"Ne pas la combattre. *Do not fight it," he whispered, his breath hot on my neck. I wanted to close my eyes again and allow myself to succumb to whatever he had in mind for me, but I resisted the urge.*

"No, Drake, there's more. I need to tell you what happened."

"What happened?" he repeated, pulling away from me, disappointment overcoming his features.

"With the board."

It seemed to take him a minute to remember what we were talking about before he replied. Men!

"The Ouija board," I clarified.

"Priez continuer. *Pray continue," he answered, becoming suddenly unsettled, and probably realizing whatever I was about to say wasn't going to be good. I cleared my throat and watched him walk to the fireplace, where he leaned his arm against the mantel and studied me, patiently waiting for me to begin.*

"I read all the articles you requested," I started. He immediately nodded as if he were happy to hear it. I swallowed, knowing he wouldn't be happy to hear the rest of my story. "So I am pretty familiar with what happened in regard to the Axeman."

"Très bien. *Very good," he answered quickly. "What does the board have to do with this, ma minette?"*

I inhaled, knowing I needed to get to the point. "While Trina and I were using the board, we asked it questions." Drake kept nodding, as if to say this were commonplace. "And when we asked whom we were speaking with, the board started spelling out the names . . . of the Axeman's victims."

Drake's expression completely changed. His lips tightened and his eyes narrowed. I glanced down at his hands and saw he was fisting them at his sides. It was uncanny to watch the complete change in his demeanor—from sensual to seething, all in the course of a few seconds.

"Drake?" I started, only slightly unnerved at the expression on his face.

He immediately shook his head, as if to say he wanted the complete story. "Go on."

His obvious agitation about the entire thing was making me nervous. I glanced down at my lap and realized I'd picked all the nail polish off the fingernails of my right hand. I looked back up at him and felt myself withering beneath his stringent gaze. "That's all there really is to say."

"Which names?" he demanded.

I took a deep breath and tried to remember. "Joseph was first. I figured that could mean either Joseph Maggio or Joseph Romano." The Axeman had attacked two Josephs. "Then I think the board mentioned Charles Cortimiglia, and Louis Besumer, and Anna . . . Lowe." I swallowed and felt the quiet of the room overcoming me. Drake didn't move, or even blink. He just stared at me. "Do you think Trina and I were in contact with the victims?" I asked sheepishly, not sure what to make of his tacit scrutiny.

He immediately shook his head and his eyes were piercing when they settled on mine. "No."

"Then who?" I started.

"Je ne sais pas. *I don't know," he replied immediately, his hands still fisted at his sides and his eyes still dangerous. "Is there more?"*

"No," I started, feeling like I didn't want to continue talking about this subject. Not without any idea what was going through his mind. Was this way worse than I'd previously thought? Had we somehow opened a demonic portal with the board, allowing the Axeman to come through and possibly do me in with an ax?

"Nothing?" he affirmed.

Then I remembered there was more. "Oh, um, yes, there is actually."

"Quoi? *What is it?"*

I tried to remember everything that happened that night. I could feel myself starting in on the fingernail polish of my other hand. "The board began to count chronologically, so Trina had to turn the board upside down." Drake's lips continued to tighten until they paled white, but despite my anxiety, there was more I had to tell him. "And it started to repeat the words that were written in chalk on the sidewalk right before the murder of the Maggios."

"Mrs. Maggio is going to sit up tonight just like Mrs. Toney," Drake repeated, as if he'd been working on the case only yesterday. I simply nodded, hating the words as he uttered them. They were so filled with obscene mystery that went way beyond ominous. He took a deep breath, finally releasing the tension in his lips. He started to zone out on the floor, and just when I wondered if our conversation was over, he looked up at me. "I received the call about the message," he started, his voice sounding far away. "Upperline and Robertson Streets. It was just a block away from the Maggios' home." I nodded and listened, intrigued by his story . . . fascinated by him. "No one could make any sense of it. At first, we thought it was a simple schoolboy prank. He inhaled deeply and then shook his head. "Merde."

"So what did it mean?"

He cocked his head to the side and shook it, as if to say he didn't have an answer for me. "It was only after the attack on the Maggios that we decided it was a warning to Mrs. Maggio because it was discovered mere hours before her death."

"Who was Mrs. Toney?"

He shrugged. "No one knows for certain, although some thought she was a woman who foiled the attempts of the Axeman, only much earlier, in 1911."

"So why did that message come through the board?" I asked, completely baffled as to what it all could mean.

Drake faced me and the color drained from his face entirely. "Just as it was meant to warn Mrs. Maggio, you must consider it a warning to you, ma minette."

Once I woke up from my dream about Drake, I couldn't get back to sleep. I still wasn't convinced whether he was truly a spirit reaching out to me, or just a figment of my overactive imagination. Either way, though, I figured it was better to think he *was* real because if my house had to be cleansed from harmful spirits, poltergeists, or demons, better to be safe than risk becoming possessed, or even dead, right?

I woke up at the crack of dawn and slammed down a few cups of coffee while I tried to derail my muddled thoughts with something on television—which didn't work. Figuring Trina might assist me with my quest to find someone to cleanse my house (since she'd performed that little candle cleansing ritual and the Ouija board was *her* idea), I gave her a call and explained my dilemma. Although less than thrilled, since she had to work and therefore couldn't accompany me, she directed me to Marie Laveau's House of Voodoo, the best place she could think of to find what I was looking for. The House of Voodoo specialized in "spiritual and religious ceremony" as claimed by their website.

Now with a clearer sense of purpose, I had to bide my time while the early morning faded away. Once nine thirty rolled around, I hightailed it from the Omni hotel and walked down St. Louis Street until I reached Bourbon Street and hung a right. Then it was maybe three blocks to Marie Laveau's House of Voodoo. I only hoped that someone there might be able to help me. And if they couldn't, ideally they would direct me to someone who could.

When I arrived, I was fifteen minutes early. I just hung outside of the smallish store and people-watched as I wondered if this visit would solve my problem. The humidity was high and the air fairly warm, considering it was springtime. I watched groups of overweight tourists walking by, all looking like extra-large Skittles, with their incredibly bright T-shirts, capri pants, and Bermuda shorts. At least one person in every group had a camera around his or her neck, but all of them had adventure in their eyes. Interspersed between them was the occasional drunk, who'd clearly partied too hard the night before. In general, Bourbon Street smelled of alcohol, vomit, and sewer.

As to Marie Laveau's House of Voodoo, it looked like something you'd see on the bayou. It was a single-level shack of a place, perched on the corner of Bourbon and St. Ann Streets. The lean-to looked as if it were constructed of plank boards. Some of the boards were painted white, others unpainted, and still others gray with mold. Faded black plantation shutters covered the windows. A white portable air conditioner hung out of one window, the only thing lending the store a modern vibe. While the overall look of Marie Laveau's was distressed, the sign—a circle painted black, looming above the walkway, proclaiming in bright white letters, "House of Voodoo"—looked fresh and new. I gazed at the sign for a few seconds, hoping it would do its namesake proud, the most infamous Voodoo Queen, Marie Laveau.

I heard the sound of the front door being unlocked from the inside. When the door opened, I smiled at the woman who appeared. She looked like she was in her early thirties. Her hair was cut short with a bright red stripe running down her center part. She wore a bull's ring through her nostrils, and had sharp-looking triangular metal cones jutting from each of her ear lobes. Her black tunic reached her upper knee, and she wore a pair of black-and-red webbed leggings that were actually sort of cool. As she walked, her incredibly heavy-looking military-issue boots sounded loudly beneath her.

"Hi," I said with a big smile. I wondered if she'd take offense to my tight pink T-shirt, platinum blond hair, or cutoff jean shorts. Clearly, we were from different fashion planets.

"How's it goin'?" she asked with a genuine smile. I took a deep breath and she laughed. "That bad, huh?"

"Could be," I answered as I started up the stairs behind her. Once inside, I immediately noticed all the stuff hanging from the walls, even on the ceiling. On the wall nearest the cash register were masks of all sorts. Most had a tribal look to them, rather than something you'd see in a Mardi Gras parade. Next to the masks was a shelf of spiritual books, and directly in front of the register was a litany of baskets filled with so much junk, I had a hard time focusing on any one thing. I glanced around and took in myriad candles on the shelf behind me (I could have sworn a few of them were in the shape of penises, but didn't want to stare) surrounded by beaded jewelry.

"You look overwhelmed and confused," the girl continued, offering me an encouraging smile. "What are you looking for?"

I faced her and hesitated for a few seconds as I tried to postulate the best way to explain why I was here. Finally, I just figured I should come out with it—if anyone would understand, it would be someone working here . . . or so I hoped. "Well, I think there's a chance my house might be haunted by . . . bad spirits, and I was told to cleanse it." I took a breath and glanced down at my hands absentmindedly. "I'm not even sure what that means."

The girl nodded and didn't look the least bit surprised, to my intense relief. Then she sidestepped around me and walked to a shelf directly behind me, next to what it took me a few seconds to realize was an immense altar, complete with a painted portrait of what looked like a witch. The witch lady, who had snakes in her hair, was surrounded by fake flowers, beads, masks, cards, and signs warning visitors not to touch anything. I looped my fingers together behind my back . . . just in case I accidentally bumped into something and became cursed for all eternity (which wasn't a stretch, considering how much crap was stuffed into the tiny space).

"Hmm, what you need is one of our ritual bags," she said, more to herself than to me as she bit her lip, apparently determining which ritual bag would do the trick. She reached out and picked up a black velvet sack and handed it to me. I didn't accept it because I wasn't convinced a do-it-yourself cure was what I was after.

"Um," I started as I worried my lower lip. "I was sort of hoping you could direct me to some*one* who could do the cleansing for me?" I cleared my throat, feeling like maybe I needed to explain myself better. "I don't know anything about this sort of stuff, so I'd rather just find someone who does."

She shrugged. "Why have someone else do it when you can do it yourself? It'll save you a ton of money too." She glanced at the price tag of the black velvet bag. "I mean, thirty bucks versus at least a few hundred, right?"

It was my turn to shrug because I wasn't sure if in this instance, it was better to take the cheap route. "And you think that black bag will do the job?" I asked doubtfully.

"Put it this way, if I were you, I'd try this first. You might be surprised by its power." She held the sack out to me. "And if your haunt still persists, you know it's time to bust out the bigger guns, right?"

"I guess," I managed. "What is this exactly?" I ran my thumb across the soft material, wondering if whatever was inside could really get rid of any bad energy in my house.

"It's a ritual bag," she repeated. "It's created by one of our local spiritualists and each one is charged to cure whatever ails you. The Dark Moon ritual bag, which is the one you're holding, releases negative energy. You can also use it for banishing unwanted connections, which, in your case, would be whatever malevolent entity is haunting your house. It calls on the moon for lunar protection. So just be sure you use it when the moon is waning."

"When the moon is what?" I asked as all hope that I might rid my house of any malevolent ghosts promptly disappeared. I had no clue what a "waning moon" was, which meant we were already off to a bad start . . .

"Waning," she repeated with a hurried smile, like she had more important things to do and my time was nearing its end.

"What does that mean?" I demanded, following her.

"A waning moon means the moon decreases in size as it moves from the full moon toward the new moon. The waning moon is the best time to use magic to banish or release energy. That's why it works with the Dark Moon ritual bag," she added before a big smile lit up her round face. "And, guess what?"

"I also get a set of vacuum bags to go with it?" I asked facetiously, regretting it as soon as her eyebrows met in the middle. Luckily, though, she dismissed the apparently unfunny comment and continued.

"It must be your lucky day because the moon will be waning this evening. That's perfect timing for your ritual."

"Oh, good," I answered genuinely, because the last thing I wanted to do was wait any longer—I wanted the house cleansed, like, yesterday. When she started moving toward the rear of the store, I followed her again, because I still wasn't sure what in the hell I was supposed to do with my Dark Moon ritual bag. "So, uh, how does the bag work?" I demanded. "What am I supposed to do with it?"

She turned around and pasted a less genuine smile on her face. "There are directions inside. But basically all ritual bags are filled with herbs, flowers, resins, crystals, ritual salts, sage, and a gris-gris.

You just fill your empty mojo bag, which is also included, with whatever items you need in your ritual spell."

A mojo bag? Was that a joke? I took a deep breath and exhaled, shaking my head and wondering what in the hell I'd just gotten myself into. "What's a green-green?" I asked, not remembering the way she'd just pronounced the word.

She swallowed and there was a slight twitch in her left eye, which hinted that she was growing impatient with all my questions. "Gris-gris," she started, enunciating the word and giving me a snide look as if to say, you pronounce it *gree-gree*, stupid, "is a huge part of New Orleans voodoo."

"Okay."

"It's basically a small bag that you fill with magical ingredients for whatever purpose you're after," she finished. She turned her back toward me again as the sounds of footsteps announced that she had more customers. As soon as she saw she had an out, she left me standing there like an ugly dog with fleas, halitosis, and gas. I frowned but, figuring this was all the help I was going to get, worked my way up to the register where she rang me up as quickly as humanly possible.

As soon as I stepped onto the sidewalk, my cell phone rang. Reaching into my purse, I saw Ryan's name on the caller ID. "Hi," I said.

"Hey, neighbor, what are you doin'?"

I glanced up at Marie Laveau's and sighed. I didn't have a good feeling about everything that had just happened. Call me lazy, unimaginative, or just plain stupid, but I was really hoping someone would do the cleansing for me. "Um, I bought a ritual bag to cleanse my house of any negative energy that might have been left over after the Ouija board incident."

He chuckled. "Nice."

"So, what's up?" I asked as I wondered why he was calling me. It was Saturday, so it wasn't like he was working at my house and might have questions for me. No, this had to be a social call . . . well, maybe. Hopefully.

"Oh, I, uh, wanted to ask you if you'd be up for a dinner date this evening?" His voice was hopeful, but calm all the same. Didn't this guy possess a nerve in his body? I had to smile as I thought if the tables were turned and I was the one asking him out, I'd be a nervous wreck. But not Ryan. Nope, he was the epitome of composed and collected.

I wanted to immediately say yes, that I would love nothing more than to go out on a date with him, until I remembered the waning moon, my haunted house, my mojo, and my bag of grease, or whatever the hell it was called. "I would love to, but I have to do this ritual thing tonight while there's a waning moon."

"If I didn't know better, I'd say that was the king of all disinterest lines," Ryan said with another chuckle.

"No, I'm being serious. I really have to do this ritual thing tonight while there's still a waning moon out . . . before it crosses the sky and becomes new or whatever."

"As opposed to a waxin' moon?" I could tell he was shaking his head as if he were at a loss, like he often did in my company.

"I guess," I answered with a little laugh. "I'm so confused about all of this stuff, I have no idea what I'm doing . . . waning, waxing . . . and what in the hell is a new moon?"

"You got me." He was quiet for a few seconds. "Well, does your wanin' moon ritual require that you be alone? Or can you have company?"

I shrugged because I didn't know the answer. "I guess I can have company. I mean, the super-informative and helpful girl working at the House of Voodoo didn't say anything about me needing to do the spell or whatever the hell it is alone." And the truth was, I much preferred the idea of having Ryan with me. At least that way if something went wrong, I'd have the large barbarian there to protect me . . .

"Okay, let's have dinner first and then we'll do your ritual," he said, a smile lighting up his voice. "Sound like a plan?"

I couldn't restrain my happy smile. "Sure, sounds like a plan, Stan."

Ryan picked me up from the Omni hotel at seven p.m. for our 7:15 dinner reservation. He was dressed in dark jeans, black dress shoes, and a light-blue short-sleeved button-up, which made his olive complexion appear even tanner. I'd never seen him dressed to impress before, and impressed was an understatement. He was stunningly handsome. And showing up with a dozen red roses was merely icing on the cake.

When I opened the door, he didn't say anything for a while, but simply looked me up and down before smiling broadly. "Wow, Peyton, you really look lovely . . . no, you look beautiful," he corrected himself and handed me the flowers. "These pale in comparison."

The roses actually did pale in comparison (well color comparison anyway) because I was dressed in a dark crimson fitted dress that ended just above my knees. The bodice was low and tight and did wonders for my bust. I'd accessorized with four-inch black strappy stilettos and pulled my hair into a chignon. I thought I looked the part of sexy and glamorous mixed with classy and feminine.

I immediately smelled the flowers and beamed up at him. "Thank you, Ryan, that was really nice of you." Then I turned toward my makeshift kitchen, and eyeing a large glass tumbler, went for it. I released the doorknob and called over my shoulder, "Come in while I put these in water."

Ryan obeyed, closing the door behind him as I filled the glass and arranged the roses inside it, admiring them as I turned back toward him. I was more than a little surprised to find him right behind me. "Oh," I started, taking a step back.

"Sorry, I just wanted an up-close whiff of your perfume. It smells," he inhaled deeply, "delicious."

"Thanks," I answered with a smile as I leaned in and smelled his neck, suddenly needing to be near him. "So is yours." And I wasn't lying—his cologne smelled of something soapy and crisp, but masculine all the same. When I pulled away from him, we both just stood there awkwardly for a second or two, staring at each other as if waiting for the other to make the first move.

"We should go," Ryan said hurriedly as he started for the door. "Don't want to be late."

"Yes," I said quickly, bringing up the rear, remembering my room key at the last minute before the door closed behind us. We didn't say anything on the walk down the hallway, or in the elevator. Even though it was just the two of us on the ride down, neither of us uttered a word. When the elevator doors opened, I had to conceal my smile as I watched two women who were waiting to take our elevator gawk at Ryan as he strode by.

"Have you been to Antoine's before?" Ryan asked, completely unaware that he was the source of so much female attention. We waited just outside the front entry doors to the Omni hotel while the valet retrieved Ryan's truck.

"No, I haven't," I answered as the valet pulled Ryan's white Ford F350 up to the curb. After tipping the man, Ryan held the passenger door open for me and I hoisted myself into the raised cab.

"Antoine's is just down St. Louis Street," the valet said. He had a look of puzzlement as to why we would drive when we could walk just as easily.

Ryan nodded fervently. "I'm aware of that, but did you see the heels on those shoes she's wearin'?" He motioned to me with a laugh.

"Ah, good point, sir, enjoy your evening," the elderly man said with a large smile.

Ryan bid him the same and we started down the street, with me feeling idiotic that we were driving such a short distance. "You know, I am capable of walking a few blocks?"

Ryan immediately shook his head. "Nope, tonight isn't about what you're capable of. It's about what you're comfortable with." I smiled at him. Sometimes he was just so damn nice.

The drive to Antoine's took maybe five minutes. Though I'd seen the restaurant from the street and never ventured inside, I was aware that Antoine's was really a household name all around New Orleans. At one hundred sixty years old, it was also one of the oldest if not *the* oldest restaurant around.

Once we parked and made our way into the main dining room, I took in the white table linens covering square tables, which all had four wooden chairs. The dining space was incredibly open, with high ceilings, columns, and French décor. Once Ryan gave his name, the host showed us to our table, which was in the far west corner and decently set apart from the rest of the tables. Whether by accident or design, I didn't have a clue. Ryan pulled my chair out for me and I sat down, accepting the menu as the waiter handed it to me. When the man took our drink order and retreated into the kitchen, I faced Ryan with a large grin. "So, what sort of food do they serve here?"

"French Creole," Ryan answered as he took a swig of his ice water and leaned back into his chair, looking slightly ridiculous in the undersized seat.

I glanced down at the menu for a few minutes before deciding I had no clue what to order. I looked up at Ryan again, my eyebrows reaching for the ceiling. "Um, what would you suggest?"

He laughed. "Do you want to try somethin' new? Or stick with somethin' tried and true?"

I cocked my head to the side as I considered it. I mean, the right answer was to try something new, especially when I hadn't really done a great job of sampling all the Louisiana specialties offered in New Orleans. "Why don't you pick for us? I feel like being surprised." It wasn't the total truth, but I figured when in Rome, or in this case, New Orleans . . .

"Roger that," Ryan said with a smile as he inspected the menu for another few seconds. Closing it, he studied me, an expression of amusement on his lips.

"What's that look for?" I asked as the waiter arrived again.

"Do you know what you'd like to order?" the older man asked as he poured us glasses of sparkling Perrier per Ryan's request. "Or do you need more time?"

Ryan shook his head and leaned forward, as if this ordering stuff were important business. "The lady has left the orderin' to me."

The waiter glanced at me and smiled. With an overbite, beady eyes, and long, crooked teeth, he reminded me of a large rodent. "Brave young woman!"

I just shook my head and laughed while Ryan glanced over at me with a smile before facing the waiter again. "We'd like to start with the gumbo."

"Very good," the waiter nodded as he scribbled on his pad and faced Ryan again expectantly.

"And the crevettes rémoulade," Ryan continued in a flawless French accent, which immediately made me think of Drake. I pushed the thoughts of my ghostly housemate to the back of my mind and focused on my corporeal dinner date.

"The what?" I asked with a muffled laugh.

"The dish is a very famous one, consisting of our shrimp in a special rémoulade dressing," the waiter answered, pronouncing every word as if he had a spoonful of peanut butter stuck to the roof of his mouth.

I just shrugged, since the waiter's description didn't really clear much up for me.

"For our main courses, I would like the filet de truite amandine and the pommes de terre soufflées," Ryan continued as he narrowed his eyes at me. It seemed he was trying to decide just what dish would suit me most. "For the lovely lady, the poulet sauce Rochambeau."

"Very good, sir, and are you happy with your Perrier? Or would either of you prefer another beverage this evening? Perhaps something alcoholic?" the waiter continued his efforts to persuade us.

Ryan nodded immediately. "I'd like a double Jameson served neat, please." Then he faced me. "Peyton, what do you drink?"

I glanced up at the waiter and smiled. "An amaretto sour, please."

Ryan nodded like he was pleased with my choice. "How very Southern of you." I didn't respond but watched the waiter walk away as I wondered what in the world Ryan ordered for our dinner.

"To answer your question," he said, interrupting my thoughts as I took a sip of my Perrier before focusing on him again.

"What question was that?"

"The one about why I was givin' you the look I gave you," he answered while doing it again.

I nodded, blotting the water on my lips with my linen napkin before returning it to my lap. "Ah, yes, why was that?"

Ryan chuckled and shrugged. "Because you took me by surprise and I was surprised by my own surprise," he finished with another hearty chuckle as he shook his head and leaned back into his chair, appraising me silently.

"I've taken you by surprise?" I repeated, frowning because I wasn't really sure what to make of Ryan. I mean, I figured it was fairly obvious that we were both digging each other—well, that is to say this wasn't just a friendly date. No, there had to be more going on between us. We had chemistry for sure.

"Yep, you have," he answered immediately. He continued to gaze at me and I felt like I might lose myself in the low-lit amber of his eyes. "Little did I know the night Hank called me and asked me to check on you durin' that storm that you would later convince me to repair your house and, now, expel your ghost."

I smiled and shrugged. "You make it sound like the expulsion of my ghost is going to be a big deal. I mean, what's a little exorcism, really?"

He chuckled and shook his head, his eyes still on mine. "You're really somethin', you know that, Peyton Clark?"

I didn't really know how to respond so I figured a good old-fashioned thank-you worked best. "Thanks, Ryan."

He just nodded, taking another sip of his Perrier, his eyes never leaving mine. "Your ex-husband was a fool to let you go."

I swallowed hard at the mention of Jonathon. I hadn't thought about him in a while, but whenever I did, a sinking sort of feeling took hold of my stomach, making the rest of my body feel tight, constricted. "He was a lot of things."

The waiter returned with our drinks and said nothing as he served them on the table. Ryan nodded his thanks and took a sip of his whiskey. I stirred the ice cubes in my amaretto sour while I tried to banish thoughts of Jonathon from my mind.

"Peyton?"

I glanced up at Ryan and nodded. "Hmm?"

"You've never really talked much about your marriage or your ex-husband," he commented. "Actually, I think you've mentioned him once."

I bit my lip, not exactly happy at where this conversation was headed, but I could understand why it needed to come out, all the same. Ryan clearly wanted to know more about me, and my marriage was something that had defined me for the last five years. "I generally try to avoid talking or thinking about him," I answered honestly.

Ryan nodded. "If it's painful, we can drop the subject."

I reminded myself what this conversation really was—a way for Ryan to get closer to me, to learn my background, in order to understand me. "No, we can talk about it," I answered quickly, even though there was a part of me that definitely didn't want to. "What would you like to know?"

"Did you leave him?"

I nodded. "Yes, but I took way too long to do it."

He took another sip of his Jameson. "Why did you wait so long?"

"That's the twenty-million-dollar question," I answered as I took a deep breath and slowly released it, taking a sip of my sour before facing him again. "I don't really know. I guess he just had a way of zapping my self-confidence."

"What do you mean?"

I shrugged. "Jonathon is a very wealthy lawyer, and his public image always has and always will mean more to him than anything else. I think he considered me to be a good move where his image was concerned."

"Why?" Ryan asked.

"He is all about community service—showing the public that he cares in order to woo big clients, blah blah blah. Everything Jonathon ever did had to benefit him in some way." I dropped my gaze to my amaretto sour because I wasn't exactly thrilled admitting this next part. "When he met me, I was a mess."

"A mess?" Ryan scoffed, as if the thought were completely ridiculous to him.

I glanced up at him and nodded, sighing. "I was living with a friend who was a drug addict." I watched his eyes go wide just like I knew they would. "So, as you can imagine, my life started to spiral out of control."

"But you were in college, studying history?" Ryan asked, his eyebrows meeting in the middle.

"Yes, I was . . . Let's just say it wasn't easy to balance school life with a robust partying life."

"Were you an addict too?"

"I came close but something always held me back. I mean, don't get me wrong, I dabbled, but no, I wouldn't say I was an addict." I took a sip of my drink and wondered if all I was doing was scaring perfect Ryan Kelly away. Well, the cat was way out of the bag now, so there was no going back.

"So?"

"So I met Jonathon while I was working part-time as a cocktail waitress in this hoity-toity club in Los Angeles," I said with a strange little laugh. "He immediately knew that I was going nowhere, that I was a mess and in need of direction. So he recognized his opportunity."

"I don't understand," Ryan said while shaking his head.

"What better form of public service than to rehabilitate some poor, hopeless girl and then marry her? All his clients, the press—they ate it up. It was like this fairy-tale, rags-to-riches story, and of course, he's the one who came out on top!"

Ryan frowned. "You think he married you as a career move?"

"I know he did." I took another sip of my drink. "And I was the model wife for a while because I believed his charade just like everyone else did. Until one day it dawned on me that I was living a completely inauthentic life and I'd lost myself in the process."

"Lost yourself?" Ryan repeated.

"Yeah," I said and nodded. "It's a very strange thing when you wake up one day and realize you aren't the person you thought you were."

"What sort of person did you used to be?"

I started to answer the question but then closed my mouth as I realized the answer wouldn't come quite so easily. Instead, I pondered it for a few seconds before responding. "I used to be fun," I finally said. "I used to be carefree, outgoing, and spontaneous. I was up for anything."

"And you weren't up for anything when you were married?" Ryan asked.

I shook my head. "It was like that part of me died, like I just became this automaton to Jonathon. I was like this yes-man, or woman, who basically did whatever he told me to. And then once I realized I'd become his puppet, I decided to try to be myself but that didn't go over well because Jonathon didn't like anything other than the Stepford Wife Peyton."

"So why did you stay so long?"

I cocked my head to the side as I pondered the question. "I guess I stayed because I was too afraid to leave."

"You don't seem lackin' in self-confidence to me," Ryan answered as he continued to study me, his eyes narrowed and his jaw tight. It was pretty clear that he didn't like what I was saying.

I nodded. "I'm a different person now than I used to be." I focused on my amaretto sour and pushed each of the ice cubes down with my straw before I looked back up at Ryan.

"I like the person you are now," he said softly. "In fact, I like her a lot." He was quiet for a few seconds as he studied me. "I don't see anythin' Stepford in you at all. You're strong, capable, funny, char-min', sweet, and you're beautiful."

I could feel myself beaming as tears suddenly threatened my eyes. I glanced down at my drink and blinked them away. I just felt so incredibly close to Ryan, grateful to him because he accepted me for who I was. I looked up at him again and smiled. "It's funny to say, but I feel like I'm home here, you know? I'm happier now than I've been in a very long time."

"Glad to hear it," he answered, holding up his glass with a broad grin. "To Peyton findin' herself . . . and me in the process."

I smiled and clinked my glass on his. "Cheers."

Chapter 10

When we found ourselves back at my house, I couldn't help wishing we were still at dinner. It was just so easy to enjoy Ryan's company. We talked, joked, and laughed as if we'd known each other all our lives. The drive to my house was a fairly informative one, with Ryan pointing out various homes he'd renovated, along with the homes of the rich and famous. We parked alongside the crumbling curb and Ryan was quick on his feet to open my door for me, ever the gentleman. He held my arm as we walked up the pathway, and I couldn't deny how good it felt to have him so attentive, not to mention so close to me.

As soon as I unlocked my front door, the contrast in ambiance between the ethereal airiness of Antoine's restaurant and the darkness of my house wasn't lost on me. The brightness, soft chit-chat of guests, and coziness of the restaurant starkly accentuated the empty, gloomy foyer that loomed before us. I wasn't sure if it was just a trick of my mind, but it seemed like there was also a shadowy, ominous feeling to the walls and the broad expanse of aged walnut floors.

"So, do you know what we're supposed to do for this cleansin'?" Ryan asked as he closed the door behind us.

Glancing at him over my shoulder, I frowned. "Nope, but the girl at the store said the directions were in the bag."

"Why doesn't that leave me with much confidence?" Ryan grumbled as I nodded with a small, nervous laugh. Crossing the threshold into my house, my nerves went on high alert. Even though there wasn't any proof that anything malevolent, or anything at all, really, had contacted Trina and me during the Ouija board experiment, the air felt heavy. And I also couldn't shake the feeling that we were being watched—and not just by the nosy Drake. No, this was a feeling that left me frightened. It just seemed as though the house was hiding its own secrets. The more I thought about it, the more it freaked me out.

"You good, Peyton?" Ryan asked, visible concern in his warm eyes.

I nodded immediately, trying to prevent him from getting a whiff of my overactive imagination, which was definitely running away from me. I reached inside my purse and produced the small black ritual bag, which was about the size of my palm. Untying the black satin ribbon, I took a seat on the floor, tucking my legs to the side so as not to appear unladylike in my dress.

"This house is so dusty, you're gonna ruin your dress," Ryan pointed out as he sat alongside me. I waved away his concern, and emptied the contents of the bag on the dark wood floors. There were three sacks of flower petals and herbs, another sack filled with what looked like bath salts, another with three stones or gems, a bag with a crystal in it, and finally, a plastic ziplock bag with what appeared to be sage inside. There were two more empty velvet sacks, along with a black candle that was maybe the length and width of my middle finger.

"Directions, directions," I mumbled absentmindedly as I fumbled with the wrinkled piece of paper. The print was so tiny, it was nearly illegible. As I brought the inscrutable instructions to my eyes, the sound of the door opening on its own caused Ryan and me to turn around immediately. I wasn't sure about Ryan, but the creaking sound caused my heart to leap into my throat. I even dropped the instructions as I brought my hand to my chest in an attempt to quiet my suddenly pounding heart.

"Sorry I'm late!" Trina called out, closing the door behind her and hurrying toward us. She had a red backpack over one of her shoulders and an apologetic smile on her pretty face.

"Trina?" Ryan and I asked at the same time, both of us clearly at a loss as to why she was here, although I had to admit that seeing her was a huge relief. I was worried that our visitor might have been someone or something less welcomed.

Trina nodded, a stray lock of golden hair falling into her face. She secured it back into her ponytail and walked closer to us. "I tried to get here as quickly as I could to help banish the spirit, since you both clearly have no idea what's going on." She speared both of us with a pointed expression before dropping her backpack beside Ryan and taking a seat between us. Ryan cleared his throat as if to say he'd prefer her take a seat elsewhere, but Trina didn't seem to notice. She methodically unzipped her backpack and began rummaging through it.

"First we must clear the space with a prayer to Saint Joseph," she announced matter-of-factly. She pulled out a few ziplock bags, which were stuffed to splitting with what looked like dried flower petals and rosemary. "This prayer is for protection," she added, focusing her attention on me. Opening her mouth, she was about to deliver her protection prayer to Saint Joseph when Ryan interrupted her.

"Trina, what are you doin' here?" he asked, his eyebrows bunched together in obvious puzzlement. "Peyton and I *were* on a date, you know?"

"Yes, I'm aware you *were* on a date," she started, fixing him with an exact replica of the frown he was giving her. "Which is why I didn't show up at Antoine's. But now your date is over, and we need to deal with more important things."

I couldn't stifle a slight giggle as I watched Ryan continue to frown at her. She, meanwhile, elbowed him playfully. "Come on, big brother, you're neighbors . . . there'll be plenty of time to steal sweet kisses later." Then, eyeing me, she winked. "Just call me your friendly chaperone."

I laughed again and Ryan shook his head, but there was a definite smile tugging at the corners of his mouth. "Okay, so get the show on the road," he mumbled.

She frowned at him. "An' y'all are welcome, by the way."

"For what?" Ryan demanded.

"For my showin' up here tonight! I mean, hello, it's more than a little obvious that neither one of you has any idea how to rid Peyton's house of ghostly energy. I figured it was my responsibility as a voodoo practitioner to render my skills."

Ryan chuckled and shook his head again. "A voodoo practitioner, Trina? Since when?"

"Since a couple of months ago, nosy," she replied before skewering him with a big frown and clearing her throat.

I took a deep breath and exhaled slowly. I couldn't help but wonder if this would be a repeat of the Ouija board incident, which was to blame if anything malevolent really had crossed over.

"Gracious Saint Joseph," Trina said out loud before giving us a narrow-eyed expression that inferred we should be grateful she'd arrived to help us. "Protect me and my family from evil as you did the holy family. Keep us ever united in the love of Christ, ever fervent in the imitation of the virtue of our Blessed Lady, your sinless spouse, and faithful in devotion to you. Amen."

"Amen," Ryan repeated. Assuming I was supposed to participate, I responded in kind.

Apparently satisfied, Trina reached into her backpack again and produced what looked like two bricks of charcoal. She placed them in front of her while eyeing the sage from my Dark Moon ritual bag and pointing to it. I handed it to her and watched as she opened the bag and placed the sage on top of the two charcoal briquettes. She then pulled a lighter from her backpack and lit the sage.

"The sage purifies the air," Trina explained. "It's used for protection, cleansin', and blessin'."

Reaching inside her backpack yet again, she produced a white candle. She held it in one hand while she dug inside the small pocket on the front of her backpack. She produced a tiny vial with what looked like yellow oil inside of it. Pulling off the top of the vial, she placed a few drops of the oil on her palm and also coated her fingertips. Then she gripped the candle and started anointing it upward, from its middle, while she closed her eyes and chanted something. After a few seconds, she opened her eyes, placed a few more drops of oil in her palm, and started working the candle from the middle downward. When she was finished rubbing oil all over the candle, she opened her eyes again and inspected what remained of my Dark Moon ritual bag. She spread it out on the floor and pointed to the bag of herbs and flower petals closest to me. I handed them to her and watched as she unwrapped the satin ribbon from each gossamer bag. She examined the contents with little interest before turning up her nose and reaching for the ziplocked bags that she'd brought with her. I could only guess what they were filled with.

Rummaging through her backpack again, she pulled out a mortar and pestle, placing them at her feet. Then she turned her attention to the bags before her, opening three of them and extracting a pinchful from each. She placed each pinchful into the mortar and, using the pestle, ground the contents into a fine powder. She then sifted about a tablespoon of the powder into her palm and picked up the candle. She rolled the candle in the fine dust, being careful to ensure that it was thoroughly covered.

"I just dressed the candle with Curse Reversal oil," she announced to the room. "Then I rolled it in a mix of cedar, bay, and eucalyptus leaves; garlic powder; lilac petals; and mint leaves. All aid in protection as well as releasin' negative energy and bad spirits." She pulled the two charcoal bricks apart and wedged the white candle between them so it would stand up, before reaching back inside her backpack and producing a black candle. Just then, she spotted mine and waved at it. "I need that."

I said nothing but dutifully retrieved it for her. I watched her pop it in place next to the white one. Then she lit both and looked up at me. "The white candle is for purity and cleansin'. The black candle is for removin' evil and for protection."

She eyed my bag of tricks again and motioned for the small, sheer bag that held three stones or gems. I handed her the bag and she removed the stones, studying each one before closing her eyes. Chanting something only known to her, she then deposited each gem beside the candles. "Amethyst, petrified wood, and quartz crystal—all for protection." She reached inside her backpack and produced a piece of jade, which she lined up next to the other three. "And jade, since the House of Voodoo is too cheap to include it."

Ryan and I laughed before she gave us a discouraging look, which made us immediately go silent. Reaching inside her backpack again, she took out what looked a pair of the swamp man's feet.

"Good Lord, Trina, what in the hell are those?" Ryan roared as he stared at his sister with a mixture of interest and offense.

"Alligator feet," she answered noncommittally. "For good luck and protection."

"Gross," I muttered. Ryan continued frowning at the ugly, webbed, and shriveled-up things, but Trina ignored us, placing the alligator feet alongside her other odds and ends.

Then she started reciting Psalm 23, after first informing us that it would serve as a blessing for my home. "The Lord is my shepherd, I lack nothin'."

After she finished, she checked the candles to make sure they were still burning, and continued. "Now for the hefty stuff . . . the demon-purgin' and exorcism of evil spirits," she continued. All we were missing was a drumroll to aid in the unveiling. She started reading Psalm 29, followed by Psalm 10, then 19. When I thought she was going to take a breather, she burst into Psalm 40.

Neither Ryan nor I said a word. We just sat there and listened to Trina as she repeated the Bible passages. She only stopped after both of the candles burned out. Pulling out a brown paper bag from her backpack, she placed the remains of the burnt candles into it. She folded the paper bag, put it in her backpack, faced both of us again with a big smile, and clapped her hands together.

"Voilà! Your house is cleansed!"

"That's it?" I asked, frowning skeptically as I glanced over at Ryan in question. He simply shrugged.

"Well, I've gotta deposit those candle remains at a crossroads, but other than that . . . Yeah, that's it," Trina said with another big smile as she started to collect her things and put them all into her backpack. She eyed the remains of my Dark Moon ritual bag and faced me with a sweet smile. "Are you goin' to keep that stuff? Or could I have it?"

"Take it," I answered quickly, figuring there wasn't anything more I could do with it.

The day finally came that I moved back into my house, or more specifically, the guest bedroom and bathroom on the first floor; but it wasn't all rainbows and butterflies. Yes, I was very excited to be out of the Omni hotel and back into my own personal space, but I was also apprehensive. How could I be sure that all that negative spiritual energy was properly purified from my house? I had to admit I wasn't entirely convinced about the efficacy where Trina's voodoo skills were concerned . . .

Four days had passed since Trina, Ryan, and I performed the cleansing ceremony in the living room, and as far as I could tell, the house seemed unoccupied by anything paranormal. 'Course I hadn't yet spent the night, which meant I could've been completely wrong. Tonight marked my first sleepover in my house since all the spirit stuff went down. To say I was nervous was an abject understatement.

"Are you happy with how everythin' looks?" Ryan asked while examining his handiwork before turning back to face me. We were standing in the guest bedroom and I happily agreed he'd done a miraculous job in restoring it.

The walls were painted buttercream with white decorative casing molding around every window, as well as around the door and in the corners where the walls met the floors and ceiling. The floors had been sanded, stained, and sealed, now closely resembling the walnut floors I saw in my dreams when I was visited by Drake.

As to the furniture, I'd ordered the entire Sofia bedroom collection from Pottery Barn, which evoked the style of Swedish furniture. It didn't so much speak Swedish to me—but I was pretty happy that it matched the room so well. The queen-size mahogany headboard was painted white and the coved corners and posts matched perfectly with the ornate molding in the room. I'd also ordered the matching bedside table, dresser, and armoire, which only aided the airy, bright space. Completing the look was a light-blue wool rug and paisley bed linens of the same hue.

"You really did a beautiful job, Ryan," I said with a big smile as I hung up another of my sweaters in the undersized closet. I'd managed to hang up about half the contents of my closet so far, with Ryan's help.

Picking up a lemon-yellow chiffon blouse, Ryan studied it for a second before reaching for a hanger on the bed. "This is see-through," he said.

"Yep, it is," I answered with a nod, adding without a pause, "that's the blouse I wear on all my second dates."

Eyeing me with what looked like surprise on his face, he chuckled once he realized I was pulling his leg. He shook his head and hung the blouse in the proper section. "I'm really happy you approve of everything so far," he answered as he faced the bathroom. "I have to admit, I wasn't convinced about the navy blue, but now I like it."

He was referring to the navy-blue paint I'd chosen for the walls in the bathroom. Even though the color was pretty dark, when juxtaposed with the white wainscoting it neither confined nor overwhelmed the small bathroom. The cabinets were a crisp white as well, with black pulls. The bathtub also served as a shower with only a sheet of glass to keep the water inside the tub. Everything had a clean, modern feel to it.

"My favorite is the floor," I told him as I inspected it, then smiled, appreciating the view once again. The newly tiled floor was comprised of twelve-by-twelve-inch white porcelain tiles, offset with two-by-two-inch black diamond tiles that were interspersed between every second tile.

"Maybe you should consider becomin' an interior designer?" Ryan suggested when I turned back and found him hanging up my fire engine–red pencil skirt. It struck me as both amusing and heartwarming to have such a man's man standing here, helping me hang up my clothes. I could honestly say that I'd never met a man like Ryan before. He was a true original.

"Hmm," I started, thinking the idea didn't sound half bad.

"I think you have an eye for it, Peyton," he continued, reaching for an extra-short gold-sequined halter dress. After studying it for a moment, he sighed, as if he had no words. Then he asked, "Goin' for disco ball?"

"I'll have you know that is very cute on!" I replied, even going so far as to stick my tongue out at him while unfolding my pink angora sweater and hanging it on a hanger. I had to admit that I enjoyed hanging up all my clothes simply because I liked reminding myself that everything in my closet represented the new "me" and was free from the tarnish of my marriage. In fact, the wardrobe of the married Peyton would be shocked and abhorred to meet the wardrobe of the new and improved "real" Peyton. And that was exactly how I wanted it.

"I doubt it," he said with a frown, cocking his head to the side as he studied the dress more carefully. "Maybe if you're attemptin' to look like a Christmas ornament."

"Blah," I answered as I yanked it away from him. Holding the dress up, I admired it. "It goes well with my hair," I finished as I took a few steps toward the closet, intending to hang it up.

"Somehow, I don't believe you," Ryan interrupted as he blocked me from hanging it up. "I think you should go try it on."

"What?" I asked, frowning at him. "After you pooh-poohed it as a disco ball or a Christmas ornament? I think not! Instead, I'm going to hang it up and let it lick its wounds in peace." I started to hang it up again, but he stopped me.

"I think it prefers the option of showin' how *cute* it is on you, rather than bein' shoved into the darkness of your closet to forever live in obscurity."

I faced him and narrowed my eyes as a smile formed on my lips. "Forever live in obscurity? Wow, impressive words there, Ryan. Did you just come up with that by yourself?"

He took a few steps toward me, his smile turning devilish. He didn't say anything but reached for the dress. He slipped it off the hanger, threw the hanger on the bed, and pushed the now wadded-up dress toward me. "Ha-ha, smart-ass." His Southern accent suddenly seemed more pronounced. He was standing about a foot away from me; and when I saw the undisguised expression of pure sexuality in his eyes, I felt my heartbeat race and butterflies start in my stomach. "Try it on."

I didn't say anything else but simply offered him a raised brow, suggesting I wasn't amused, but I started for the bathroom all the same. When I shut the door behind me, I exhaled a deep breath. I dropped the dress on the granite countertop and faced myself in the mirror. My cheeks were flushed, making it more than obvious that Ryan was having an undeniable effect on me. It was also more than obvious that there was a reason he wanted me to try on the dress—the idea of it must have turned him on. Because regardless of whether the thing looked like a disco ball or not, there was no way anyone could deny how revealing it was.

I took my shoes off and started to undress. My nerves were still very much present and accounted for, and a big part of me just wanted to forget the whole thing. I mean, what in the hell was I doing? And, more importantly, what would Ryan do or say once he saw me in it? I felt unbelievably, undeniably awkward, but before I could change my mind, I pulled the dress over my head.

Seeing myself in the mirror, I sighed heavily and leaned forward. I reached inside the halter top to adjust my breasts to make sure I was showing some cleavage. Then I smoothed down the bottom half of the dress, which ended mid-thigh, before trying to talk myself out of walking through the bathroom door.

"What's takin' so long?" Ryan demanded.

"Calm yourself!" I called back as I gathered my last shred of confidence and walked barefoot to the door. I paused for a few seconds with my hand on the doorknob as I tried to quiet the thrumming of my heartbeat, which kept echoing through my ears. Without another thought, I pulled the door open.

Ryan didn't say anything at all. He was standing maybe four feet from me and as soon as I met his eyes, I had to strain to hold his gaze. I knew I was blushing from my head to my toes because I was so embarrassed, I didn't know what to do with myself. The longer he stared at me unabashedly, the more I felt like a horse at auction. I cleared my throat and forced a grin. "Christmas ornament or disco ball?"

But Ryan's expression didn't change—no hint of a smile, nothing. He had the look of a deer caught in headlights . . . make that a really, really horny deer.

"Neither," he said in a husky voice.

"So, I guess I win the argument." I laughed nervously as I dropped my eyes to the ground because I felt like a total idiot standing there. I wasn't prepared when I found Ryan standing in front of me. With a gulp of air, all I could comprehend was the sensation of his arms around me, pulling me into him, as he brought his mouth to mine. When I wrapped my arms around him and closed my eyes, I felt his tongue inside my mouth, which I eagerly met with my own.

Even though I'd imagined kissing Ryan many times, it was one of those moments that surpasses everything you dreamed it would be. Still so overcome with shock at him kissing me in the first place, I couldn't fully absorb the situation. I had to kick myself to remember Ryan Kelly was standing in the middle of my guest bedroom, running his hands through my hair, while his tongue mated with mine.

"I'm sorry," he suddenly said as he pulled away from me and caught his breath, shaking his head as he apparently thought better of what had just happened between the two of us. "I . . . I shouldn't have done that . . ."

He ran his hand through his hair and took a few steps away from me. I immediately closed the distance between us and reached for his arm. "Ryan, it's okay."

"No," he interrupted and pulled away from me. "It's not."

I shook my head, not understanding him at all. "Why?"

"Because you and I are friends," he answered immediately, as if having to remind himself of the same fact.

I felt the frown working on my lips. "I don't understand," I started, shaking my head as I figured I was about to put myself out on a limb, but I was so dumbfounded by his reaction that I couldn't even say I cared. "Didn't we just go out on a date a couple of days ago?"

He nodded and glanced at me quickly before returning his attention to the ground. "Yes and I don't . . . I don't know what the hell I was thinkin'," he finished.

"You regret our date?" I asked, my voice trembling.

"Yes," he answered before shaking his head. "I mean, no, I don't regret it." He cleared his throat and finally brought his gaze to mine. "This isn't easy for me, Peyton. I can't deny that I'm attracted to you. I am." His eyes searched my face as he paused for a few seconds. "God, am I attracted to you, but I also haven't allowed myself to feel close to any woman since . . . Elizabeth died."

"Oh," I said and dropped my attention to the ground.

"Every time I start to think somethin' can happen between you and I," he started, reaching for my hand but then pulling back at the last minute, as if he thought touching me might burn him. He shook his head. "I don't know . . . I just get overwhelmed with feelings of guilt." He took a deep breath and ran his hands through his hair. "I haven't fully dealt with Elizabeth's death, Peyton, and until I can, you and me . . . just can't happen."

I swallowed hard as I realized I empathized with him. Even though my feelings were hurt and I was still reeling from his announcement that we were just friends and that he basically wanted things to remain that way, I couldn't really be angry with him. Not when I could see the battle brewing in his eyes. "I understand, Ryan," I said softly.

"I'm sorry, Peyton," he responded and offered me a hurried smile. "I thought I was ready for this, for you." He shook his head as if he were angry with himself or the situation. "I really felt like I was ready to put the past behind me and move on, but kissing you . . ." His voice trailed as he focused on his calloused hands.

"Kissing me what?"

He shook his head and brought his stricken expression to my face. "Kissin' you reminded me of the last time I kissed her."

I was spared the need to respond when it sounded like an explosion came from the bathroom. At first, it was a low zapping noise, which erupted into something that sounded like it came from Dr. Frankenstein's laboratory. A high-pitched electrical hissing sound eventually gave way to the noise of a lightbulb exploding with a final, bright burst of light.

The only thought in my mind was that maybe Trina's cleansing hadn't worked.

What the hell was that?" Ryan shouted as he reached out and gently pushed me to the side as if the bogeyman was lurking in the bathroom and he didn't want me to go anywhere near it.

"I think a lightbulb burst," I answered, coming up behind him. He thrust the bathroom door open and, apparently not finding what he was looking for, scratched his head in obvious wonder. His head moved in a perfect circle as he took stock of all the light fixtures in the bathroom, finally settling his attention on the ceiling. What was left of the two lightbulbs that had been sticking out of the sockets was now reduced to nothing more than the filaments, wires, and the screw caps. The rest of the lightbulbs lay in shards of glass on the floor.

"Well, they definitely burst," he announced, cocking his head to the side.

"Thanks for that, Captain Obvious," I muttered with a small laugh as I tried to renew a sense of lightheartedness after the disaster that was our first kiss and now these blown lightbulbs, which seemed, in a word . . . suspect.

He glanced back at me and simply raised his left brow as if to say he didn't approve of my name-calling. I shrugged and played innocent. "Maybe if you'd put the ceiling fixture up, they wouldn't have burst?" I asked.

Ryan narrowed his eyes so he looked all the more sarcastic. "Maybe if you'd chosen a ceilin' fixture for me to put up, they wouldn't have blown."

It was more than obvious that we were both ignoring the enormous elephant in the room. But it was just as well because I had bigger things to worry about than bemoaning a lost relationship with a still-grieving Ryan, which had never really even had the chance to become anything.

"Hmm," I grumbled and bit my tongue because I figured he had a point. Instead of arguing, I watched him turn the light switch off and then step onto the lip of the bathtub; owing to his incredible height, he was able to reach the lightbulbs, which he then unscrewed. I started forward, intending for him to hand the remains of the lightbulbs to me, but he glanced back at me sharply and adamantly shook his head. "Go put some shoes on so you don't cut up your feet."

"Okay, Dad," I answered with a mock frown and, thrusting my hip out in a decidedly attitudinal way, returned to the bedroom, where I spotted my sneakers sitting beside the bed. Once I was out of his line of sight, I exhaled, feeling like it was next to impossible to wear the façade that everything was fine when I felt like crying inside.

Putting my shoes on, I tried not to focus on the fact that they looked ridiculous when paired with my gold-sequined halter dress. Just looking down at the dress made a lump form in my throat. Ryan had gone from hot to cold in a matter of minutes. To say I was frustrated was an understatement because I completely understood where he was coming from. Even though I'd never had to suffer the death of a spouse, I could easily put myself in his shoes and, in so doing, I understood his hesitation.

Try as I did, I couldn't concentrate on much more than the memory of Ryan's kiss. Much though I didn't want to admit it, I could still feel the warmth of his lips. His kiss had been so soft and yet so demanding at the same time, like he wanted to yield to his more wild side but also thought better of it. Kissing Ryan had just felt so natural, so right, and yet the situation had ended so wrongly. I shook my head, forcing myself to stop thinking about it, to just accept it for what it was—Ryan obviously wasn't over his grief—it was pretty apparent that he couldn't move on. Those had been his own words. So what did that mean for me? That meant that I needed to get over this crush I had on him because it would only lead to disappointment and pain.

Focus on yourself, Pey, I told myself. First and foremost, though, I needed to refocus on the current question plaguing us both—why the lightbulbs had exploded.

The more I thought about it, the more worried I became. It just didn't make sense—as far as I could tell anyway—that brand-new lightbulbs would just blow up . . . and for no good reason. Once I laced my sneakers up, I headed into the hallway, where I remembered seeing a broom leaning against the wall.

"How long does it take to put your shoes on?" Ryan called from the bathroom.

"I'm getting a broom!" I yelled back and, retrieving it, returned to the bathroom. Ryan had stepped down from the tub and was now studying one of the broken lightbulbs in his palm as if it had an answer for him as to why it had blown up in the first place. It wasn't lost on me that there was a definite sense of unease existing between us, which we both were doing our damndest to conceal by acting as though everything was just the same as it always had been. But it wasn't.

"What do you think?" I asked as I started sweeping the broken glass that was scattered clear across the bathroom floor. Ryan stepped out of my way and headed for the bedroom, where he turned around and watched me sweep all the pieces into a pile.

"I don't know," he answered and shook his head, his eyebrows crossed in clear confusion. "Everything looked like it was wired correctly, which leads me to believe it could have been a power surge."

"Would a power surge actually blow the lightbulbs up though?" I asked, my tone of voice clearly displaying the fact that I wasn't convinced. "I mean, of course I've seen lightbulbs go out before, but actually exploding?"

Ryan frowned. "It would be incredibly rare but it's possible."

I took a deep breath, the words "incredibly rare" sticking with me. Given everything that had been happening to me lately, "incredibly rare" seemed too coincidental to believe. Instead, I was beginning to worry that something not of this earth was responsible for the blowout. And, yes, it wasn't lost on me that a month ago I did believe in coincidence, whereas now I was starting to blame just about everything on those things we can't explain.

"Where's the dustpan?" Ryan asked me, interrupting my worry.

I glanced down at the glass I'd swept into a mound and suddenly realized I'd been standing there, doing nothing, like someone had simply pressed "pause" on me. It was because I was fully enveloped in my apprehensive thoughts. As to the dustpan, I hadn't even considered where it might be. "I don't know."

"I think I saw one. Just a second," he answered and then called out over his shoulder, "I've gotta throw what's left of these bulbs out too!"

Then he started for the hallway and disappeared through the doorway. I glanced up at the empty ceiling socket and shook my head as I wondered what could have caused the lightbulbs to burst. I just couldn't get away from the idea that something within my house was at fault—that some sort of ghostly energy was the answer. And that would have to mean that Trina's cleansing hadn't worked. I felt slightly guilty about the fact that I wasn't *that* surprised that Trina's attempts might not have worked. She just didn't really scream "voodoo priestess." So that meant that if there really was some sort of negative energy in my house, my next hope was that Drake was the one behind this poltergeist activity. Granted, I still wasn't completely sure that Drake was even real, but at this stage, I was beginning to wager he was.

"Here you go," Ryan said as he handed me the red dustpan, and I nearly leaped right out of my skin because I'd been so consumed by my thoughts, I hadn't heard him come back into the room. "Whoa, there, Peyton, it's just me," he said with a slight laugh. He placed a consoling hand on my shoulder. "I, uh, I hope what just happened between us won't change your feelings toward me," he said softly. "I mean, I hope we can still be friends like we were before. I care about you, Peyton, a lot."

I smiled up at him and nodded sadly. "Of course we can still be friends, and I care about you too."

He studied me, and his eyes were so searching, I felt naked. "Thank you," he said finally. "And, for what it's worth, you have no idea how much you've helped me get through the pain."

"I've helped you?" I asked, obviously surprised.

He nodded and smiled down at me. "Your smile is therapeutic, Peyton." He reached for my hand and squeezed it. "Actually everything about you is therapeutic." He took a deep breath and just stared down at both of our hands for a few seconds before he brought his gaze back to my face. "I haven't been this close to another woman since Lizzie. I don't even think I've actually had fun since she died." He took another deep breath, and I could see the sheen of unshed tears glistening in his eyes. I felt a lump forming in my throat. "So, yes, bein' around you is therapy of its own sort," he finished. "Thank you."

I didn't say anything but simply nodded, wishing I didn't have the feelings I did for this man. Was I in love with him? I wasn't sure but it wouldn't have surprised me if I were. Really, it would be very easy to fall in love with Ryan. I took a deep breath and forced myself to concentrate on other topics, topics that didn't hurt so much. "Do you think there's a chance that the whole lightbulb thing could have something to do with this house being . . . haunted?" I asked.

"Maybe," he said and then shrugged like he wasn't convinced. "While I definitely don't discount things that go bump in the night, I think it's best to first approach everythin' with scientific reasonin'. If that method fails, then you consider other alternatives, includin' the unexplainable."

"Okay, so that's a no?" I asked, not meaning to sound so disappointed but I was beginning to think scientific reasoning had betrayed me a long time ago—right about the time I'd accepted the fact that ghosts were real. Now there was no room in my life for the scientific process, not when lightbulbs were randomly exploding overhead.

"Peyton, power surges happen," he started.

"But you said yourself that they are incredibly rare and it's even rarer still that a power surge would blow out two lightbulbs!" I railed back at him, getting downright frustrated that he was trying to take the cool, level route when everything that had just happened seemed completely counter to anything rational. And, yes, I was also pretty sure that my frustration wasn't just owing to the lightbulbs blowing out.

Ryan crossed his arms against his chest and smiled at me, like I was a little kid afraid of the dark or the Big Bad Wolf. "What do you want me to say?"

"Nothing," I answered quickly and realized I was trying to back him into the corner of admitting what I was thinking. Maybe it was just to lend credence to the idea that I wasn't being completely ridiculous. "It just seems odd to me, that's all."

"And odd things happen."

I simply nodded, but that didn't mean I was buying any of it. I crossed my arms against my chest and regarded him with frustration. "I know."

"Peyton," he started, but I shook my head and interrupted him.

"You're right, I'm just being silly. Science dictates that a power surge could be responsible."

"You realize that I'm not fallin' for that, right?" He chuckled. "Especially with your arms crossed against your chest and your nose in the air?" He shook his head. "That's the ticked off Peyton right there . . ."

"I'm not ticked off!" I yelled back at him and suddenly wished I were anywhere but here at the moment. I just felt as if I needed space and time to myself. It was just so difficult to stand here, looking up at him while knowing he didn't or couldn't care for me the way I wanted him to. It was almost too much for me to take.

"Really?" he demanded and leaned against the wall as he studied me, looking incredibly sexy with his rakish smirk and the way his eyes lit up.

I cleared my throat. "I'm just . . . passionate, that's all."

"Yes, you are," he answered without pause.

I didn't know what to make of his answer so I quickly moved onto my next question so I wouldn't be plagued by the silence in the room. "So we're going to go with power surge, right?"

He nodded. "For now. I'm not rulin' anythin' out, but that makes the most sense to me."

It was my turn to nod. "Okay, then power surge it is." I definitely didn't sound convinced.

He took a few steps toward me and smiled as he glanced at the darkness outside my window. He pulled the linen curtains to the side and was suddenly bathed in moonlight, looking like some ethereal creature. "I think we've both had a long night," he started as he turned to face me again. He dropped the curtain and approached me, wrapping his arm around me as he led me to the door. "You just need to focus on restin' and stop thinkin' about ghosts and goblins."

"I'll think about science," I answered with a smile that I didn't really feel.

He laughed. "I'll come by first thing tomorrow and I'll fix the lightbulb issue. I can even stop and pick up a lightin' fixture if you trust my taste."

"Sure, I trust your tastes," I answered honestly. I didn't say anything more as I walked alongside him down the hallway that opened into the foyer. He stopped walking when he reached the front door and turned his body to face mine. He put both of his hands on my shoulders and forced me to look up at him. "Peyton, if you're scared and you don't want to stay here alone, you can always come and stay with me. You know that."

"I'm not scared," I said automatically, although I didn't believe myself. I wasn't even sure why I felt the need to pretend that I wasn't scared—maybe it was due to the fact that I was trying to convince myself that I believed in power surges and science. But, regardless, there was no way I wanted to be around Ryan any longer. I needed to be alone. "I'll be fine," I finished.

"I had a really wonderful evenin' with you," Ryan continued and smiled down at me so sweetly, I felt my stomach begin to turn to mush.

"I did too," I answered honestly as I wondered if he would ever be able to move past his grief. The silence echoed between us until it was almost uncomfortable. Ryan cleared his throat and looked decidedly discombobulated as he ran his hand through his hair.

"About earlier," he started and then cleared his throat again. "I want you to know . . ."

"It's okay, Ryan," I interrupted. "You don't owe me any explanations. I understand."

"I know I don't," he answered. "But that doesn't mean I don't want you to know how much you mean to me."

"Thanks," I responded meekly.

He nodded and dropped his attention to my hand, which he held clasped in his. He glanced up at me again and smiled. "Good night, Peyton," he said as he opened the door and, with a sad smile, closed it behind him.

Drake was definitely ticked off. Again.

As I was beginning to expect, he was pacing back and forth, his hands stuck in the pockets of his police uniform pants. At first he refused to even look at me, let alone speak to me. But after a few minutes whereby I studied my nails distractedly, he cleared his throat and offered me a polished frown. I didn't say anything but smiled as I sat in one of the club chairs facing the fireplace in "our" bedroom, and simply watched him continue to walk to and from the window. He finally faced me with an air of aggravation.

"Vous devez prendre cela plus au sérieux!" *he yelled at me.*

"Um, excuse me, what?" I asked, reminding him that I couldn't speak French.

He huffed out a breath of impatience and then frowned at me. "You need to be entirely more serious about your approach to this matter," he said at last, his lips tight and his jaw even tighter.

"So I don't even get a hello?" I asked with a smile that I wasn't really feeling. Apparently in dreamland, I was still pretty depressed about the whole Ryan situation.

But Drake wasn't having any of it. He simply frowned and cocked a brow as if to show me how irritated he was. "Bonjour," he managed at last—merely grumbling the word beneath his breath.

"Well you definitely didn't *have me at hello!" I said in response, knowing the joke would be lost on him but not caring. His eyebrows met in the middle but he didn't bother asking me what I was talking about.*

Instead, he started pacing again, shaking his head like I was one big, royal screwup.

"Je ne comprends pas. *I do not understand, ma minette," he said at last as he turned on his heel and faced me. "Why do you not believe me when I tell you that this matter is a severe one?"*

"What matter?" I asked, even though I knew what he was talking about. Even so, there was something within me that enjoyed ruffling Drake's feathers.

"The matter of ensuring the safety of our home!" he railed back at me as he started another lap across the bedroom. The heels of his shoes tapped against the hardwood floors, and the swish of his pant legs rubbing against one another was somehow relaxing and made me want to drift into a much more effortless sleep. "Ma minette!" he reprimanded me when it appeared I was doing just that. "Stay with me!"

I shook myself back into awareness and then tried to focus on the conversation. It was difficult, though, because I was suddenly exhausted. I had to wonder, even though I was asleep, if whatever sleep this was wasn't very restful for my body. I couldn't imagine it was because every time I woke up from one of Drake's dream visits, I never felt restored. "So I guess Trina's cleansing didn't work?" I asked, frowning as I realized my suspicions had been right on.

"Non, il ne marchait pas! *No, the cleansing didn't work!" Drake yelled and, throwing his hands in the air, marched back toward the bank of windows again. He turned on his heel and glared at me. "Banishing the energy of something this grandiose requires the aid of a skillful and experienced practitioner. All you managed to do was goad it with your silly candles and your imitation sorcery!"*

"Well excuse the hell out of me!" I yelled back at him, finally having had enough of his foul mood. "You told me to cleanse the house and that's what I did!"

He shook his head and then held his forehead in his hands like he had a headache—something I imagined was impossible considering he was dead. "Perhaps I was not explicit enough in my instructions," he said underneath his breath as he shook his head again. "Je ne sais pas. *I don't know."*

"So if the cleansing didn't work, what's the answer then?" I demanded, feeling incredibly frustrated and defensive all at the same time.

"The answer is that you find a voodoo priestess who knows what she is doing!" he bellowed at me, his eyes about bugging out of his head. "And you must do so promptly!"

"I'll do the best I can!" I yelled back, although I thought I'd already done the best I could and look where that had gotten me . . . Nowhere. Now I was fresh out of ideas.

Drake walked over to the club chair beside mine and collapsed into it, settling his feet on the coffee table as he exhaled heavily. "I can feel the presence growing stronger day by day, and my own hold on this property dwindles." He glanced over at me, and his eyes seemed heavier somehow, more weighted and serious.

The idea that whatever this thing was growing stronger sunk into my stomach like a sack of rocks, and I gulped down a sudden rising fear. "So this thing is centered here? In my, er, our house?"

Drake nodded and gritted his teeth. "Oui, and it is powerful enough that it is usurping my hold."

"Wait, I don't understand," I said and shook my head as if to prove it. I sat up straight and moved my legs to the side so I could face him fully. "Usurping your hold?" I repeated. "I don't know what that means. You have control over this house?"

He nodded again and stood up, pausing momentarily at the fire-place mantel before he shoved his hands back into his pockets and started pacing. When he reached the windows, he turned back toward me. "As this house belonged to me in life, my power is strongest here."

"Okay, so what does that mean exactly?"

He swallowed, then pulled his hands out of his pockets and crossed them against his chest. "Other entities cannot exert their control over this property as my power is too great."

"Why would another entity want to exert control over this house?" I asked, frowning.

"There are spirits who are vagabonds, who are not tethered to any one place. They simply move from location to location, searching for a place to anchor themselves. They would certainly think well of this property, and were it not for my authority here, you would find yourself entertaining more spirits than you would care to!"

I didn't have much time to consider the fact that Drake had some sort of control or authority over the house because I was more concerned with the fact that whatever this entity was, it was able to threaten that power. "But, this being is able to exert its control over you?" I asked, just to make sure I was following along accurately.

"Oui!" he responded in such a way that I could tell he was getting frustrated with my questions. "It is powerful; hence, I can feel my own strength fading," he finished as he stopped walking and exhaled deeply. He leaned against the wall and stared out the window, taking in a view that had long since faded with time.

"What will happen if it continues to grow stronger and your power continues to grow weaker?" I asked, afraid for his answer.

He shook his head. "Je ne veux pas l'apprendre. *I do not wish to find out." He glared at me again. "That is why it is your responsibility to see to it that this is nipped in the bud now!"*

"But I don't know any professional voodoo priestesses!" I cried as I stood up and thrust my hands on my hips. I'd had enough of his bad mood mixed with the impending sense of doom that seemed to have cast itself over our heads.

"Then find one," Drake replied indifferently.

"That's easier said than done!" I railed back at him. "I already tried

to find one and ended up with a ritual bag from the House of Voodoo! Clearly, I have no idea where to even begin looking!"

But the severe expression on Drake's face didn't change. Clearly he wasn't interested in excuses. He cocked a brow at me and shook his head. "If you want to find one badly enough, you will."

I frowned but figured arguing with him was useless. Maybe the yellow pages listed advanced voodoo priestesses, because if not, I had no clue where to even start in my search. But that was a thought for later on. Right now I had to understand what Drake meant when he said his power was fading—that this thing, whatever it was, was somehow exerting itself where it should not have been able to. "So what does this thing, this entity, want?" I asked, my tone of voice now calm.

Drake shook his head. "I don't even know what it is. It's not something I can see. I can simply feel the drain on my power, which is the only reason I know there is malevolent energy within this house."

I nodded but didn't really know what to make of what he was saying. I glanced up at him when something occurred to me. "The lightbulbs in the bathroom just randomly exploded earlier," I started. "Do you think that had anything to do . . ."

But Drake shook his head, the expression on his face difficult to read. "No, ma minette, ça n'était pas l'entité. *That was not the entity."*

It was my turn to shake my head, and I could already feel my temper growing when I considered what the alternative might be. "I know it wasn't a power surge!" I protested. "So don't think for even one minute that I'm going to buy that answer!"

He frowned. "That was the answer given to you by the barbarian."

I almost smiled at the resurgence of Ryan's new nickname but was struck dumb when something occurred to me. "Wait, were the exploding lightbulbs . . . you?"

Drake cleared his throat but didn't say anything. Instead, he looked decidedly guilty. I stood up and marched over to him. "Okay, Drake, you better have a very good reason as to why the hell you blew up my lightbulbs and, in the process, scared the hell out of me!" He didn't say anything for a few seconds but just continued to scowl at me. "Well?" I demanded.

"I didn't like watching him kiss you," he answered defensively, his chin jutted out, his eyebrows furrowed, and his arms crossed against his chest.

"You were jealous?!" I roared at him, throwing my hands on my hips. "That is the most ridiculous thing I've ever heard!"

"Pourquoi? *Why?" he insisted. "This is my house and I do not appreciate you inviting random men over and then indulging in acts of fornication!"*

"Kissing is hardly fornication! You're so dramatic!" I snarled at him.

"Well, I didn't enjoy playing witness to it all the same," he answered defiantly. "And, in the wake of whatever this malevolence is, you shouldn't be bothering yourself with that man. You should *be focused on finding a way to stop this entity!" He shook his head and then ran his hand over his forehead as if he were feeling ill.* "Vous allez me conduire à la folie!" *he grumbled. "You will drive me to madness!"*

I decided to ignore the fact that I was, apparently, having a serious effect on his sanity. "I am *focused on finding a way to stop it!" I screamed at him. "And not that it matters, but I guess you didn't stick around for the aftermath of our kiss?"*

He frowned at me. "I decided I had seen quite enough!"

"Well, if you'd stayed true to your nosy self, you would have stuck around to watch him pull away from me because he still isn't over his grief of losing his wife!"

"Humph," Drake said, jutting his chin out. He inhaled deeply and then exhaled again, looking suddenly exhausted.

"Drake?" I asked as worry began to gnaw at my insides. "Are you okay?"

He exhaled again and waved away my concern. "I am fine."

But I didn't believe him. Especially not after learning that this entity was making him weaker. I took a few steps closer to him but didn't say anything as he watched me. Instead, I studied him, looking for signs that he wasn't as "fine" as he'd just insinuated. I found the proof I was looking for in his eyes. They were just a bit duller, less lively than usual. "You're not fine," I said in a small voice as I took his hand and watched the surprise register in his eyes. I suddenly felt guilty—guilty that he was surprised when I acted kindly toward him. "I care about you, Drake," I said softly as I squeezed his hand in mine. Even though he was just a spirit, he felt so whole, so real.

He didn't break his gaze from mine. "I care about you, ma minette."

I could tell he wanted to kiss me—the look was there in his eyes. And, who knew, maybe if Ryan weren't in the picture, I would have succumbed to the idea of making out with a ghost. But as it was, I was still pretty heartbroken about Ryan, so kissing Drake was the last thought in my head. Instead, I dropped his hand and wrapped my arms around him, squeezing him tightly as I inhaled his clean but spicy scent. He hesitated only momentarily before clasping his arms around me.

"Vous ne comprenez pas à quel point je tiens à toi," *he whispered into my hair as he rubbed my back up and down. It wasn't lost on me that he didn't translate his sentence, so I figured it was something he preferred to keep to himself.*

Just as I was about to respond, he suddenly released me and cocked his head to the side as if he'd heard something. He held his hand up as if to say I should be quiet. I stopped short and simply watched him as his eyebrows met in the middle and then his eyes narrowed as he took a few steps toward the door. "Il y a quelque chose ici. *There is something here," he whispered.*

I felt my heart plummet to my feet. "What?" I whispered, but he held his hand up even higher and then faced me fully, his eyes dark orbs. Seconds later, his eyes widened with what looked like fear or maybe concern. He thrust himself toward me . . .

I sat up with a little scream wedged in my throat. I blinked a few times against the darkness in my bedroom and glanced around myself, trying to understand why I'd awakened and what Drake had been in the process of trying to tell me.

But I never had the chance to further ponder the subject because I was suddenly overwhelmed by feelings of nausea. I swallowed hard as I closed my eyes and tried to fend off what felt like a bout of advancing vomit. Just as suddenly as the feeling came on, though, it vanished, to be replaced with a multitude of tiny pinpricks all over my body. It took me a second or two to realize the stinging sensation was actually goose bumps covering every inch of me. I eyed my breath, which looked like wispy white clouds expelling from my mouth every time I exhaled. I was shivering—the temperature in the room had to have dropped thirty degrees in a matter of seconds and by now I knew well enough what that meant.

I wasn't alone.

As soon as the thought crossed my mind, I attempted to sit up but found myself restrained. But it wasn't like someone was holding me down—there were no touch points that might signal someone's hands or someone's body. Instead, it was more of the feeling that my brain's messages weren't reaching my extremities. That even though I wanted to stand up, the rest of my body wasn't getting the memo.

I was paralyzed. That was the only condition I could liken it to. I couldn't move—I had no control over my own body and what was more, my teeth were now chattering given how cold the room was. Fear began to spiral through me as I realized I was basically a sitting duck. I closed my eyes and tried to force the message to my body that I needed to get up and flee, but nothing.

Instead, it started to feel like the air was suddenly constricting in my throat. I turned my head to one side and then the next, hoping to release the tightness in my throat but to no avail. The pressure continued to build until it felt like invisible hands were wrapped around my throat and squeezing the air back out through my mouth.

Peyton, get up! I screamed at myself. *Make your legs move, dammit!*

But nothing. Instead, my heartbeat slammed through my body, echoing in my head as I fought to take a breath but failed. The pain in my throat had now doubled, feeling like an immense weight had descended on it and was slowly crushing my windpipe.

Feeling increasingly light-headed and dizzy, I closed my eyes. As soon as I did, I saw Drake. He was wrestling with something just above me—something that I couldn't clearly delineate. It just appeared as a shadow, black air that was thick and billowing in some areas, sparse in others. But it was all concentrated just above me, as in a couple inches above me.

Drake appeared to be consumed by a whitish light that kept flickering brighter and then would fade away again as he struggled with the black cloud. Perspiration dotted his hairline, and with the way he was panting, it was pretty clear he was exhausted. He didn't look at me once, just continued to battle whatever was on top of me, the light surrounding him starting to grow dimmer. But the shadow was also beginning to dissipate, and the wrenching pain around my throat began to let up.

I opened my eyes at the exact moment that I sucked in a breath and sat bolt upright in my bed. I immediately brought my hands to my throat in an attempt to ward off the intense burning sensation that plagued me, becoming an all-out incendiary whenever I swallowed.

Fear continued to beat a wild path through me, and the only thought in my mind was that I needed to get out of my bed and, more so, my room. I didn't understand what had just happened to me but of one thing I was certain: The malevolent energy in the house had attacked me. The presence was growing stronger and bolder. Now this situation had become personal.

I pushed the duvet cover off and started to stand up, when I heard something. I stood stock-still and craned my neck in the direction of the noise—something that sounded like chipping. With my heartbeat ricocheting through me, I tiptoed to the doorway and poked my head out, noticing that the sound seemed to be coming from the end of the hallway, where the hallway met the kitchen. I didn't know what compelled me to follow it, but I did. I tiptoed down the dark hallway and paused once I hit the kitchen.

The sound was definitely emanating from the rear of the kitchen, where the back door led out into the small garden. I took a few steps forward and then noticed the sound dissipated completely until I was left listening to my own shallow breathing. My throat still burned like a son of a bitch but I couldn't even say I was really all that aware of it. Instead, I was wholly focused on what I should do—whether I should stay where I was and continue to listen for . . . I didn't even know what. Or was it better to open the door and find out what was responsible for making the sound in the first place? Maybe it was a stray animal or a raccoon or something trying to make its way inside.

The more I considered it, the more plausible that reasoning seemed to be. I took another few painstaking steps toward the door and then paused, listening for the sound again. But there was nothing. It was so dark, I could only see the gleam of the reflection of the moonlight on the brass doorknob. I reached for it, and once I felt the cold metal in my palm, I took a deep and painful breath. I turned the knob and pulled, but the door wouldn't budge. That was when I realized it was locked. Taking another deep breath, I unlocked it. It felt like eons passed as I watched my hand turn the knob and open the door. My gaze shifted from the darkness of the interior of my house to the darkness of the exterior. I dropped my gaze to the concrete steps just outside the door and felt my breath catch in my throat.

Lying on the top step was a chisel. In the area surrounding the chisel were myriad wood shavings, all of various sizes. But the shavings didn't arrest my complete attention. That was reserved for the ax, which lay innocently on the second step.

I *have to get out of the house.* That was my first thought. Even though I was barefoot and wearing pajamas, I tore down the stairs, jumping over the chisel and the ax. With only thoughts about escaping, I ran down the narrow, overgrown cobble path that led to the decrepit gate in my backyard. All I could think about was reaching Ryan. I knew if I could get to Ryan, I'd be safe.

The latch on the gate was broken, but it didn't discourage me—I was running on pure adrenaline and, what was more, I was very determined. I wrestled with the ancient latch until it gave way, then I thrust the gate away from me and felt a sharp, shooting pain in my palm. Glancing down only momentarily, I noticed blood was already filling my palm where a splinter of wood impaled it.

"Shit!" I cursed and immediately regretted it because my throat suddenly started to burn even worse than it had been.

Even though I hoped whoever or whatever had left the ax on my doorstep was now long gone, I couldn't be sure he wasn't hanging out in the nearby bushes, waiting for me . . . stalking me? Suddenly angry that I didn't plan my escape route better, I wiped my bloody palm against my pajama T-shirt and figured there was only one option left—escaping through the backyard, which wound around the house and led out onto the street. I ran as quickly as I could, a difficult task considering I was barefoot and my backyard was a minefield of rocks, pinecones, pine needles, overgrown tree roots, and broken cobbles outlining what was once a path.

I cried out when I stubbed my big toe against the curb in front of my house, but seeing the asphalt of the road renewed me with hope. I took a right and ran down the street as quickly as my legs could carry me, ignoring the throbbing anguish in my toe. I strained to look for Ryan's white truck, which was always parked outside of his house.

What if he isn't home? I asked myself but forced the thought out of my mind. It was incredibly early in the morning—maybe two or three a.m. He had to be home.

I recognized his white truck a few seconds later and tore up his driveway with a renewed sense of purpose. I was almost there! The moonlight lit my way, and as soon as I felt the cold, wet grass of Ryan's perfectly manicured front lawn, I wanted to sing. Instead, I took the steps to his front double doors two at a time. Trying to catch my breath, I pounded on one of the doors before noticing the doorbell off to the side. I slammed my index finger into the doorbell and secretly prayed that Ryan wouldn't take long to answer the door. Almost immediately, the sound of barking dogs came from inside as well as the sound of canine nails tapping against the floor as Ryan's two Saint Bernards scrambled to see who was visiting.

I wasn't sure why, but hearing the dogs barking made me suddenly feel like a stranger who had no business standing on Ryan's oversize porch, demanding to see him. Even though Ryan and I were friends, I'd actually never been to his home before—usually passing by while en route to some other destination. In any other instance, I no doubt would have inspected Ryan's house more carefully, trying to decide what his style and tastes were. But since this wasn't a social call, I couldn't take stock of my surroundings. Instead, I just shivered in the cold night air, clad only in my skimpy charcoal-gray pajama shorts and a coordinating white cotton T-shirt.

The dogs continued to bark, but as far as I could tell they were the only creatures stirring inside his house. I knocked again, this time with a bit more desperation. Then I heard the sound of bare feet shuffling across the floor. One thing I was now sure of was that Ryan had hardwood floors because they were way beyond noisy.

Once I heard his footsteps reach the door, they fell silent. There wasn't a peephole in either front door, so he peered at me through one of the beveled glass sidelights on either side of the immense entry doors. He immediately opened the door once he recognized me.

"Pey—" he started as he turned on the light in the entry and blinked a few times, obviously trying to adjust his eyes to the sudden brightness. I was so overwhelmed with happiness and relief, I rushed him before he could finish saying my name. In response, he threw one arm around me while using the other to hold both of his enormous dogs back so they wouldn't attack me. "No!" he yelled as the larger of the two dogs persisted in growling and barking at me. "It's okay, Stella, go to bed!"

But Stella didn't look completely convinced that everything was okay. She glared at me with rather large, droopy eyes and continued to bare her impressive set of very sharp teeth. "Go to your bed!" Ryan ordered again, closing the front door behind us. This time, both of the dogs obeyed and disappeared down the hallway.

Once the dogs were no longer a concern, Ryan turned toward me and opened his arms, apparently seeing how badly I needed a Ryan Kelly hug more than anything else at the moment. Just the sight of him completely overwhelmed me with feelings of relief and safety. Before I knew it, tears rolled down my cheeks as I lost control of myself and began to sob. I threw myself against him and he wrapped his big arms around me, nestling me into him as he petted my hair and kissed the top of my head.

"What's wrong?" he asked in a soft voice. I couldn't answer because I was crying uncontrollably. "Peyton, tell me what's wrong," he repeated, his tone of voice more serious. "Did someone hurt you?" He pushed me away from him and appeared to inspect my bloodied T-shirt, as if seeking clues as to what happened.

I gulped, feeling the sting in my throat all over again as I forced myself to look up at him. I tried to catch my breath at the same time that I attempted to hold off my unending tears.

"Just take a breath," Ryan consoled me. "Take your time."

I nodded and closed my eyes, breathing in deeply as I tried to regain control of myself. When the tears finally subsided, I opened my eyes and faced him. "Something attacked me in my bed . . . and . . . and then s-someone left an . . . an ax outside my back door," I managed at last, wiping my runny nose against my other arm.

Ryan shook his head as if he wasn't following. "Something attacked you?"

I nodded and could feel my eyes going wide at the memory. "It was the entity in my house, Ryan, I know it was."

"A spirit attacked you?" he repeated, frowning at me.

"I know it sounds crazy!" I said as my voice started to shake. "But I was asleep and then I suddenly couldn't breathe. It was like something was choking me!" I took a deep breath, feeling the burn in my throat. "I couldn't move, Ryan; it was like I was paralyzed. And it was deathly cold in the room."

Ryan just nodded but his lips were tight and I couldn't read his expression. "And you're sure there wasn't anyone in the room with you? No one could have broken in?"

I immediately shook my head. "I was by myself."

He took a deep breath and cocked his head to the side. I could see his battle over whether or not to accept my explanation as the truth raging behind his eyes. I knew it sounded completely absurd but it *was* the truth.

"And the ax?" he prodded in a soft voice.

I shook my head. "I don't know how it got there but it was there . . . right on my back stairs as soon as I opened the door."

He didn't respond right away and seemed to be absorbing the information, trying to make sense of it all. "I don't understand, Peyton," he said at last, his voice and his eyes revealing his concern and his confusion. "I don't understand how a spirit could attack you, but leavin' that question aside for the moment, why would someone leave an ax outside your door?"

"As a warning, I think," I said. I shook my head again because I wasn't convinced that was the reason why.

"Tell me what happened from the very beginnin'," Ryan continued as he draped his arm around me and shuffled me into the living room. "You're freezin'," he added before squeezing me a little more tightly.

Leaning into him, I allowed him to lead me to a plush, oversize brown leather couch. He sat me down and reached for a brown-and-blue blanket, which he draped over my shoulders after he sat beside me. Then he pulled me into the warmth of his arms and held me while I tried to get my thoughts together.

"Peyton, tell me what happened," he repeated.

I exhaled and then told him exactly what had happened, minus the part about Drake because I wasn't sure if I was even coherent at that point. I had to imagine that no oxygen to my brain for at least a few seconds could have caused me to hallucinate. Instead, I focused on the part about the ax because I figured that was the most concrete. "I heard a sound coming from the back door in the kitchen," I started. "It was like this weird scratching sound, so I got up to find out what it was." Just remembering the instance sent another wave of fear ricocheting through me. "I thought it was an animal or something . . . maybe a raccoon trying to get in."

"Okay," he said, prompting me to get to the point.

"So when I opened the back door, I saw the ax."

"It wasn't there before?" Ryan asked. He further explained himself once he saw the befuddled expression on my face. "I mean, it wasn't an ax that you kept around the house for choppin' firewood or somethin'?"

I didn't bother admitting that I'd never chopped firewood in my life and probably never would. Instead, I just shook my head. More tears started in my eyes so I dried them off on my arm. Ryan's gaze followed my arm to my hand.

"You're hurt," he said, gripping my wrist and turning my hand around to inspect it. Then his eyes moved up the line of my hand to my arm to my shoulder and then to my neck. By the fact that he gulped and then brought his fingers to my neck, I had to imagine I had a bruise or something from my run-in with the entity.

"Who did this to you, Peyton?" he asked immediately, his eyes suddenly turning hard and angry. His lips were as tight as his jaw. It was the first time I'd ever seen Ryan angry, and I pitied anyone who was on the receiving end of such hostility. If I didn't think Ryan was fiercely protective of those he cared about before, it certainly dawned on me now.

I shook my head when I realized where his line of thinking was going. "I can't tell you who or what is responsible for whatever's on my neck," I started. "But, as to my hand, I cut myself on the gate while I was trying to get away. The latch was busted and the wood splintered and sliced my hand."

"Come on," he said, standing up and offering his hand to help me from the couch. I didn't argue but allowed myself to be led from the living room to a bathroom just down the hallway. "I have to admit I'm havin' a very difficult time imaginin' a spirit is responsible for your injuries," he said after a protracted silence.

"I'm not lying to you, Ryan."

He nodded immediately. "I'm not inferrin' that you are. It's just difficult for me to wrap my mind around the idea that something ethereal could have actually attacked you." He held up his hands in mock surrender. "Don't get me wrong, I believe in spirits and the like but I've never heard of one actually makin' physical contact with someone."

"I have no other explanations for you," I said and then sighed.

"Then let's focus on topics that are more easily explained," he started. "What do you think it meant that someone left the ax on your back steps?" he asked while glancing down at me.

"I think someone was trying to break in," I answered with no pretense.

"With an ax?"

"No," I responded, shaking my head, while Ryan instructed me to sit on the lip of the bathtub as he flicked on the light. It was intensely bright and I immediately crossed my arms over my chest as I realized how see-through my white T-shirt was. I wasn't wearing a bra. I watched Ryan open one of his cabinets and fish inside it for something. He returned with a brown bottle of hydrogen peroxide.

"That stuff hurts," I protested, bracing my arms around myself.

"We need to clean it out, Peyton," he answered before unscrewing the cap and reaching for my hand. I gave a theatrical sigh but allowed him to take my hand and hold it over the bathtub. It wasn't lost on either of us when I freed my arms from in front of my chest that his eyes settled on my breasts like a lion's on a baby gazelle. He immediately redirected his eyes to the wound on my hand and even cleared his throat uncomfortably. I felt myself instinctively hunching over, trying to make my nipples a little less protrusive. But, since it was basically freezing in the bathroom, they stood at full attention. Ryan pretended not to notice as he poured the bubbly liquid over my wound.

He tipped my chin back and inspected whatever marks were on my neck, sighing and shaking his head as he ran the pad of his finger across my skin. "There's nothin' I can do for the bruises," he admitted.

I just nodded, making the decision then and there that I didn't want to see the bruises. Somehow I felt it was better not to be confronted with them.

"Why do you think someone was tryin' to break in?" Ryan asked, his gaze traveling from my palm to my feet. He was pretty good at completely avoiding my chest. "Jeez, Peyton, it looks like you banged up your feet too. Your toe is a bloody mess." He reached for my foot and held it over the bathtub, rinsing it with the hydrogen peroxide as well.

I winced in expectation that the peroxide would sting but tried to remind myself not to be such a big baby. I mean, there were way bigger issues for me to be concerned about—like stray axes. "Because on the step above the ax, there was also a chisel and a bunch of wood shavings from where someone tried to chisel out one of the panels in my back door."

I heard his swift intake of breath. He didn't say anything as he recapped the bottle of hydrogen peroxide and patiently placed it on the counter beside the sink. When he turned to face me again, his expression was dour—all business. "We need to call the police."

I knew there was more to it than simply calling the police on a failed robbery attempt. Especially because this was something far more ominous. "Ryan, no one was trying to steal from me."

"Why else would they try to break in?" He did a good job of keeping his eyes riveted on mine, although somehow, I could tell he was itching to see my breasts again. He just seemed nervous, fidgety.

I shook my head. "This wasn't a robbery, I'm sure of it."

"So what—" he started.

"It was exactly the same thing that happened to the victims of the Axeman," I blurted out, my tears suddenly returning full stream. I realized how ridiculous it sounded, but I was convinced it was the truth.

"The Axeman?" Ryan repeated, clearly at a loss as he shook his head and furrowed his eyebrows.

"Yes," I insisted. "During the hysteria of the Axeman's attacks, a few people reported finding the aftermath of attempts on their homes. They found chisels and axes left outside and gouges in their doors from where he'd tried to force his way in."

"So you think a crazy person is tryin' to recreate the scenes of some of the Axeman's attacks?" Ryan asked, taking a deep breath as his eyebrows reached for the ceiling. "That's a big leap to take, Peyton. It could just be that someone found the ax and thought they could break in and rob you with it."

"Then why not break a window? Why bother with the arduous task of chiseling out my back door?" I shook my head adamantly.

"And someone breakin' in makes a hell of a lot more sense where the bruises on your neck are concerned."

I shook my head and sighed, knowing I needed to tell him the whole story to try to make him understand exactly what was going on. "I haven't told you everything," I started as I took a deep breath and told him about the dreams I'd had about Drake. I also told him how Drake figured into the Axeman's murders and how he'd appeared in the vision I'd had while the dark, shadowy figure had been choking me.

"He was the police officer in the newspaper clippings that were on the wall in the guestroom?" Ryan asked, piecing the puzzle together for himself.

"Yes," I admitted, nodding ardently. "He worked on all the cases, as far as I know."

"And you think he's visitin' you in your dreams?" Ryan continued. Although his question made it sound like he doubted my sanity, his expression wasn't quite as oppressive.

"I'm sure of it," I answered immediately. "And I'm convinced he's also haunting my house." I took a big breath, then let it out. "He was the one whose footsteps I heard that night."

Ryan nodded and looked like he was trying his damnedest to suspend his disbelief for a minute to hear me out. "Okay, I can accept the idea that your house is haunted and you're havin' dreams about the ghost. Whether or not the ghost . . ."

"Drake," I corrected him.

"That *Drake* is contactin' you through your dreams is a harder pill to swallow." He paused for a few seconds. "I have to admit, I still can't fully buy into the idea that you were attacked by a spirit, and believin' the same spirit was responsible for the ax on your doorstep is even harder for me to wrap my head around."

"I was dreaming about Drake at the same time someone or something attacked me," I continued, trying to stress how everything was linked. "Drake was the one who first noticed that something wasn't right and he tried to warn me! But, instead, whatever this thing was . . . it attacked me." I took a deep breath as I continued to remember the details. "Then I heard that strange scratching noise and I followed it to the kitchen and found the chisel outside my door."

"Those are just dreams, Peyton," Ryan started, obviously trying to soothe my frazzled nerves.

"No," I said, shaking my head immediately. "Drake speaks French and translates it for me! If he weren't real, it would be impossible because I've never studied French!" I finished, jutting my chin out. "So, no, they aren't just dreams. He *is* contacting me; I know it."

I sighed, realizing how completely insane I sounded. "Ryan, I know this sounds absolutely crazy. I know you think I've really lost my mind—"

"I don't think that at all," he interrupted. "I do think you've got a lot of weird stuff goin' on in that house and it's makin' you lose sleep and jump to conclusions."

But I shook my head again. "I'm not jumping to conclusions. I know there is a ghost in my house and I know it's the ghost of Drake Montague. And what's more, I am completely convinced that he's reaching out to me in my dreams because, currently, that's the only way he knows how." I dramatically inhaled and then exhaled. "What's even more important is that he can feel the energy of this entity, whatever it is. And he says it's draining his power."

Without saying anything, Ryan just stared at me and slowly swallowed. "You don't have any way of provin' to the police that this incident is tied to the Axeman. Most everyone wouldn't even remember who the Axeman was, since it was nearly one hundred years ago," he said in a low voice.

"It doesn't matter because we aren't calling the police," I answered with my mouth in a stubborn frown.

"What do you mean, Peyton?" Ryan demanded, his lips tight. "We have to tell the police! Someone tried to break into your house!"

But I emphatically shook my head. "Not someone. Something."

"The police need to be notified," Ryan insisted. I knew he still wasn't exactly convinced that something spiritual was to blame.

"And what will the police do?" I parried. "They won't believe there's an otherworldly connection to any of this!"

Ryan narrowed his eyes at me. "How are you so sure there's an otherworldly connection?"

"Because!" I roared back at him. "This is not a case of coincidence! Drake was one of the officers working on the Axeman case! And it's a well-documented fact that the Axeman left behind axes and chisels outside of people's homes when he wasn't able to get inside. And think about all those articles I found in my guest bedroom! Every single one had to do with this case! Do you think it was just coincidence that someone posted them all over the room?"

He shrugged. "Maybe it was Drake who left them there. Have you asked him?"

I didn't think he intended for his question to sound so sarcastic, but it came out that way—or maybe I was just overly sensitive. "I haven't asked him about the clippings yet. We've been too preoccupied with trying to get the house cleansed of the malevolence that won't leave it."

"Trina's cleansin'—"

"Didn't work," I interrupted. "Drake said it simply goaded the entity."

Ryan shook his head and sighed long and hard. I knew this was difficult, if not impossible, for him to come to terms with and accept. "Peyton, step outside of the situation for a moment and listen to yourself. You're talkin' about Drake, a ghost, as if he were real. I think you're takin' all of this a little too far."

I felt my lips tighten. "I'm not taking it too far, Ryan." I stood up and hobbled to the door, but he grabbed my hand.

"Let me bandage that hand up," he offered. He pulled a bandage, scissors, and medical tape from his cupboard. I took a seat on the lip of the tub and allowed him to perform his ministrations on my toe. He was very gentle as he applied the bandage and taped it in place.

"So you think it's a ghost that left the ax outside your back door?" he asked, with no tone of condemnation in his voice.

"I don't know," I responded as I watched him carefully tending my toe. "All I'm saying is that I don't believe in coincidence. Not in this case. Not when I know better."

He tightened the tape around the bandage on my toe and stood up, returning all the items to their proper places in the cupboard. Then he turned around again and faced me, his arms crossed against his chest as he leaned against the counter. He didn't say anything for a few seconds but just looked at me with an unreadable expression on his face. "I'm tryin' my best to suspend my own disbelief so I can be here for you. And I'm really tryin' to see the advantage of *not* notifyin' the police about this."

I smiled up at him, genuinely appreciating his concern with all my being. "I know this all sounds very far-fetched, Ryan, but please know that I appreciate your help more than I can say."

A slow smile took hold of his lips. "So the cleansin' Trina, the not-so-effective voodoo priestess, performed didn't work?"

"According to Drake, no."

He dropped his attention to the floor and shook his head as he sighed. "It's gonna take me a while to get used to you referrin' to a ghost as if he's a friend of yours—I mean, a corporeal one."

I smiled but held my ground. "I'll grant you as much time as you need."

Silence stretched between us as we both just looked at one another. Ryan was the first to break it. "So if the cleansin' didn't work and the entity's power is growin' stronger, what's next?"

I nodded as I took a deep breath and focused on the chipped paint of my toenails. I'd intended to repaint them days ago but just hadn't gotten around to it. I picked at the baby-pink lacquer while I tried to remember what the next step was, according to Drake.

"Our next step is to find someone who can cleanse the house. Drake said something about finding a voodoo priestess who was well versed in magic." I paused for a second before smiling. "I don't think we should tell Trina her cleansing didn't work."

"Good idea. She's already done enough damage," Ryan agreed before his smile vanished and he scratched the back of his head contemplatively. "As to voodoo priestesses, that isn't my realm of specialty. I have no idea where to start."

"That makes it problem number one because neither do I."

We were both quiet again for a few seconds when Ryan glanced up at me and suddenly smiled. "Well, I might not know any voodoo priestesses, but I do know a warlock."

"What?" I asked with a laugh.

"I headed a construction project for him. It was an old convent he purchased in the French Quarter, which we remodeled into a house," Ryan said with a knowing smirk. "Christopher Raven Adams. He's a warlock for hire."

"I don't even know what that means," I answered, shaking my head.

"He practices witchcraft but he's a *he,* so he's not exactly a witch. I don't know if he'll be able to help us, but it won't hurt to find out."

I nodded and couldn't stifle the sense of relief that was already welling up inside me. I couldn't think of a better place to start other than a witch, er, warlock. "When can we go see him?" I asked.

Ryan chuckled and glanced at his watch. "For one thing, it's three in the mornin'. Although he's probably awake and more than likely performin' some sort of séance, propriety dictates that I call him at a reasonable hour." He quirked an amused brow. "And three a.m. doesn't constitute a reasonable hour."

"Okay," I answered with an air of disappointment as I glanced down at the floor and tried to talk myself into being patient.

"Hey," Ryan started, offering me a smile as he closed the gap between us and tilted my chin up. "We're in this together, Peyton. I don't know if this thing is a spirit, a demon, or just some psycho human, but whatever or whoever it is, it isn't gonna hurt you again," he said, his lips tight and his voice strong. "Not on my watch."

We're in this together. Ryan's words echoed in my head and I couldn't help but smile. "Thank you," I said and tried to hold my tears back. I just felt like I'd been through so much in the last few hours, and my ability to cope had definitely taken a toll.

Ryan shook his head, and his eyes burned into mine. "Don't thank me, Pey," he insisted. "I care about you . . . I care about you in a way I haven't cared about a woman in a very long time."

At that precise second, the screeching sound of breaking glass interrupted an otherwise perfect moment. The barking cacophony of Stella and Ralphie as they tore down the stairs was the next assault on my ears. Ryan's eyebrows furrowed as he glanced down at me in startled wonder. A split second later, he jumped up and headed for the stairs. I was quickly behind him, as were Stella and Ralphie, but instead of following him up the stairs, they both stopped short at the foot of the staircase. Ralphie continued to bark while Stella whined and pawed at the ground.

"Come on you two," Ryan said as he patted his thigh. But neither of them budged. When he stepped onto the first stair, Ralphie lunged forward and barked with even more ferocity while Stella clawed at Ryan's pant leg. He eyed me and shrugged. "I have no idea what's gotten into them."

But I did. I stepped beside him and took a deep breath. "They don't want you to go upstairs."

He shook his head like it sounded silly to him and started for the second step. Ralphie lunged again and Stella continued to whine. "Go to your beds then!" Ryan roared at them. Neither made any motion to leave; instead, they watched their master take the next two steps. Ralphie's bark grew increasingly louder and more determined while Stella dropped onto her stomach in submission. I took the first step but paused, feeling like neither of us should venture upstairs. I couldn't explain why, but there was a feeling deep in my gut—something warning me to stay where I was. I'm sure it also had something to do with Ryan's enormous dogs cowering in fear, their tails between their legs.

Ryan took the next two steps before I stopped him. "I don't . . . I don't think we should go up there," I said in a trembling voice. "The dogs must have sensed something, Ryan."

He glanced back at me and his expression was determined. "I need to find out what that shatterin' sound was."

I swallowed and watched him take the next few steps. That voice in the back of my head warned me not to follow him, but there was no way I could let him investigate by himself. What if something happened to him? I glanced back at the dogs, who both stared at me from their droopy eyes, imploring me not to allow their master to continue. But I had no choice; he was already halfway down the hallway while I was still stuck on the stairs. I took a deep breath, turned around again, and shot up the remaining steps, easily catching up to him. He turned around to face me and shook his head.

"Peyton, I can check things out myself. I know you're scared—"

"I'm not scared," I interrupted, trying to convince myself. "I just think your dogs are acting weird and it has me concerned."

He looked down at the dogs, who hadn't budged from the bottom of the stairs, and shrugged. "They've never acted like this before." Before I could respond, he was already moving down the hallway, his footsteps heavy on the buffed wood floors. He stopped in front of the first door and pushed it open, revealing a bathroom. He turned the light on as I came up behind him.

"Shit!" he yelled as we both faced the mirror above the sink. It had a crack in it that must have been an inch wide, running down the center from top to bottom.

"How could that have—?" I started.

"I don't know," Ryan interrupted, shaking his head. "Maybe the dogs somehow jumped up and broke it?" But as soon as he finished his sentence, I could tell he didn't believe it, not for a second. And neither did I.

He stepped out of the bathroom and started down the hallway again, this time ducking into the next room, which was a bedroom. The room was comprised of a queen-size bed with a black headboard and footboard, a matching chest of drawers, and a square wall mirror, which had to be five feet tall. It, too, was broken. But instead of a long fracture in the glass, it looked like someone had taken a blunt object to it. The mirror had a circular smashed area in the middle of it, with weblike fractures radiating outward.

Ryan didn't say anything but ducked back out of the room with me on his heels as he started down the hallway again. He paused to open the double doors that led into a wood-paneled home theater. The flat-screen television, which hung on the opposite wall from where we stood, looked like it had been blown from the inside out. The screen was completely missing and scattered in sharp fragments all over the hardwood floors. Some of the pieces littered the plush, black leather movie theatre–style seats.

"Oh my gosh," I said in complete shock as I brought my hand to my open mouth. But Ryan still didn't say anything and, instead, turned around and closed the doors behind us. His silence was beginning to make me very uncomfortable because I didn't understand it. If my house had been vandalized in such a bizarre way, silence would not have been my reaction.

With every step we took, the feelings of dread, which had first accosted me on the staircase, increased tenfold, and my instinct to turn around and escape became increasingly difficult to ignore. But Ryan didn't seem to share the same sense of self-preservation. Instead, he ambled forward, throwing open the door to another bathroom where the mirror on top of the sink was also cracked, this time in an "X" formation.

He didn't hesitate, but continued down the hallway until it ran into a set of double doors, those of the master bedroom. Glancing back at me only momentarily, his face was completely emotionless. It was like he went on autopilot or something. He opened both of the doors and walked into the room, while I took up the rear. Once we were in his room, he stood stock-still. Following his gaze, I noticed an ornately carved mirror that was so large, it took up half the wall beside the attached bathroom. The mirror appeared to be an antique, judging by how cloudy and gray the glass was.

Ryan breathed out a sigh of relief, probably because, strangely enough, this mirror was completely intact. He started for the bathroom and I followed him, both of us taking in the two wood-framed mirrors that hung above each of the sinks. They, too, were broken, each with cavernous cracks running from top to bottom.

"Why do you think the mirror in your room isn't broken?" I asked in a small voice.

Ryan shook his head as he started for the bedroom again, and I followed him. We both stood in front of the mirror and studied it. Ryan crossed his arms against his chest, looking completely troubled and puzzled. "I don't know," he answered, continuing to shake his head. "None of this makes any fuckin' sense at all," he admitted finally.

I nodded and didn't know what more I could say because he was right. Whatever had happened completely defied logic. As we stood there, staring at the mirror, my attention started to wander around the room as I took in the furnishings that all reminded me of Ryan. Next to the bed was a nightstand and on it, a picture. I took a few steps closer and picked up the frame, realizing it was Ryan standing next to a woman I didn't recognize.

They were both laughing and both beautiful. Ryan's hair reflected the sunlight, his crisp white shirt almost glowing in the sunlight. His arms were wrapped around the woman's waist and she was facing him, her left cheek buttressed against his chest and her arms clasped around his middle. Her long, dark hair was pulled back into a low ponytail, and with her olive complexion, her happy brown eyes, and her long, slim body, she was stunning.

I couldn't help but feel a twinge of sadness, envy, and guilt as I stared at the picture, which represented a much happier time in Ryan's life. I sighed as I turned to face him and found him staring at me, his expression unreadable. I offered him a slight smile and propped the picture back on his nightstand. "She was really beautiful," I said.

He nodded. "That was taken on our first anniversary."

I wanted to say something but didn't really know what to say so I just stood there instead, looking up at Ryan while he stared back down at me.

"Sometimes when you laugh, you remind me of her," he continued.

"I do?"

He nodded. "When you're embarrassed about something and you laugh, you cover your mouth with your hand. She used to do the same thing."

I wasn't really sure what to make of the comment but figured it was simply an observation that didn't really require a response. Instead, I just smiled at him and hoped he understood that this was difficult for me too. After another protracted silence, I took a few steps toward the double doors, figuring it was best to go back downstairs so we could try to piece the puzzle together, although I felt like we were missing most of the pieces.

When I realized Ryan wasn't following me, I looked back only to find him still standing in the same position, staring at the mirror. "It belonged to Elizabeth," he said in a hollow voice.

I walked back toward him and we stood side by side. I reached over and slipped my hand into his to let him know that I understood why the mirror was so important to him. I had to imagine it was one of a few reminders of the way his life used to be. He watched me with heavy eyes and I smiled as a popping sort of noise suddenly came from the mirror. It felt like slow motion as Ryan and I turned toward it. Then, like the earth separating along a fault line, the glass cracked straight down the middle. I was only slightly aware of my own scream, but Ryan didn't make a sound. He just stood there, unmoving. My heart pounded through me and the urge to leave the room almost suffocated me. I glanced at Ryan and followed his gaze back to the mirror where the glass continued breaking. It was like watching ice cracking on a frozen lake, the sound just as eerie. It seemed like someone was using an invisible diamond on the glass, outlining where each new crack would begin and end.

"Ryan," I started as I grabbed his arm, my need to escape the room now my primary concern.

But Ryan shrugged me off and stared at the mirror as it continued to break.

"Ryan, we need to go!" I begged him, focusing entirely on his profile because I couldn't look at the mirror. I only knew we needed to get away from it. Whatever was happening, it wasn't good. "Please!"

But he ignored me and continued watching the mirror until every inch of it was broken into small squares, rectangles, and triangles. I pulled on his arm again, but he wouldn't budge.

"Ryan!" I yelled at him. Suddenly, I felt an incredible blast of air against my face and the sound of glass exploding from the mirror. I felt Ryan's body on mine as he shielded me and knocked me off my feet, slamming us both into the floor to escape the flying glass. When I hit the ground, the impact knocked the wind right out of me and it took me a few seconds to restore my breathing. Pieces of glass rained down against the wood floors, and I covered my head with my arms to protect myself.

"Peyton!" Ryan's voice sounded panicked as he rolled me over and stared at me with wide eyes. "Are you okay? Are you hurt?"

I coughed and forced myself into a sitting position before eyeing the mirror, which was now devoid of glass.

Christopher Raven Adams, the warlock-for-hire, was not what I'd expected. For one, he was much younger than I thought a necromancer would be. He was tallish—maybe six feet or thereabouts—and had a general doughy appearance to him, both in the color of his skin and his musculature. Although I'd guess he was in his early to mid-thirties, his hair was completely gray, even white in some parts. His face possessed a certain warmth to it with large brown eyes. He was dressed, as I supposed befitted a warlock, in black—long pants, large boots, and a long-sleeved, billowy shirt that reminded me of Jerry Seinfeld's puffy pirate shirt.

"Please come in," I said, smiling as I opened my front door wider for him.

"Christopher, it's good to see you again," Ryan greeted him with a hefty smile at the smaller man. Christopher didn't say anything to either of us but half smiled at Ryan before sweeping theatrically into my house. That was when I saw the black cape. He looked like a chubby, goth superhero.

Closing the door, I hoped the various shop lights suspended randomly around the house were bright enough to conduct the "testing." Christopher explained to Ryan that it needed to be done immediately. After the breaking mirror incident at Ryan's house, Ryan hadn't seem as concerned about the time and, instead, had immediately phoned Christopher. The warlock-for-hire had instructed us to return to my house where we were to wait for him to test the energies in my house so he could evaluate just what we were up against.

Christopher removed his cape and handed it to Ryan, who took it with a slight smile, folding it over his arm. As Christopher sauntered past me, I noticed the tiny Chihuahua that was clutched underneath his left arm and dressed in a black sweater. I glanced at Ryan, who just looked back at me with a shrug. We both followed Christopher through the foyer, down the hallway, and into the kitchen.

"Mmm-hmm," Christopher kept saying along the way as he glanced left and right, as if inventorying valuable artwork. But the walls were bare, some of them even without drywall, depending on the progress of the demo work.

When we reached the kitchen, which was still mostly intact, Christopher spun around a few times and leaned against the kitchen counter. He closed his eyes and continued to nod as if someone were talking to him and he wanted to signify he was listening. When he opened his eyes, they narrowly focused on me.

"You've got yourself quite a big problem, missy," he said.

I felt my heart plummet to my toes. "What do you mean?"

"What do I mean? What do I mean?" he answered, tapping his index finger against his mouth and eyeing the ceiling, as if the answer was up there. Then he retrieved his strange little dog from under his arm and held it up to his eyes. "What do I mean, little Esbat?"

I glanced at Ryan again, who simply shrugged at me like this was standard procedure. Christopher faced me again as he rolled

Esbat back under his arm. "There are two powerful, strong energies here," he started. "One seeks to nurture you, and the other is more nefarious."

"Are they energies from people?" I asked, leaning against the kitchen counter beside Ryan. I was convinced that one of the energies was Drake, and I was worried about him. Since the last encounter I'd had with him, when he'd warned me that this entity was draining his power, I'd come to realize how much Drake meant to me. Even though he only existed in my dreams, he'd become my friend. Yes, it sounded crazy even to me but the more I considered it, the more I couldn't deny that I cared about Drake—just as much as he cared about me.

"One is," Christopher answered immediately. "A young man associated with this house."

"Drake Montague," I finished for him eagerly. He scowled at me, apparently miffed at my interjection. "Sorry," I offered, biting my lip while Ryan chuckled and squeezed my upper arm, trying to comfort me.

"The other energy is less easily explained," Christopher continued, dropping his gaze to the floor as he sighed. "It is dark, no doubt, but as to its nature and evo-lu-tion, I am less certain."

I was quiet for a few seconds as I wondered if I was allowed to ask a question yet. Still uncertain, I raised my hand slightly like I was back in grade school. Christopher saw me and arched a perturbed brow before he simply nodded. "Are you able to see Drake or talk to him?" I asked, taking a deep breath. I figured it might sound crazy to Ryan, but I was concerned all the same and decided I should just come out with it. "I'm worried about him."

Christopher nodded as if he understood my concern. "His power is fading and he grows weaker." He started petting his dog. "The entity has attached itself to him as a parasite attaches itself to a host."

I felt myself gulp as a lump formed in the back of my throat. The idea that this thing was hurting Drake made me feel sick to my stomach. Even though Drake was just a spirit, he was real to me and the thought of losing him made me suddenly want to cry. "How do we stop it from happening?" I asked. Ryan shifted uncomfortably next to me but didn't say anything.

Christopher furrowed his brows, no doubt irritated that I couldn't resist interrupting him. "*We* do not stop anything from happening." I shook my head and was about to argue, but Christopher stopped petting his dog and held up his hand in a gesture that I should shut up. I bit my lip as he continued. "This benevolent spirit, Drake, as you call him, has formed an association with you," he said, eyeing me placidly. "As he has made contact with *you*, so *you* shall be the vessel through which he again can taste the richness of life."

"Huh?" I asked, not caring if I pissed him off or not.

"You lost me on that one as well, Christopher," Ryan admitted, crossing his arms over his chest. Apparently, he didn't like what he thought Christopher was saying.

Christopher sighed as he shook his head like both of us were stupid. "What does a spirit lack?" he asked me in particular.

"Life," I answered almost immediately.

"Ah, yes," he said as he held his index finger up like he was about to scold me. "The power of life, the blood of life, is an immense power, an all-encompassing current of energy. If you lend your life current to the deceased, their power and energy shall increase."

"Lend her life current to the deceased?" Ryan repeated, frowning all the while as he narrowed his eyes. "What are you suggestin'?"

Christopher scowled at him. "I suggest nothing!" he called out histrionically. His silly shirt billowed as he lifted his arm and did a strange little wave thing. He looked like a lost Pirate of Penzance. "I am merely responding to the lady's question," he added after calming down.

I wasn't sure what I thought about lending my life current to Drake. I didn't even really know what that meant, but based on Christopher's reaction to Ryan's inquiry, I also didn't dare ask. Instead, I thought about the alternative. "If everything continues as it is now, what will happen to Drake?"

Christopher nodded as if the question were a fair one and faced me, pausing for a few seconds. He sighed as if it were a difficult answer for him to explain, and dropped his eyes to the ground before looking at me again. He exhaled heavily. "He will simply be absorbed into the power of the entity, thereby further strengthening it."

I nodded in silent understanding, promising myself and Drake that I wouldn't allow that to happen to him. Because at the end of the day, it didn't matter if Drake was alive or dead, a ghost or corporeal; he was my friend and that was all that mattered to me. And now that Christopher had more or less provided proof that Drake wasn't just a figment of my imagination, I was even more determined. "And you don't know anything about the entity? How did it get here? How could it become so powerful?" I asked.

Christopher shook his head. "I cannot answer your questions at this stage. The threat is too great for me to drop my defenses," he said with his nose in the air. "I cannot delve too deeply for my own safety." He held up his index finger again. "But, suffice it to say that whatever this threat is, it is quite a hefty one." He checked around himself and reached out as if he were pointing at or touching something only seen to him. "I can feel rivulets of its energy flowing through the air, the ground." He eyed me again. "It tries to attach itself to you, but as of yet, it is unsuccessful. This Drake spirit purports himself to be your . . . protector of sorts." He nodded while saying this, as though someone were streaming the information to him as he said it to me. "The entity realizes this, which is why it attacks Drake. It seeks to remove him as an obstacle." He fell silent for a moment and peered at me again. "Ultimately, however, it wants you." He was quiet again as he nodded and then faced me. "It has already attacked you, left its mark." Then he brought his fingertips to his neck while he spied mine, nodding once he saw the bruise. "This Drake character protected you, stopped this entity from further harming you."

I nodded immediately. "Yes." I swallowed hard and made the decision that I would fight for Drake. In the same way that he had taken it upon himself to be my protector, now it was time to return the favor.

"Then the answer is simple," Ryan interjected, shaking his head like he'd heard enough. "She won't live here anymore! She sells this house and she moves!"

Christopher shook his head and chuckled mirthlessly as he paid attention to petting his dog. "The answer is not quite so easy, I'm afraid," he said to Ryan.

"I can't move," I answered at the same time. This house was a part of me and no matter how diseased it was, I wouldn't flee with my tail between my legs. I would fight this negative power, if not for my own sake, then for Drake's. Just as Drake had come to my defense, I needed and wanted to come to his.

"The entity has targeted her, seeking her out for a purpose only known to it," Christopher continued as he closed his eyes again and started to nod. "It senses a deep-seated connection between it and you," he finished at last, opening his eyes as he focused on me.

"A connection to me?" I repeated, completely failing to see how that could be. What was worse, the very idea made me feel sick to my stomach. "How is that even possible?"

Christopher raised his left brow and cocked his head to the side. "You might be surprised."

"Then how do I find out what this connection is?" I continued.

"Perhaps it is time to research your genealogy," Christopher responded, his tone of voice and his general air one of boredom.

"My genealogy?" I repeated, shaking my head. "I don't even know where to start!"

"I always suggest Ancestry.com to my clients, as the answers can usually be found there," Christopher answered before he turned to face Ryan. He motioned for Ryan to hand him the black cape that still hung over Ryan's arm. Ryan handed it to him, and Christopher simply shook his head and motioned to his back. He asked, "Would you kindly do the honors for me?"

Ryan smiled and laid the cape across Christopher's shoulders as the smaller, pudgier man started for the hallway. "I am beginning to tire, which means I must leave this place to ensure my safety." He turned back toward me and cleared his throat. "Find the answers you require regarding your connection to this home and this malevolence," he started. "When you have found the information you seek, I will instruct you on your next action."

Chapter 14

I spent the next morning on my laptop at the neighborhood Starbucks. I hopped on Ancestry.com and started my search. After entering my first and last name, my age, and my e-mail address, I decided to skip the free trial and pay the twenty bucks for one month because I figured I'd probably need it. I mean, who knew how long this research would take me?

I entered my mother's full name, her date of birth, and her birthplace, then was prompted for information regarding my maternal grandfather that I didn't have. Great, I was off to a wonderful start . . . I skipped that field and clicked "Enter" and was bombarded with a list of names that matched my mother's. The first one had a little green leaf in the corner which was supposedly the closest match to my mother as far as the website was concerned, so I clicked it. And wouldn't you know, it was right. I added my mother's profile to my family tree and started a search on my grandmother.

I didn't get far. And I wasn't very surprised. As far as my mother's family went, I didn't know much about them. All I did know was that my mom had left home at the age of seventeen, never to return again. She and her family weren't close by any stretch of the imagination, which meant I knew next to nothing about any of them. I'd never even met my grandparents, but I did know my grandmother's name was Esther and my mother, who had never married, carried the last name of Clark, so I figured Esther was Esther Clark.

I entered as much into the space provided and the website returned a long list of what seemed like a million Esther Clarks. I clicked on the first few links but couldn't make any associations with the information returned. Stumped for a few seconds, I then decided to do a search on someone I did have a bit of information on: my Great-Aunt Myra. From all the paperwork on the house, I remembered that Myra's full name was Myra Jennings.

I entered her name, estimated her date of birth, and then entered "New Orleans" into the search parameter. Then I clicked "Search." My query returned another long list of names but the closest matches were at the top, so I clicked the first listing. It returned a census from 1940 and I clicked the link to find out more. I was taken to a page that listed other residents who were at the same address on the day the census was taken. They included Esther Jennings, my grandmother, who was listed at the time of the census as being eighteen years old; Myra, who was listed as being twelve years old; and Sarah Laumann Jennings, who was listed as being forty years old. I could only imagine that Sarah was both Myra and Esther's mother. And for some reason I couldn't quite pinpoint, the name Sarah Laumann Jennings seemed familiar to me.

I noticed in the upper right-hand corner of the page, I could click a link that would take me to a scanned copy of the census from 1920 so I did just that. It returned a handwritten document that was difficult to read. I scanned the myriad names scribbled down until I reached the line with the Jennings. Further studying it, I learned that Sarah was, indeed, the mother of Myra and Esther. Furthermore, there didn't appear to be a head of household, aka a man, in the picture. Instead, there appeared a "D" as a line item next to Sarah's name, which meant she had been divorced. The census also noted that Sarah apparently owned her home.

I clicked the next census, which was from 1960, and learned that in that year, only Myra had lived with Sarah in the house I now called my own. According to the records of history, my grandmother, Esther, had married John Clark and had had my mother.

"Sarah Laumann Jennings," I said to myself, shaking my head as I tried to figure out why the name sounded so familiar to me. Maybe my mother had mentioned my great-grandmother in one of our very rare discussions about her side of the family?

I opened another browser window and typed Sarah's name into Google. What Google returned made my breath catch in my throat.

"The Axeman and the unsolved murders that terrorized New Orleans," I read. My heart now pounding in my chest, I clicked on the link and scanned the page until I reached Sarah's name and came to learn that she'd indeed been one of the victims of the Axeman:

> Wednesday, September 3, 1919, marked the day a young woman, living alone, was attacked by the Axeman. The nineteen-year-old woman, named Sarah Laumann, was assaulted in her bed by a man wielding an axe. She sustained several head wounds but survived and recovered from her attack at Charity Hospital. She could offer no description of her attacker other than that he came in the dark and appeared as a dark and shadowy figure. A bloody axe was found in the grass just at the rear of Sarah's back door.

I took a deep breath and brought my eyes to the ceiling as I ran my hand through my hair and realized what this meant—I was related to one of the victims of the Axeman. Sarah Laumann had been my maternal great-grandmother and from what I could glean, she was also one of few survivors of the Axeman's attacks.

There was the connection Christopher had told me to find. But there was one piece to this puzzle that still didn't make any sense to me—how Sarah Laumann had ended up purchasing Drake's home.

Figuring the Internet would lead me to my answer, I opened yet another new tab and entered my address as a search parameter.

The first responses were mainly real estate–related sites offering house values and the like. Once I noticed a link purporting to be a listing of public property records, I clicked on it. The first line item referenced my taking over ownership of the house but previous to that, it appeared the house had only changed hands once before—in 1969, when it appeared Myra took over ownership from Sarah. But prior to that, there wasn't any other information. I figured it was because the information predated the available public records. It was something that would probably require a trip to the courthouse.

Instead, I returned to Ancestry.com and continued researching Sarah Laumann, learning that she died in 1969 at the age of sixty-nine. When my head started to ache from information overload, I turned the computer off and decided to give myself and my research a rest for the time being. What I really needed to do now was establish the connection between Drake and Sarah, and the easiest way to do that was to discuss the subject with Drake himself. But, of course, that would have to wait until later tonight when I went back to my house and went to sleep. Something that didn't exactly fill me with the warm and fuzzies.

"Drake!" I yelled his name as soon as I recognized my surroundings. I was in the dining room, only it was the way it had looked in 1919. I found myself alone and seated at the end of a long, rectangular wooden table. I immediately stood and started for the hallway, barely even registering the pain when I rammed my hip against one of the chair backs.

The hallway was empty. An errant breeze fluttered the white gauze curtain that hung alongside the window at the end of the hall, exposing the pristine gardens below. But I wasn't interested in any bygone view. I needed to find Drake.

I sailed down the hallway, feeling as if I were flying rather than running. The impact of my footsteps on the hardwood floors was loud and echoed through the house, reminding me that I was the only one in it. The first doorway I reached was the kitchen. Peering in, I saw it was empty, so I continued down the hall until I reached the next door. Pushing it open, I found a room full of floor-to-ceiling bookshelves, stocked neatly with leather-bound volumes of what I assumed were the classics. In modern times, this was my laundry room. Somehow, I preferred it as a library.

A lone ladder was attached to the bookshelf and stood at the far corner of the room. There was a fire blazing in the hearth, the smell of wood smoke and warm leather somehow comforting.

"Bonjour, ma minette," Drake said from where he reclined on a brown leather settee in the middle of the room. His voice sounded as stricken and exhausted as he looked. His head was propped up on a pillow and a dark-brown blanket covered the lower half of his legs, which were motionless. Blue plaid pajama pants peeked out from underneath a blanket that matched the navy blue of his loose-fitting robe. It did little to cover what I could see of a very well-defined chest, lightly peppered with dark-brown hair. When my wandering eyes returned to his face, I noticed he appeared to be suffering from the flu or something. But I was acutely aware that the reality was far worse than just a simple virus. As ridiculous as it sounded, his soul was in jeopardy, not his life.

"Drake," I said, choking on his name as I approached him. I kneeled down so our faces were level. "What's happening to you?"

*He cleared his throat before taking a deep breath, which seemed to sap all his energy. "*Je perds. *I am losing," he responded quickly, shaking his head as if he were angry over it.*

I reached for his hand, which felt ice-cold when I touched it. I massaged his fingers and smiled at him, hoping I could invigorate him and breathe some warmth back into his bluish countenance. "I won't let this thing beat you," I said with steely resolve, feeling my words echoing through me.

Drake shook his head like he appreciated my enthusiasm but wasn't buying it. Then he gave me a quick but pained smile before he eyed the ceiling and seemed to zone out. It was another few seconds before he spoke. "I still cannot see what this being, or thing, is," he said slowly, but I could see the confusion in his eyes just as clearly as I heard it in his tone. "But it feels as if it grows stronger with each passing second." He took another deep breath and fell silent for a few more seconds as if speaking took everything out of him. "And with each moment, I grow wearier, plus faible . . . *weaker."*

He turned toward me and smiled sadly again, his eyes empty orbs and his skin sallow and lifeless. His ordinarily thick, full head of hair took on a grayish hue except where it was wet from the sweat that beaded along his hairline. He seemed weak, frail, and small—nothing like the handsome, charismatic, and robust man I recognized from my dreams. I felt like I wanted to cry but held my tears in check, knowing they wouldn't do either of us any good. Drake needed my strength, not my sadness.

Even more alarming than Drake's current condition was the time it had taken for him to get there. I just couldn't understand how it happened so quickly! One night had passed since the last time I'd seen him, and even though he'd seemed tired, his condition in no way resembled the broken man lying before me now.

"Everything is going to be okay," I said, even though we both remained unconvinced. It just seemed a stupid thing to even think when everything was so far from being okay. "I found someone to cleanse the house," I added quickly, hoping to imply the situation wasn't exactly as bad as it seemed. And while Christopher the warlock never exactly agreed to cleanse the house and, actually, hadn't agreed to do much of anything at all, I didn't want Drake to know that. Besides, I had no one else but Christopher. He was my golden ticket, the only arrow in my quiver that could possibly defeat whatever this entity was. So, despite

any reluctance on his part, Christopher would *cleanse the house, as far as I was concerned.*

"Le sorcier . . . *the warlock," Drake said, breathing out shallowly. He nodded, and his eyes revealed some recognition. "He visited me, but I was too weak to interact with him."*

"I don't understand," I said, shaking my head. "Did you see him?"

Drake shook his head while recalling the event. "He existed merely as a strange voice, disembodied. Our connection was spotty at best so I couldn't understand what he said or what his intentions were."

"We asked him here to determine what the entity is," I answered. "I think he can help us, Drake," I finished with a heartfelt smile. I began stroking his hair and wiping the sweat from his forehead with the cuff of my shirt. "He's not a voodoo priestess, but I bet he's just as powerful. He's a necromancer. He said I can help bring you back to health again."

Drake didn't say anything and his expression was unreadable. "Was he able to connect with the entity?" he asked, turning to face me with sudden interest. "Could he see it? Did he know what it was?"

I shook my head. "He said it was too dangerous for him to attempt reaching out to it. But he recognized its malevolence immediately."

"Does he know why it's here or what it wants?" he continued, his interest obviously piqued.

I cleared my throat because I knew Drake wouldn't take my answer well. Even I still wasn't taking it very well. "He says the entity wants me," I finished, my voice dropping lower with resignation.

Drake nodded as if he weren't surprised, which worried me. Frowning, he settled his lifeless gaze on me. "I figured that part out too late, I'm afraid." He shook his head and bit his lip. I could see his frustration and it was a difficult thing to watch. "I tried to protect you, ma minette, but I am afraid I've failed you."

"You haven't failed me," I said with watery eyes as I remembered him battling the entity when it was choking the life out of me. "You've kept me safe this whole time. If it weren't for you, I wouldn't even be here right now."

He gripped my hand and stared at me, a sudden urgency in his expression. Maybe it was with the realization that he couldn't keep me safe any longer, not when his vitality was fading so rapidly. "Il faut que vous quittiez cette maison! *You need to leave this house," he said, his eyes boring into mine. "Get as far away as you can."*

I shook my head, remembering how Christopher said that it wouldn't do any good. For whatever reason, this entity had its sights on me and I doubted it would care what zip code I lived in. And seeing how quickly it had drained Drake's power and vivacity convinced me it could locate me wherever I tried to hide. I had a feeling the fact that Sarah Laumann was my great-grandmother had something to do with it.

I smiled down at my friend and continued running my fingers through his hair, trying to console him. "I need you to hold on for me, Drake," I said softly. Bringing my mouth to his forehead, I kissed him gently. I pulled away and saw his unbridled affection for me reflected in the chocolate of his irises. "I need you to resist it just for a little while longer," I finished. But I already knew that waiting to see Christopher wasn't an option. Drake was too far gone already. Time was of the essence and I had to act now.

He simply nodded and smiled up at me as I wondered how much longer he could hold this thing off. "Ma minette, ma belle, my beautiful," he whispered.

But before I left Drake to visit Christopher, I needed some information. "I need to know if you were ever in contact with Sarah Laumann."

He closed his eyes and took a deep breath before nodding. "Oui. She was one of his victims," he said in a far-off voice.

"Yes, how did you know her?"

"I was working on her case," he answered immediately before taking another deep breath and finally opening his eyes. "She was so young. When I visited her at Charity Hospital to question her as to what had happened,

she was so frightened she was barely able to speak. Her head was bandaged but the bandages did nothing to detract from the beauty of her face."

I swallowed hard as I started to guess where this conversation was headed. "Were you and my great, er, Sarah, involved?"

He sighed and then nodded, glancing up at me briefly. "Pour un temps. *For a time." He cleared his throat and I could see the exhaustion beginning to build in his eyes. It was time for me to go.*

"I need you to wake me up now, Drake," I said in a soft voice. "Wake me up."

I came to almost immediately. Sitting up with a start, I glanced around and found I was back in my bed, in my guest bedroom, in my house. I wiped my eyes as I pushed the duvet off and immediately turned to the task of getting dressed. I was more than sure that Christopher wouldn't appreciate a phone call at midnight, but this was an emergency. I'd never seen Drake so infirm, so vacant and sickly. It scared the hell out of me.

Pulling on my bra and panties, I slid the pair of jeans I'd worn earlier in the evening on and wiggled into a white sweatshirt. Then I fished out two balled-up socks that had never made it to the hamper and hoped they didn't smell too bad. Throwing on my sneakers, I picked up Christopher's business card from my side table and dialed his number.

"Warlock-for-hire, Christopher Raven Adams here," he answered on the second ring in a blasé tone. He didn't sound like he'd been sleeping.

"Hi Christopher, this is Peyton from Prytania Street."

"Mmm-hmm."

"Um, I'm sorry I'm calling you so late."

"It's okay. I don't sleep. What do you need?"

I took a deep breath and heaved out a sigh. "I just made contact with Drake and, uh, he's really not doing well. I don't think he'll last much longer."

He grumbled something unintelligible and groaned before becoming quiet for another few seconds. "Very well, I shall arrive within the hour."

He was off the phone before I could thank him. Hanging up my phone, my thoughts switched to Ryan. Yes, I did consider calling him to let him know what I was up to. Ultimately, however, I decided against it. First of all, I'd had a hell of a time convincing him to let me continue sleeping in my house, after everything that had gone down. But I was determined to make contact with Drake if only to check in on him. And my chances of reaching him were better when I was in our house.

Second, it wasn't Ryan's problem; it was mine. I didn't want to ask for Ryan's help again and possibly put him in any more danger. That was a thought I wanted nothing to do with.

I started to pace my room back and forth, thinking of Drake. I refused to sit still, not while I was worried to death that Drake might not last however long it took Christopher to arrive. Within the hour? An hour was a long time to wait! Could Drake last another hour?

I walked out of my room and started for the hallway. I intended to plug in all the overhead shop lights and brighten the place up. After completing that task, I kept busy by inspecting each of the downstairs rooms to see how much progress Ryan's men had made. That took all of ten minutes and I was left twiddling my thumbs again. But I was spared from inventing another mindless task to keep my thoughts off the slow, molasses dripping of time when I heard a steady stream of water coming from the guest bathroom.

Narrowing my eyes, I tried to remember if I'd turned off the faucet and eerily recalled that I'd never even turned it on. Gulping down my surging fear, I prodded myself forward to investigate. I didn't race to do it by any stretch of the imagination, but tiptoed toward the bedroom, where the sound of water became more audible. Now closer, it didn't sound as though it was coming from the sink faucet, but more like someone had turned the bath on.

When I reached my bedroom, the bathroom door was shut, and I definitely remembered leaving it open. A steady flow of steam emerged from beneath the door, illuminated by the bathroom light.

My heart climbed into my throat as I approached the door. When I reached for the doorknob, I feared I might just seize up and suffer a stroke right there. But I didn't. Grasping the knob in my palm, I turned it and felt like I was in slow motion. I pulled the door toward me and became momentarily blinded by the overhead light, which seemed much brighter when combined with the enormous amount of condensation in the room. The steam hit me full force in the face like a slap and I blinked against it. It was just like walking into a sauna.

Incredibly, the air was so thick, I couldn't even see through it. Taking a few small steps forward, I shielded my face with my arm so the scalding mist wouldn't scorch my eyes. They were already tearing up, and I had difficulty breathing the inexplicably searing air. I tried to fan the steam, but it was like dense, white smoke, and so cloudy and heavy, it was opaque.

Following the sound of rushing water, I stumbled through the haze until I inadvertently kicked the bathtub with my toes. I slid the glass door to one side and reached into the bathtub, gripping the hot water knob and turning it off. Standing up again, I turned back around and noticed the steam was dissipating so quickly, it was almost as if an invisible vacuum were sucking it up from the middle of the room.

When I looked up, I was standing in front of the mirror above the sink. The steam seemed to cling to the mirror, keeping the whole thing cloudy. As I watched the vapor slowly dissipate, I could see it was leaving something behind on the mirror—words.

Taking a few steps closer, my eyes went wide and my fight-or-flight reflex was on high alert. Somehow, I couldn't retreat, not until I read what the mirror said. The steam continued to dissipate, revealing paragraphs of text. The font was so small, I had to take a few steps closer in order to read it.

Hell, April 15, 2014

Esteemed Mortal:

They have never caught me and they never will. They have never seen me, for I am invisible, even as the ether that surrounds your earth. I am not a human being but a spirit and a fell demon from the hottest hell. I am what you Orleanians and your foolish police call the Axeman.

When I see fit, I shall come again and claim other victims. I alone know who they shall be. I shall leave no clue except my bloody ax, besmeared with the blood and brains of him whom I have sent below to keep me company.

If you wish you may tell the police not to rile me. Of course I am a reasonable spirit. I take no offense at the way they have conducted their investigation in the past. But tell them to beware. Let them not try to discover what I am, for it were better that they were never born than to incur the wrath of the Axeman.

Now, to be exact, at 12:15 (earthly time) on next Tuesday night, I am going to visit again.

The Axeman

It was the Axeman's famous letter that first appeared in the New Orleans *Times-Picayune* newspaper in 1919. Only now it was on my bathroom mirror and it had today's date. I heard myself screaming at the exact time that I twirled around on my toes, before running headlong into Christopher's black cape.

"Yow!" he yelled. He spun around to face me, his cape catching air and billowing over my head. I screamed again, thinking the Axeman was enveloping me in his darkness. Then I felt cold hands on my upper arms as the cape fell away and I looked up at an enraged Christopher.

"You nearly gave me a heart attack!" he screamed at me, his eyes popping out of his head.

But I was too breathless to think, and much too overwhelmed and terrified to make a sound. Instead, I shook my head as I turned around, pointing to the mirror. Christopher gave me a bizarre expression, which I didn't understand, before entering the bathroom and approaching the mirror. He stood there for a few seconds while he read the Axeman's message.

That was when I noticed his companion—a slightly overweight African American woman with a beautiful face, full lips, and wide brown eyes. She was maybe in her late forties or early fifties. She wore a red-and-purple head scarf thing that looked like a turban, based on the way she'd wrapped it on her head. Her blouse was red and white and matched the floor-length skirt that billowed out from her waist.

Her eyes were closed as she hummed something to herself. Then, she turned around and held her arms out before her as if she were blindly groping toward the door. Moments later, she opened her eyes and looked at me as she shook her head.

"This is no good, Christopher," she said in a Southern accent. That really threw me because, judging by her appearance, I figured she was Jamaican or Haitian.

Even though she spoke to Christopher, her eyes remained on me. I heard the sound of Christopher's footsteps as he walked back into the bedroom.

"It's far worse than not good, Lovie," he answered with a deeply heartfelt sigh. He spun on his toes and stared at me. "It's a demon," he announced, as if I hadn't already read the letter and figured that much out for myself.

"Did you notice the date?" I inquired, wondering if my heartbeat would regulate anytime soon.

"Today's date," he answered. Lovie started for the bathroom, her curiosity no doubt piqued by what we'd said about the letter.

I nodded. "It says he's going to visit again next Tuesday night . . .," I started. Taking another deep breath, I began to feel dizzy. "Based on the fact that it's dated with today's date, do you think it's safe to assume he means this coming Tuesday? April 22?"

"I believe in instances such as this one, it is always better to assume the worst and plan accordingly," Christopher answered. I figured that was a yes. Christopher chewed his lip. "We must act quickly, then," he concluded.

At that moment, Lovie returned from the bathroom and faced us both with a worried expression. "This demon is growin' stronger," she announced. "I can feel its energy pulsin' throughout this house. I'm havin' a difficult time keepin' my psychic walls up."

"If you need to take a break, Lovie, go outside," Christopher answered matter-of-factly.

I faced him and from the corner of my eye, caught Lovie shaking her head. My heartbeat started to pound again. "Can you tell if Drake is still here?" I demanded. "Is he still with us?"

Christopher closed his eyes, and moments later they started to twitch like he was in REM sleep. When he reopened them, he eyed me and simply nodded. But his expression didn't bring me any sort of comfort. "He is waning rapidly."

"Then we have to get on with it!" I announced, throwing my hands in the air like we'd spent too much time gabbing when we should have been focusing on Drake. "Whatever we have to do to keep him safe, we need to do it now!"

Lovie glanced at Christopher with a dubious look on her face. "Have you explained to her," she started, but Christopher's crisp shake of his head interrupted her.

"I have not," he answered as they both turned their eyes from each other to me.

"Explained what to me?" I demanded.

Christopher arched one eyebrow, which lent him a serious expression. "Explained what is involved to save your friend from this entity."

"I don't care!" I rebutted. "Whatever it's going to take, we need to do it and we need to start now!"

Christopher cleared his throat as Lovie frowned. "In order to save him, you must make a very personal sacrifice," he said.

I shook my head in wonder, because I had no clue what he was talking about. "A personal sacrifice? What does that mean? Like donate some blood?" For some reason, the image of a ritual involving a few drops of my blood was playing through my mind.

"Blood is not enough," Christopher said between tight lips. "You must share your body with him."

"Huh?" I managed, thinking this was sounding like we were delving into some weird ghost-sex area that I found not only uncomfortable but also unfeasible—at least, as far as I knew.

"You gotta allow his spirit to possess you!" Lovie exclaimed impatiently. She sounded both frustrated and amused as she shook her head at Christopher.

"Possess me?" I repeated, thinking maybe I should have read the fine print before I signed myself up for saving Drake's soul.

"It wouldn't be like *The Exorcist*," Christopher said. Waving a hand at me, he implied that I was overreacting. "You both would simply share the same body."

"Share my body?" I repeated again, thinking the idea sounded completely unattractive.

"It's not as bad as you're thinking," Christopher continued. "My domicile has been shared with many spirits over the years."

I supposed "sharing a domicile" was the euphemism for demonic possession. Although it didn't exactly surprise me to learn Christopher had been possessed; based on his career as a warlock, it sort of seemed par for the course. I also had to wonder if he was possessed now, because the way he dressed and spoke seemed anachronistic, to say the least. As far as my willingness to allow *myself* to be possessed, now that was an altogether different subject.

"Yer soul would have priority ova yer body," Lovie interjected. "It wouldn't be as though the foreign spirit could control you."

"Oh, yes, of course," Christopher agreed. "All it really means for you is having an extra voice in your head." I wasn't exactly happy with the current voices I heard in my head.

"An' you would also share his power," Lovie added. "That could be a big benefit when dealin' with the spiritual world." She started to nod as if she were in the midst of convincing herself. "The other thin' ta consider is that this spirit, Drake, has been protectin' you from the malevolence o' this house all along."

Christopher nodded. "True, Lovie, true."

"What's the importance of that?" I asked, shrugging.

"His power must be strong, considerin' how long he fended off the entity's advances. If you allow him ta join you, he can continue protectin' you, only now he'll pull more strength from yer life energy, which will make his own power that much stronger," Lovie answered.

Hmm, I couldn't say it sounded too bad especially when I remembered when the entity had attacked me. If not for Drake, I probably would have become a member of the spirit world myself. So there were some pros to this possession thing buried in the cons. "The entity already attacked me but Drake was able to fend it off," I said before taking a deep breath.

"It already gone after you?" Lovie repeated, eyeing me spearingly.

I simply nodded as she turned her attention to Christopher and both her eyebrows shot toward the ceiling. Christopher returned her knowing expression before resting his eyes on mine. He then closed his eyes and reached out to me, touching my arm. He was quiet for about seven seconds as he nodded and his eyelids started twitching again. When he opened his eyes, his mouth was caught in a straight white line. "Were it not for Drake, you would not be standing here now," he said with certainty in his tone. Then he turned toward Lovie. "This possession needs to take place for her own protection. The entity is increasingly gaining strength and dominion over her and this house. If we do not buttress her defensive aura with Drake's strength, this malevolence will most definitely be able to claim her."

Lovie just nodded before they both faced me. "Is possession the only way to ensure that Drake doesn't get killed, for lack of a better word, by this demon?" I asked, setting my own needs aside for the moment.

Both of them nodded. I felt a little sick as I quickly weighed my options. Drake was losing his battle with the demon. Even worse, if it did eliminate him, it would come after me. And apparently according to Christopher, the only thing standing between this demon and me at the moment was Drake. If his power could be enhanced by my life energy and he could better protect me, then why wouldn't I agree to it? And, really, how bad could possession be?

Famous last words.

I took a deep breath and then exhaled it. "Okay, what do we need to do?"

Christopher inhaled deeply and then exhaled before he faced Lovie, his expression hard. "Are you ready for this, Lovie? I, for one, certainly did not prepare myself for a possession when I received her phone call." He glanced back at me with a raised brow like it was my fault I hadn't warned him that he might be possessing me with Drake's soul. Then he returned his attention to Lovie.

She quietly nodded. "I attempt ta prepare mahself for all varieties o' unexpected situations."

"Do we have everything we require?" Christopher continued as he tapped his fingers against his other arm and glanced around himself as if expecting to find a list of useful items for possession on the walls of the guest bedroom.

Lovie nodded again. "I believe so."

Christopher chewed his lower lip. "Did you bring Raven or Claude?" he asked, before cracking his knuckles. "I really hope you brought Raven."

Lovie beamed up at him, apparently pleased that he would be pleased by her information, and nodded. "I got this feelin' before we left that Raven would be our better choice."

"Very good, Lovie, very good," Christopher responded with a genuine smile.

"Raven?" I asked, glancing between the two of them. "Who is Raven?" I couldn't say I was exactly thrilled by the idea that there might be one other witch, warlock, fairy, vampire, or werewolf to witness this possession.

Christopher faced me with the expression of someone who'd just remembered I was still in the room. "Raven is a human skull," he answered matter-of-factly as my mouth dropped open in accordance. "Raven is the better skull to have brought with us for the purposes of your situation because her lower jaw is still intact as well as all her teeth, which means she is truly a necromantic skull and will be able to converse with us and your spirit far better than Claude could, owing to the fact that he's missing his jaw."

I reminded myself not to ask any more questions because I was pretty sure I wasn't going to be prepared for Christopher's responses. I was spared the need to say much more as Christopher immediately started for the hallway. Lovie was right behind him. He glanced back at me and called out over his shoulder, "We shall return momentarily after we retrieve our things."

"Okay," I responded as I wondered if I'd just gotten myself in over my head. Human skulls? Was it even legal to own a human skull and, furthermore, how in the hell had Christopher and Lovie procured one? I suddenly had an image of the two of them digging one up and hoped that scenario was as far from the truth as possible. And, really, there was no way I was going to broach the topic with the reluctant warlock so I figured I'd never know.

Christopher and Lovie were gone for maybe ten minutes before I heard the sounds of their footsteps on the pathway up to the front door, which Christopher had left open. I met them in the foyer. "Do you need help carrying anything?" I offered.

Christopher immediately turned his nose up at me. "We can manage," he answered succinctly before glancing around himself.

"You must direct us to the space where you believe Drake's energy is at its strongest."

"The master bedroom," I answered without pause. Then I led them both upstairs and pushed open the double doors, watching them place their numerous boxes and bags in the corner of the room. Christopher rummaged through one of them and produced an oatmeal-colored, waxy, oblong piece of something that resembled soap. He handed it to me.

"While we are setting up, you need to wash yourself with this. Wash every inch of your body as well as your hair. Allow yourself to air-dry." He bent down again and thrust his hand into what looked like a black velvet satchel, producing a white garment of some sort, which he then thrust in my direction. "When you have air-dried, put this on."

I accepted the garment and nodded. "Why do I have to shower?"

"To ensure your body is clean before Drake takes possession of it. The soap is made with purifying and cleansing oils, and the gown is made of pure cotton," Christopher answered before turning his back on me, which I imagined signified that our conversation was over and I needed to go "purify" myself in the shower. I didn't say anything more but started for the double doors and headed down the staircase, feeling only slightly nervous about showering in the guest bathroom where only minutes earlier, I'd witnessed the Axeman's message displayed across the mirror.

Hoping I was safer now that two witches were in my house, I decided to leave the bathroom door open as I turned the water on in my shower. Once it was warm, I hopped inside and was careful to lather myself with the cleansing soap from head to toe. Fortunately the soap had a nice scent to it—of rosemary or something similar. Wanting to be as clean as possible, I even repeated my ministrations a second time just to make sure I hadn't missed any part of me that might taint Christopher's ritual. Yep, Drake was going to have one hell of a clean host.

I turned the water off once I was happy with my cleanliness and then stepped onto the bath rug, remembering Christopher's instructions to allow myself to air-dry. I tried to ring the water out of my hair to aid in the drying process and then shook myself off like I was a wet dog. Even though I tried to keep myself from doing it, I glanced across at the mirror only to find it completely clean. There were no ghostly words formed from the steam of the room, and the only thing reflected back at me was my dripping self.

After another few minutes, during which time I squeegeed the water off my body with my hands and then rung out my hair once more, I figured I was as dry as I was going to get. I plopped the nightgown over my head and pulled it down over my body, the hem just dusting the floor. If not for my bobbed hair, I would've looked like a character from *Little House on the Prairie*.

Starting for the door, I made my way down the hallway and up the stairs, taking a deep breath before I walked through the double doors of my master bedroom. As soon as I did, I immediately noticed a card table in the center of the room with a white sheet covering it. On top of the table were various white bowls of God only knew what, as well as a black and a white candle, an incense burner, a bell, what looked like a dagger, and something else that looked like a small cauldron. My breath caught in my throat as soon as my gaze settled on the human skull sitting off to the side on the table. I couldn't seem to pull my attention from the cavernous holes where its eyes had once been or the long and square teeth that decorated its jaw, making it look as if it were smiling at me.

"Lovie, are you ready?" Christopher asked. I then noticed Lovie was sitting to the right of the table, her attention on me.

She simply nodded and held out both of her hands to me. I placed my hands in hers and allowed her to pull me closer to her. She stood up and smiled at me warmly, but even so, my body was a nervous, fidgety mess. I was scared. There was no use in trying to deny it because my hands were shaking.

"We must first contact Drake so we can walk him through the ritual. We have ta have his permission before we can begin the possession," Lovie said.

I simply nodded and wondered how in the world we were going to reach Drake. Up until now I'd only been able to converse with him in my dreams. But I had a feeling that was about to change.

"You an' I are gonna contact him together," Lovie continued. "Ordinarily I would contact him mahself but because you two have such a strong connection already, I believe we'll have more luck doin' so together."

That made sense. "Okay."

She led me to the chair that she'd previously occupied and pushed lightly on my shoulders to suggest that I should sit down. I did as I was instructed and folded my hands in my lap as I faced her for further directions.

"You need ta be in a receptive state," she started, her voice lullaby soft. "In order ta do that, I want you ta close yer eyes." I did as I was told. "Very good. Now, Peyton, I want you ta breathe slowly an' deeply. Breathe in for a count o' five an' breathe out for a count o' five. Imagine takin' in the air that is full o' Drake's spirit as you expel yer spirit, which he then breathes in. You are unitin' yerself with the air, becomin' one with the air, such that Drake can inhale an' exhale yer life force an' become one with you."

I didn't point out the fact that as a spirit, I didn't think Drake could breathe. I figured it was a moot point. Instead, I did as she instructed and started to feel light-headed. The more I breathed in and out, the more light-headed I became until I felt almost delirious.

"Yer fingers an' toes, yer arms an' legs, will begin ta tingle as you open yerself ta the spirit world. Don't be afraid if you begin ta feel numb an' dizzy. Trust in yer safety here. Continue ta breathe even more slowly, more deeply as you fall into the spirit trance. I want you ta now count backward from ten ta one. When you reach one, I want you ta tell yerself you are now ready ta accept Drake's spirit, that he will flow through you," Lovie continued in her singsong voice.

I nodded and started counting backward, my entire body feeling incredibly heavy, and then the pins and needles started in my appendages, the feeling working its way inward, up my arms and legs until it reached my core. The numbness set in by the time I reached number five and when I got to number one, I said to myself that I was ready to accept Drake.

"Are you prepared to receive him?" Lovie asked.

I simply nodded and heard the tinny sound of a bell ringing. "We have created a sacred space," Lovie said in her strong yet beautiful voice. "Drake Montague, we are ready ta make contact with you." She touched my hand then. "Peyton, you can open yer eyes."

It felt like it took me seconds to open them but when I did, I watched Lovie reach for and light first the black candle and then the white one. She then placed each of them back on the table and closed her eyes as she said, "This black candle draws the spirit o' Drake Montague that he may converse with us while the white candle shall allow him ta feast upon the energy created here."

She then reached for a piece of paper and scribbled Drake's name on it, placing it on what appeared to be a large pentacle that had been painted in black on the white sheet atop the table.

"As I have written Drake's name, I summon his spirit here!" She then reached for a bottle of oil and, unstopping it, anointed her wrists, the area above her heart, her throat, her forehead, and the crown of her head before turning to me and repeating the process on me. "I consecrate mahself an' this woman, Peyton Clark, an' ask that Drake Montague come forth an' receive us both!"

She then reached for a small sack and, unwinding the ties from it, bent over and sprinkled white powder on the floor around each of us and the table in a counterclockwise circle. When she was finished, she stood up and, with her face to the ceiling, announced, "This powder shall protect us from all evil an' harmful energy. Let no spirit enter here who wishes ta do us harm. We seek only the spirit o' Drake Montague." She glanced back at Christopher who stood in the corner of the room, watching us. "Do you have yer protective defenses up, Christopher?" she asked.

He simply nodded so she turned to face me again. This time she reached for the dagger and, holding it with her right hand with the blade down, reached for my right hand. She wrapped my hand around the handle of the blade. "Trace a circle 'round yerself," she instructed. As I did, she said, "By the bronze o' this dagger, Peyton casts this circle ta defend her from any evil intentions. Let only the spirit o' Drake Montague come forth!" She then took the dagger from me and drew a circle around herself, repeating the same mantra. She lit a stick of incense that smelled pretty musty, and we both watched the stick burn, the remnants twirling into a spent cocoon that dropped onto the holder. Once the incense had burned about halfway, she sprinkled the burnt remains onto a hunk of charcoal sitting on the tabletop. She then raised the charcoal brick directly in front of her, then to her right, then to her left before she turned around and held it up once more. Each time she switched directions, she said, "Let this sacred incense summon the spirit o' Drake Montague. Come forth!"

Then, using her right hand, she picked up what looked like a branch of a tree and tapped the crown of the skull three times, saying, "We conjure the spirit o' Drake Montague ta come forth with this branch o' the yew tree!"

She placed the yew branch onto the table and then picked up a glass of water, pouring it into the cauldron that was sitting on the table. She opened a jar of honey and plopped a wooden spoonful into the water, following suit with what looked like a small bowl full of olive oil, milk, and red wine. Then she sprinkled a handful of barley into the cauldron and said, "Let these offerin's please the spirit o' Drake Montague so he shall come forth!"

Then she reached for my index finger on my right hand and, at the same time, grasped a lancet from the tabletop. Before I could pull my hand away, she pricked the end of my finger. She reached behind her for the small black cauldron and held it underneath my hand as she squeezed out three drops of blood, which landed inside. What was strange was that my body was so numb, I didn't even feel the prick of the lancet.

"I make this offerin' o' Peyton's blood, that it may feed you, Drake. Come forth!" Lovie called out.

She then gripped my left hand and, overlaying it with hers, placed them both on the top of the skull as she closed her eyes. I followed suit and could only hear the sounds of her breathing deeply so I figured I should probably do the same. Almost immediately there was a vibration in the palm of my left hand, where it touched the top of the skull. The vibration climbed up my arm and seemed to reverberate through my entire body.

"The spirit current is flowin' through us," Lovie said, obviously explaining what the vibrations were. "Drake Montague, are ya there?" she asked in a loud voice.

There was nothing but silence for a few seconds.

"*Oui.*" I heard his voice as clear as day inside my head and I nearly opened my eyes in response but then reminded myself to keep them closed.

"Is that his voice?" Lovie whispered to me, which I guessed meant she must have somehow heard his voice inside her head as well.

"Yes it is," I answered.

"I want you ta introduce me ta him an' tell him not ta be frightened. He will only be able ta hear you," she continued. "An' you must converse with him in thought only. He will not be able ta hear yer voice."

I simply nodded. "*Drake,*" I started. "*It's me, Peyton. Can you hear me?*"

"*Oui, I can, ma minette. Are you well? Is everything okay?*" he answered immediately, his voice laced with worry. "*I do not understand how we are conversing as I cannot see you. I can only hear your voice.*"

"*Yes, everything is okay,*" I answered in thought. "*I want you to know that I have two people here with me. Lovie is a witch and she is the one who is doing this ritual so you and I can speak. She isn't going to hurt you.*"

"Je comprends. *I understand.*"

I took a deep breath. "*The other person is Christopher. He's the warlock who came to visit you earlier, do you remember?*"

"*I recall,*" Drake responded. His voice suddenly sounded tired, exhausted really, and I had to wonder if he was in even worse shape than he had been the last time I'd seen him.

"You must explain ta him that we are gonna attempt a possession unitin' the two o' you," Lovie interrupted. "You must git him ta agree ta it before we can attempt it."

I nodded. "*Drake, we are going to do a ritual whereby you are going to . . . to possess me. It's the only way to ensure this entity doesn't defeat you, and at the same time, it's also the only way to ensure that it doesn't . . . hurt me.*"

"*Are you certain, ma minette?*" he asked, his voice reflecting alarm. "*Do you understand what this means for you?*"

"*I do,*" I answered immediately. "*It's the only way to ensure both of us are safe, Drake. But before we move forward, I must have your permission.*"

He was quiet for a few seconds. "*Ma minette, if you are doing this to spare me, I do not give you my permission.*"

"*No, Drake, it isn't just for you,*" I answered immediately, knowing that if I tried to convince him to do it in order to save himself, he wouldn't go for it. Nope, the only way Drake was going to agree was if I built up the case that my safety was on the line. "*If the entity defeats you, I have no defenses against it.*"

"*If what you say is true and this will be of benefit to you, then I absolutely grant you my permission,*" he answered automatically.

I opened my eyes and simply nodded at Lovie, who offered me a relieved smile. "Tell him he needs ta stay with us, that the rest o' the ritual won't take long."

I informed him of as much and then watched as Christopher pushed off from where he'd been leaning against the wall at the far side of the room. He stepped over the powder circle that surrounded us and then, taking up the bronze dagger, circled it around himself, repeating the same words about protection. He nodded to Lovie who then looked at me and smiled.

"I'm gonna retreat out o' the circle now, Peyton," she said and suddenly seemed incredibly tired. "Do not remove yer hand from the skull or we will lose our connection ta Drake."

I simply nodded and watched her pull her hand away from mine as she picked up the branch of yew and circled herself with it in a clockwise direction. She said out loud, "I hereby relinquish mahself from this sacred circle. Let no harmful entities or powers follow me."

Then she placed the branch back on the table and stepped over the circle of powder, retreating to the far side of the room where she took a seat on a makeshift chair they must have brought with them.

She reached inside a bag nearby and pulled out a bottle of water, which she downed in almost one gulp.

"Peyton, are you ready to move on?" Christopher asked, studying me intently from where he stood in front of me. "Do you feel strong enough to continue? Because the rest of this ritual will require your strength."

I swallowed hard but then nodded, figuring there was no time like the present to get possessed. He didn't say anything more but simply nodded and turned toward the table where he added a small palmful of salt to a bowl of water. He mixed it with the index finger of his right hand. Then he drew something in the air above the bowl of water and then made what appeared to be a cross in the air. "I bless this water by the power of Michael the Archangel as well as that of my own that it shall purify this space and rid it of all malevolence." He said the words with such authority that he almost seemed angry.

He then drew the same image (which I was beginning to think might be a pentacle) in the air and repeated his comment over the incense and over both candles. Stepping out of the circle, he picked up a bowl of what looked like salt and walked to the far side of the room where he closed the double doors. Then he sprinkled the salt in all four corners of the room, repeating, "By the element of salt of the earth and my power as a warlock practitioner, I banish all evil and harm from this room! Let only the spirit of Drake Montague remain here with us! All others shall return whence they came!"

He then stepped back into the circle and held up the white candle, but not before first blowing out the black one and allowing the smoke to dissipate from the air. "By this sacred flame, the element of fire shall cleanse and purify this space of evilness." He stepped out of the circle again and visited each corner of the room, raising the candle up to each corner and repeating the mantra to cleanse and purify the space.

Following suit with a new stick of incense, he then did the same with a bowl of spring water. Apparently this possession ritual required calling on all the elements—fire (the candle), water (the spring water), air (the incense), and earth (the salt)—to cleanse and purify the room. When he returned to the circle, he picked up the bell and rang it four times, saying, "Let all things malevolent hear this bell and depart this space immediately! I banish all evil spirits from this place!"

Then he picked up the bronze dagger and the bowl of salt, stepping out of the circle. He approached the double doors and then each of the four windows in the room, drawing a cross with the dagger in the air just in front of them. Then he sprinkled a line of salt in front of the windows and followed suit in front of the doorway. "By this salt of the earth and the blade of bronze, I consecrate this threshold such that no malevolent spirits can pass by!"

When he returned to the circle, he placed the dagger and the bowl of salt on the table and then faced me. "Are you ready?"

I simply nodded and watched as he cleared his throat. "Begin your deep breathing in and out again. You must allow the spirit world into your lungs, into yourself. Imagine bringing Drake into your body, becoming one with him."

I nodded again and started to breath in and then breathe out again for a count of five. I watched Christopher place his hand on top of mine, which still lay limply on the top of the skull. He closed his eyes and they immediately started to twitch as he began to chant something in his head, his lips moving with the words.

He opened his eyes, and with his right hand still on the skull, he placed the palm of his left hand on my forehead. "Is Drake with us still?" he whispered to me.

Figuring that was my cue to try to make contact with Drake, I closed my eyes and thought to myself, "*Drake, are you still here?*"

"*Oui.*"

I opened my eyes and glanced up at Christopher, merely nodding. Christopher looked down at the table and, picking up the lancet, faced my hand where it lay on top of the skull. He then picked up each of my fingers and pierced the fleshy pad of each one, squeezing until a drop of blood appeared. Just as with the last time, I couldn't feel anything. Then he pushed my fingers onto the threshold of the skull, smearing it with my blood.

He faced me. "Do you, Peyton Clark, agree to open yourself up to the spirit of Drake Montague so that he shall inhabit your body?"

I figured my answer was supposed to be a "yes" so I answered in accordance.

Christopher nodded and then faced the air again, holding up his arms as he continued speaking in a loud voice, "This woman has agreed to open herself up to the spirit of Drake Montague. As she has shed her blood, so shall she offer domicile to Drake's spirit only. No other spirits are given permission to become one with her body. As administrator of this ritual, I call forth the spirit of Drake Montague into this sacred circle."

I suddenly felt a whoosh of cold air against my face, and the flame of the white candle began to flicker back and forth. I reminded myself to continue with my deep breathing even as my heartbeat began to escalate.

"Drake Montague, is that you?" Christopher called out as he glanced around himself. "If it is truly the spirit of Drake Montague, I beseech you to give us word."

"*Oui. I am here, ma minette,*" I heard Drake's voice in my head.

"He's here," I whispered, finding it difficult to speak when my heart was beating uncontrollably and I was starting to feel like I might pass out.

"Repeat after me," Christopher started as he focused on me. "I, Peyton Clark, open myself to receiving the spirit of Drake Montague."

I did as I was told and suddenly felt a wash of cold air all around my body, as if Drake had suddenly enveloped me in his cold embrace. My skin tingled all over my body as if I'd just escaped a freezing cold pool and now stood in a draft.

"Repeat after me," Christopher instructed before taking a deep breath. "I, Peyton Clark, welcome the spirit of Drake Montague to enter me and become one with me, to make my body his body, to make my home his home," he finished and I repeated the words immediately after.

The light-headedness continued to plague me, and my breathing was now coming quickly, in short gasps, as my heartbeat continued to increase. I felt my eyes close of their own volition.

"*You can still change your mind, ma minette,*" I heard Drake's voice in my head and, from the breathiness of his words, I had to imagine he was experiencing something similar to what I was.

"*No, I'm not changing my mind,*" I responded adamantly.

"Repeat after me: Enter me through the blood of my offering," Christopher continued, eyeing me speculatively as if he wasn't sure if I could handle whatever was happening to me.

"*Enter me through the blood of my offering, Drake,*" I said in my mind.

"*Ma minette,*" his voice sounded strained but exhilarated. I could feel the numbness of my fingers slowly giving way to a tingling sensation. "*I can taste your life!*" I could hear the smile on his voice.

"*Enter me through the blood of my offering, Drake,*" I repeated.

I arched forward at the same time that I yelled out as feelings of an incredible wind beat through me. It was as if the wind blasted against my face and then traveled through my fingers into my being, spreading into all the corners of my body, bonding with me, filling me until I was brimming with something that was almost impossible to explain. It felt like energy suddenly buzzing through me, only the feeling wasn't at all uncomfortable, just new, different.

"Peyton!" I heard Christopher's voice but was only barely aware of it. "Peyton!" he called out again and then smacked my cheek to get my attention.

I opened my eyes and thrust myself forward, panting as I tried to catch my breath. Once I could see clearly and once my heart stopped pounding, I sat up and took stock of my surroundings. Christopher was just staring at me while Lovie did the same from the far side of the room.

"Did it work?" Christopher finally whispered to me, his eyes wide.

"*Ma minette*," Drake's voice sounded in my head. "*Being inside you is pure bliss.*"

I glanced up at Christopher as I tried to will my pounding heart to regulate. I ran my hand across my perspiring forehead. "It worked."

I was suddenly bombarded with thoughts and images and memories that weren't my own. I grasped my head and clamped my eyes shut tightly at the same time that Christopher reached down and gripped my shoulder.

"You must control the flow of his thoughts, Peyton," he said in a firm voice. "You must be able to regulate his thoughts."

I glanced up at Christopher and frowned, part of me thinking I was seeing him for the first time. I had a feeling that part of me was Drake. "How do I do that?" I demanded.

Lovie stood up and approached us, stepping over the powder circle as she reached for my hand. I glanced up into her kind face and took a deep breath. "Yers is the more powerful spirit as yer body belongs ta you," she said tenderly. "If you want ta silence him, ta shut him out, you simply think those exact words. Whatever you want from him, envision it an' so shall it be."

I nodded and then took another deep breath, thinking to myself and apparently to Drake, "*I need to shut you out for a moment, Drake, until I can gain control of myself again.*"

As soon as I thought the words, the buzzing flow of energy seemed to die down within me and all the foreign images, thoughts, and memories that had been bombarding me simply stopped until I was left with only the quiet splendor of my own thoughts.

"Did that work?" Lovie asked.

I just nodded, feeling Christopher's eyes on me. "Just remember that whatever you want or need from Drake, you just ask him for it," he said. "It's very important that you don't allow his will to overtake yours. That's when people lose their minds."

"Nice of you to tell me this now," I grumbled, feeling suddenly exhausted.

Lovie laughed and took both of my hands in hers, squeezing them gently as if to remind me that everything was going to be okay. "You need ta sleep now, Peyton," she said in her bell-like cadence. "Yer body has been taxed, which means you will need plenty ta eat an' drink. Even though you might not realize it, you've been through an enormous experience so it's best ta imagine yer body is wounded an' needs time an' nourishment ta rehabilitate itself."

Christopher nodded as he retrieved one of his bags and started repacking the items on the table. "And Drake will push you to allow him to experience this new world he's seeing for the first time in a long time. You must remember to go at your own pace. He's tasting life again and will not want to pause in his quest for new experiences, but you must keep in mind your own needs and do not allow him to push you."

I just nodded and suddenly felt just as tired as Lovie warned me I would be. But before I took their advice and went in search of my bed, there was one question that still remained unanswered. "What about the entity?" I started, my voice coming out fatigued. "Is the entity still in my house?"

Lovie didn't respond but glanced over at Christopher, who folded the tablecloth and put it away. Then he started folding the table's legs into itself. He looked at me and his expression was one of distraction. "Yes, the entity is still here. We have not yet performed the exorcism."

I swallowed hard. "But . . ."

"It will not be able to hurt you because your psychic defenses have been buttressed by Drake's spirit," Christopher continued as he carried the now folded card table to the wall on the opposite side of the room and began folding the chairs into themselves to make for easier carrying.

"Okay," I started, not exactly thrilled with the fact that there was still a highly malevolent and powerful force in my house. "When can you perform the exorcism?"

Christopher sighed as if he was annoyed with me. "Both Lovie and I require at least a couple of days to rebuild our psychic defenses. Just as your body requires sleep and nutrition to heal its psychic wall, so will ours. If we attempted the exorcism now, the entity would be far too strong for us and the results could be disastrous."

"So should I . . .," I started.

"We will contact you as soon as we feel we are ready ta return," Lovie said in a kind voice before Christopher could blast me with another of his less than friendly statements.

Christopher glanced at Lovie and pointed to the table he held under one arm and the two chairs he held under the other. "Are you able to get the rest, Lovie?" he asked as he motioned to the two bags and the box, which sat unattended in the corner of the room.

She simply nodded as Christopher started for the door but, thinking better of it, paused and turned back to face me. "You'll be getting our bill in the mail."

Lovie offered me an apologetic smile as she followed Christopher out of the double doors and I turned to the task of getting some sleep.

I think I managed to get about an hour of sleep . . . maybe. Even though I couldn't hear Drake's voice in my head, presumably because I'd forced it out, there was a general restlessness inside of me that hinted to the fact that he was excited and wanted to be out and about exploring.

After tossing and turning for the last however long, I finally gave up and, sitting up in my bed, rubbed my eyes as I stifled a yawn and glanced at the clock. It was eight in the morning, which meant that either I'd slept longer than I imagined or the possession ritual had taken a really long time to perform.

"*Drake,*" I thought. "*Are you there?*"

"Bien sûr, je suis là*! Of course I'm here!*" came the irritated response. "*I've been here the entire time you've been asleep, waiting for you to wake up! I've been keeping myself company!*"

I laughed—I couldn't help it. He just sounded so irritated and somehow I found his irritation amusing. Feeling like I had to pee, I stood up and started for the bathroom when something occurred to me . . . since Drake was sharing my body that meant he would play witness to me peeing and, furthermore, eventually he'd also see me naked . . .

"*Ah, oui,*" he said, his voice taking on a pleased tone. "*I had not considered that absolute benefit to our arrangement.*"

"*Ugh, I need to be better at hiding my thoughts from you!*" I railed back at him as I pushed open the door to the bathroom and wondered if there was a way to keep him from seeing me during times I'd rather he not. Thinking it might work, I craned my neck upward so I could only see the ceiling as I pulled up the ridiculous nightgown Christopher had lent me and, feeling for the toilet, blindly guided myself down.

"*Do you really think this necessary?*" Drake demanded in a put out tone.

"*Yes! I need to maintain some shred of my own privacy!*" I yelled back at him.

He chuckled. "*Has it not crossed your mind, ma minette dearest, that I have already seen you in every state of your undress?*"

Hmm, I'd forgotten about the fact that Drake had already witnessed all my embarrassing moments considering he was haunting my house and he was beyond nosy. I didn't say anything but frowned as I exhaled and figured I might as well not encourage a neck cramp. After I finished my business, I flushed the toilet and walked to the sink where I glanced at myself in the mirror. I didn't look any different, I thought to myself as I washed my hands and wondered how much my life would change now that I had Drake eavesdropping on it.

"*Let's practice something,*" I thought.

"*Practice what?*" came his perturbed response.

"*What can you see at the moment?*" I continued as I stared into the mirror.

"*I see your reflection,* ma beauté. *And while I must admit I am not in the least bit fond of that nightgown the warlock lent you, I am quite fond of the way in which your nipples protrude through the very thin fabric.*"

"*Really, Drake?*" I ground out at him. But then I reminded myself that being upset with Drake for his constant suggestive remarks was like being upset with the wind for blowing. And, what was more, I had a theory to test. I focused on myself in the mirror again and then thought the words, "*I'm shutting you out so you can't see what I am seeing at the moment.*"

"Pourquoi*? Why would you do that?*" he demanded.

I smiled broadly as I wondered if my words had the desired effect. "Can you still see me?" I asked aloud. "And for that matter, can you hear me when I talk out loud like this?"

I could feel the fact that he was annoyed. "Bien sûr*! Of course I can hear you! You do possess ears, you know? And as to whether or not I can see you, when you disallow me to share in your vision, what do you expect the outcome to be?*"

So it had worked. Drake could only partake of my life and experiences when I willingly allowed him to. That was a huge relief in and of itself because it meant I could force him out whenever I wanted to. Both of us were spared when a loud knock on the front door announced we had a visitor. Not knowing who would be visiting this early in the morning, I reached for my robe, which was hanging on a hook behind the bathroom door.

"*Please enable me to see again,*" Drake announced. "*I am curious and slightly ill at ease that we have a visitor.*"

"Okay, I give you permission to see what I see," I announced out loud as I pulled on my robe and started for the front door. There was another knock on the door, which apparently meant I was taking too long to answer it. "Who is it?" I called out, my hand perched on the doorknob.

"It's me," Ryan called back.

Hearing his voice caused my entire stomach to sink in on itself, which alerted me to the fact that apparently I still wasn't over the fact that he and I had a wonderful future ahead of us as friends . . . just friends. I pulled open the door and smiled at him as he gazed down at me and grinned in turn.

"*Ah,* le barbare. *The barbarian,*" Drake muttered in my head.

"*I don't want to hear about it!*" I threw back at him. "*He's my friend, and if you don't like it, I'll just put you on mute again!*"

"*I shall bite my tongue. No need to threaten me, ma minette.*"

I didn't respond but, instead, focused on Ryan who continued to stand in my doorway, looking decidedly nervous or uncomfortable about something. "Ryan, is everything okay?" I asked.

He nodded and then shook his head, running his hand through his hair as he looked past me and into my living room. "Are you busy, Pey?" he asked, finally returning his gaze to my face. "I, uh, I was hopin' we could talk for a few minutes."

Confused as to what he wanted to talk about but undeniably curious, I held the door open wider for him. "I don't have any plans this morning so we can talk," I responded.

He didn't say anything but quickly walked inside as I closed the door behind him. When I turned to face him, he was already staring at me and his expression was one of befuddlement as he took in my robe and then my nightgown. "Where did you get that white thing?" he asked, pointing at it and obviously not appreciating it.

I was about to tell him that Christopher had given it to me but then realized that would mean I'd have to unleash the whole long story about Christopher and Lovie possessing me with Drake's soul and I couldn't say I was in the right frame of mind to explain the whole thing. Especially not when it was clearly obvious that Ryan's visit had everything to do with getting something off his chest. "Oh, around," I answered evasively before changing the subject. "So, what's up? You seem like you've got the weight of the world on your shoulders."

He chuckled as his eyebrows reached for the ceiling and then he sighed. He glanced around himself before returning his gaze to mine. "Is there somewhere we can sit?"

I smiled because he was more than aware that the only two rooms that were completed in the house were the guest bedroom and bathroom. I just nodded and took the lead down the hallway and into my makeshift bedroom where I took a seat on the bed and he sat just beside me, turning his enormous body so that he was facing me.

"Okay, so what's on your mind? Spill the beans!" I said with a laugh as I wondered if this was the point at which he was going to try to talk his way out of finishing the rest of my house. He just had a worried expression that made me fear I wouldn't like whatever was going to come out of his mouth.

"I, uh, I've been thinkin'," he started and glanced down at his lap as he rubbed the back of his head and then brought his eyes back to mine.

"About?" I prodded, wondering why he was finding it so difficult to just come out with it.

"About us, Peyton," he answered almost immediately.

I felt my stomach drop but then had to remind myself that we'd already had this conversation. "It's okay, Ryan," I said with a small smile. "I'm totally okay with us being friends."

But he shook his head, which told me he wasn't talking about the conversation we'd already had. I suddenly felt my stomach drop even further as I realized what this might mean. "Please tell me you *still* want to be friends?" I asked, hating the thought as it occurred to me.

"No, I don't want to be friends," he answered in a nearly harsh voice before he immediately shook his head. "That's not what I meant . . ." Then his voice trailed off completely as he paid attention to his knee, which was bobbing up and down as if he were overloaded with nervous energy.

"Um, what did you mean?" I asked, afraid that he did mean exactly what he'd said but didn't like the way it had sounded so abrasive and was now going to try to soften the blow.

He sighed and brought his attention back to my face. I suddenly wanted to cry. "Pey, I've been doin' a lot o' thinkin' since we last talked an' I've realized that I'm makin' a mistake."

Don't cry, Pey! I told myself. *Please don't cry!*

"*If this barbarian causes you to cry, ma minette, he will answer to me!*" Drake responded, reminding me that he was still in my body and my mind.

"*Answer to you?*" I demanded, thinking it sounded ridiculous. "*Remember, you're in my body, which means he'll basically be answering to me!*"

"*Ah,* très vrai. *Very true,*" Drake said in apparent realization and then disappeared back into the deep recesses of my mind.

"A mistake?" I repeated, placing my full attention back on the conversation as I inwardly sighed.

Ryan nodded and then offered me a genuine smile. "I have to get beyond this grief, Peyton," he continued. "An' I'll be honest with you, meetin' you scared the hell out o' me."

"But is that a good reason to end our friendship?" I asked, shaking my head against the tears that were already threatening to break their way through.

"I believe it is a good reason to end our friendship," Ryan started before taking another deep breath. "Because I want to experience more with you."

I felt my eyebrows scrunch up in the middle as he completely derailed my train of thought and I went careening into the side of a mountain. "Wha-what?" I asked, rather eloquently.

He chuckled and then took my hand in his as he leaned into me. "Peyton, I screwed up. I was afraid o' the feelin's I had for you because I haven't felt them in such a long time an' the idea o' lovin' someone is frightenin' to me."

"Loving someone?" I repeated, my voice sounding ridiculously high.

But he didn't seem frightened by the word. "Yes," he answered succinctly. "Pey, I want this to work out between us." He waved at me and then himself. "I want *us* to work out because the idea of my life without you isn't somethin' I even want to contemplate. An' the idea of another man sweepin' you up makes me want to punch somethin'."

I laughed and almost couldn't believe I was hearing Ryan say these words because they were so unexpected. I had to half wonder if I was still asleep and dreaming or maybe I'd really lost my mind and was hallucinating this whole thing.

"He *makes* me *want to punch something*," Drake muttered.

"*Oh, shut it!*" I yelled back at him. He didn't respond so I figured he'd taken my advice.

"Say somethin'," Ryan said as I realized that while I'd been having a spat with Drake, Ryan was sitting here waiting for me to come back to reality. "Please tell me I'm not too late with this or that you don't feel the same way I do?"

I took a deep breath and wasn't sure if I should just throw my arms around him and cry tears of happiness or jump up and sing "Hallelujah" at the top of my lungs. Fortunately I managed neither and instead just smiled at him while I tried to keep my tears at bay. "When you came here, I thought you were going to tell me we couldn't be friends anymore and the thought of that made my heart break in two."

He nodded and dropped his attention to his hands where they fidgeted with my duvet cover. "So you do just want to stay friends, then?" he asked quietly.

"Let me finish," I said and leaned forward while I shushed him with my index finger against his lips. "What I was going to say was that I can think of no better reason to change the scope of our friendship than by expanding it into a relationship." I felt my lips split into a huge, beaming smile. "Ryan, I've cared about you from the moment you first showed up on my doorstep in the middle of that storm." I took a deep breath and smiled again. "You had me at 'Is your roof leaking?'"

Ryan chuckled as I laughed and then he reached for me, pulling me into the cocoon of his embrace. I wrapped my arms around him and rested my head against his chest as I closed my eyes and listened to his heart beating. I couldn't remember the last time I'd been this happy.

"*Will you allow me to give you my opinion on this situation now?*" Drake asked.

"*No,*" I responded immediately. "*And don't tempt me into tuning you out completely!*"

"D'accord*! Fine!*"

"So there is one other thing I screwed up on," Ryan interrupted in a deep, throaty voice.

I glanced up at him and frowned. "What did you screw up on?"

He tilted my chin and stared into my eyes as he smiled. "Our last kiss."

I felt myself blushing all the way from my toes to my cheeks. "Yeah, you did sort of botch that one, didn't you?"

He chuckled and then stood up to his full, impressive height as he stared at me with unmasked yearning in his eyes. "I'm about to make it up to you," he practically whispered.

I nodded and swallowed hard. "I think I'm about to let you," I whispered back.

Ryan chuckled, taking the few steps that separated us until he was only a couple of inches from me. He leaned into me, but when I thought he would kiss me, he nuzzled my ear and peppered kisses down the line of my neck instead. "Do you accept my apology for nearly botchin' everythin'?" he asked.

"Yes," I answered, even though my eyes were closed and my breathing was growing heavier.

His lips found mine and he wrapped his arms around me.

"Arrêtez! *Stop this! You have no idea how completely uncomfortable this is for me!*" Drake suddenly shouted in my head and he sounded pissed. "*I have never had a homosexual experience in my life and I did not plan on starting in my afterlife!* Incroyable*!*"

Shock ricocheted through me as I realized I'd completely forgotten about Drake! "*You're tuned out!*" I said immediately. "*I don't want you to see or hear any of this!*"

I had to take a deep breath as I waited for Drake's response but not getting one, I figured my forcing him out of my head had worked. Or I hoped so.

"Pey, is everythin' okay?" Ryan asked as he glanced down at me, a wide smile on his lips. "You seem preoccupied?"

I nodded immediately. "Yes, everything's okay," I breathed and then let out a little moan as he lifted me up and, holding me in front of him, gave me no choice but to straddle him. He carried me over a few steps to the edge of the bed where he carefully deposited me on my back. Lying beside me, only a few inches of air separated us. He raised himself up on his elbows and then paused for a moment, gazing down at me with what looked like admiration in his eyes.

"Peyton, are we movin' too fast?"

I immediately shook my head as my belly clinched with the realization that what we were doing was probably going to lead to sex. I mean, we were lying on my bed and the passion between us was so thick, Christopher could have cut it with his lancet.

"Are you gonna be okay if we do this?" Ryan continued.

I immediately nodded but then I realized that maybe he wouldn't be okay with it. I cleared my throat as I gazed up at him. "Are . . . are you going to be okay with it? I don't want to rush you," I started, but he immediately shook his head.

"I've taken the last couple o' days to make peace with everythin', Peyton. I've done nothin' but think an' think some more an' I've reached the conclusion, logically an' emotionally, that I want to move forward with you." He ran his fingers through my hair and smiled down at me. "I want you more than I've wanted anythin' in a very long time."

That was good enough for me. "Then take what you want," I whispered in response.

Ryan gave me a smile that spoke volumes. Coupled with the burning passion in his eyes, I felt my breath catch in my throat. A flurry of butterflies quivered through me, fluttering on a breeze of elation. I just couldn't believe that Ryan and I were finally getting down to it, that sex was in the cards at last. It felt like such a long time coming and I'd imagined the moment so many times that it hardly felt real.

I watched him lower his body on top of mine. He was tender and careful to distribute his weight so he wouldn't crush me. He pushed his hips between my legs and the breath caught in my throat. He was so close to me! So close I could absolutely feel his excitement for me stirring against my inner thigh.

And his scent! All I wanted to do was close my eyes and inhale it—a mixture of soap, Tide detergent, spicy aftershave, and the natural aroma of his skin.

"I've never met anyone like you," he whispered into my ear as he brought his mouth to my neck after peppering kisses along my collarbone. I didn't say anything because I was too busy trying to mentally record in rapturous detail exactly what his kisses felt like. He kissed me down to the line of the top of my nightgown, and when I thought he might make a play for my breasts, he simply started up the line of my neck again, aiming toward my chin. Such a tease!

When he reached my face, he pulled away and smiled down at me. "You're beautiful, Peyton." He pushed a stray tendril of hair behind my ear and grinned broadly. "So beautiful."

I couldn't speak, and hoped the enormous grin that stretched my lips was response enough for him. His eyes crinkled at the corners and his smile broadened into a smile that was just as wide as mine. Before I knew it, his lips fastened on mine. They were so soft and moist. I wrapped my arms around his expansive chest, pulling him toward me as tightly as I could. I loved the feel of his large, warm body against mine.

I whimpered when his tongue pushed into my mouth. As soon as he heard my small cry, he responded by pushing his pelvis against me. His tongue eagerly sought mine and I ran my hands through his hair as our tongues mated. He pulled his pelvis away from me only to thrust it forward again. In glorious response, I moaned and broke the seal of our tongues. I craned my neck backward and arched up toward him, closing my eyes as I focused entirely on the tingling between my thighs. It was beginning to burn but felt delicious . . . not so much pain as it was an urge for satiation.

"Tell me what you want, Pey," Ryan groaned as he pulled himself up onto his arms and continued to grind against me with his lower half.

"You," I answered breathlessly, yanking him back toward me again. "Isn't it obvious? I want you."

"No," he chuckled, shaking his head, obviously playing with me. It was like he'd become possessed by a demon whose sole purpose was to taunt me.

"Oh my God," I grumbled.

He continued to chuckle, obviously enjoying my disquietude. "What do you want, Peyton? Tell me what you want."

I pushed up onto my elbows and narrowed my eyes as I realized his game. A smirk formed on my lips when I spotted his erection, which was straining against his pants. In response, I spread my legs wider and arched up against him, moving up and down along the length of him. I watched him swallowing hard as he dropped his head back and closed his eyes. "Now *you* tell me, Ryan, what you want," I demanded, smiling victoriously when he opened his eyes and focused on me.

He chuckled for only a moment before suddenly nodding. The expression on his face said he was meeting my bet and raising me. "I want nothin' more," he started as he pushed against me with a wicked smile, "than to be inside you."

I gulped and said nothing at all because his words were turning my lower half into a swimming pool. I couldn't remember the last time I wanted a man so badly, or the last time I'd been this turned on. After considering it, I realized I'd never been this turned on before. I wanted to feel Ryan pushing inside of me more than I'd ever wanted anything. "Kiss me," I groaned as I gripped the back of his neck, pulling him against me. His kiss was much more urgent this time. Our tongues met instantly and we groped one another blindly. Ryan ran his hands through my hair as I pushed mine underneath his shirt and was thrilled when I felt his muscular abs. I worked my way up to his pecs, which were . . . rock hard.

"Take your shirt off," I demanded. Ryan cocked an amused brow at me as he sat up and pulled his shirt over his head. I was immediately in awe. His chest looked like it could have been on the cover of *Men's Fitness* magazine. "I must have been very good in a previous life," I whispered, unable to pull my eyes from his magnificent body.

"Not as good as I was," he mumbled and chuckled as his hands found the hem of my nightgown, which he started to pull over my head. I glanced down and as soon as the white cotton material met my eyes, memories of the possession ritual began to consume me. With the remembrances of Christopher and Lovie and the ritual itself was the realization that Ryan had no idea that Drake was also playing tenant in my body.

You have to tell him! I yelled at myself. *Before this goes any further, he needs to know that Drake is a part of you!*

But I suddenly couldn't bring myself to tell him. I wasn't sure how he'd take it. I still wasn't exactly sure how I was taking it.

I took a deep breath and pushed away from him, watching his eyes go wide. "I, uh, I think that maybe this is going a bit too fast for me." I said the words even though my body fought them. The truth was that I wanted nothing more than to feel Ryan pushing inside of me but I also knew that wasn't fair to him—not when he didn't have all the pieces to the puzzle.

"Oh," he said in absolute surprise before he pulled away from me and took a deep breath. "It's okay, Pey, this does seem very fast and I, uh, I apologize. I just couldn't keep myself from you once I made the decision that this, that you, were what I wanted." He took another breath. "I'm sorry."

"Don't be," I replied immediately while wanting to smack myself across the face. "Let's just slow things down for now, okay?"

He nodded and smiled down at me, reaching for me as he wrapped me in his arms. "Your wish is my command," he said softly.

Chapter 17

TWO DAYS LATER

It was rainy, cold, and windy when Christopher and Lovie returned to host the exorcism on my house. Even though it was the middle of the day, the skies were so gray, it looked like it was closer to dusk. I'd debated the subject with myself repeatedly and even come to the decision that Ryan deserved to know, I still hadn't told him about Drake's new home. And I'd also decided that today wasn't an ideal day to tell him. Instead, I pretended I wasn't feeling well and asked him to cut his construction day short and, of course, he obliged.

But then came the difficult part of getting him to leave before Christopher and Lovie's arrival. One thing I could say for Ryan was that he gave Florence Nightingale a run for her money when it came to tending to the infirm, or the pretending-to-be-infirm. Once I made the case, though, that I wanted nothing more than to sleep for a few hours, he finally acquiesced. Well, with the agreement that I would call him as soon as I woke up. I could only hope that the exorcism wasn't going to be a long-winded one.

"*I do believe you will never inform* le barbare *about me,*" Drake said in a pouty tone. It was the third or fourth time he'd brought the subject up in the course of two days. If I didn't know better, I would've thought Drake imagined the conversation wouldn't go over well . . .

"*Don't be silly,*" I answered as I tried to multitask by checking the time on my phone for the umpteenth time. Christopher and Lovie were due to arrive in two minutes. "*Of course I'm going to tell him!*"

"Vraiment? *Really? And when would that be?*" Drake persisted. I could see him in my mind's eye crossing his arms against his chest and tapping his foot impatiently. What was interesting was that whenever Drake and I had conversations in my head, I always envisioned him in the flesh. That is to say that he wasn't just a random, floating voice. I wasn't sure if the imagery of Drake was something my own mind created or a picture he was projecting.

"*The next time I see him!*"

"*Humph!*" He ground out, the image of him in my mind frowning. "Je le croirai quand je le verrai*! I shall believe it when I see it! Quite like the fact that you still haven't allowed me beyond the periphery of this house!*"

Recently, our conversations either revolved around arguments about the "barbarian" or arguments about when I was planning on taking Drake on the grand adventure known as life beyond the confines of our home. For the last few days, though, I hadn't wanted to venture anywhere because my body was achingly tired. That and I knew I'd need to be in the right frame of mind to explain things like cars, traffic lights, supermarkets, Starbucks . . . the list went on. So far, I just couldn't find the energy so, instead, I'd basically hidden out in my house.

A determined knock sounded on the door. It was a knock that could only belong to Christopher because it was as adamant and curt as he was. Pulling open the door, the smile dissolved right off my face when I recognized Ryan standing between Christopher and Lovie. And he was frowning. "Can we come in?" Christopher asked impatiently when it appeared the cat had gotten my tongue. "We have to prepare."

I just nodded and stepped aside as he and Lovie brushed by me. Ryan took a few steps toward me and then paused when he was in the threshold of the doorway. "So much for bein' sick," he started.

"I, uh . . .," I started as I searched for an excuse. "I didn't want to involve you in this, Ryan, because I figured it was my business."

"Your business?" he repeated. "I thought we both agreed that we were a team now?" He shook his head and exhaled. "Not only that but I would've liked it if you'd talked to me first before goin' through with this exorcism." Well, that answered the question as to whether or not Christopher had informed Ryan as to why he and Lovie were at my house. "This sort o' stuff isn't to be taken lightly," Ryan finished as he exhaled heavily.

"There's really nothing to be worried about," I answered and brushed away his worry like it was a mosquito buzzing around my head.

"There's everythin' to be worried about," he rebuffed.

"Like what?" I asked, playing the role of devil's advocate because the truth was that I was nervous about the exorcism too.

Ryan cocked his head to the side and frowned. "Sometimes these things don't go as planned, an' if that's the case, all hell could break loose."

I narrowed my eyes at him and shook my head, trying my best to play the part of cool, calm, and collected. "All hell could break loose? Wait a second, I thought you were Mr. Rational, Mr. Scientific Method? Whatever happened to that?"

He cocked his head to the side and regarded me coolly. "I guess I'm a little less convinced about science in situations where you're concerned."

Not wanting to stand in the doorway any longer, I held the door open wider, hinting for Ryan to step inside, which he did. Then I closed it behind us and started down the hallway, being careful to sidestep Christopher, Lovie, and all their belongings they'd brought.

I continued into the kitchen, wanting a little privacy. "So, do I take this to mean that you finally believe that a spirit is responsible for attacking me?" I asked.

Ryan took a deep breath and then simply nodded. "I believe you."

"*You must tell him about me!*" Drake sounded inside my head. "*Now is the perfect opportunity!*"

I leaned against the kitchen wall, eyeing the myriad boxes filling up the majority of the room—they were my special order kitchen cabinets. Had I been in the right frame of mind, I might have been excited to see them. But as it was now, I was nothing but stressed out—nervous about the impending exorcism and apprehensive about telling Ryan about Drake. But I knew I had to tell him. Because now that Christopher and Lovie were here, the chances of them letting something slip were probably 99 percent.

"Um, Ryan," I started, my heart already hammering in my chest. I was afraid for his reaction because my first thought was that he wouldn't like the idea of another man interloping on our affairs and, furthermore, I hadn't really negotiated a date or time when Drake would need to vacate my body. The other part that I knew would upset Ryan was that I hadn't included him in this decision—I'd just made it for myself. And not only that, but I'd also taken my damn time about telling him.

"What, Pey?"

"Um, there was something that I wanted to talk to you about," I said, my voice quaking as I searched inside myself for the right words. Somehow they failed me.

He nodded encouragingly. "What's on your mind?"

I smiled as I tried to think of the best way forward. Was it enough just to come out with, *Guess what? Drake's soul is now in my body, which means he can see and hear everything I see and hear! And that's why I haven't had sex with you yet. But the good news is that I can tune him out . . .* Somehow I didn't think that was a good way to break the news.

"Cessez de tergiverser! *Stop procrastinating!*" Drake demanded again.

"*If you don't quit it, I'm going to permanently lock you out of my mind!*" I railed back at him. "*So unless you want to spend a hell of a lot of time in the darkness of my head, with no one to interact with, shut up!*" I yelled back.

"Peyton, what's up?" Ryan repeated, this time eyeing me pointedly. I wasn't sure if it was obvious when I was having conversations with Drake or if Ryan was just intuitive, but he seemed to always take note whenever I was carrying on with Drake.

"We are ready to begin!" Christopher yelled from the hallway.

"Okay!" I called back and breathed out a sigh as I realized my opportunity to tell Ryan about Drake was gone. "I guess we can talk about it later," I said as I started for the hallway again, Ryan right beside me.

"*I will refrain from commenting,*" Drake said, but his tone sounded stilted.

I didn't respond because I was only too convinced the subject was going to come up while Christopher and Lovie were here doing the exorcism. But it was way too late to worry about that. If the subject came up, it came up. And it was probably going to, which meant that one way or another, Ryan was going to find out about Drake by the end of the evening. Or so I imagined.

"*If I learned your secret from someone else, I would certainly be angry with you,*" Drake announced.

"*Well, now what choice do I have?*" I barked back at him. "*It's not like I can control whatever comes out of Christopher's or Lovie's mouths!*"

"*Oui, but for your sake, just hope nothing does!*"

"Lovie, let's start in this room?" Christopher asked as he spun around to face her. He was wearing the same long black cape he had the first time I'd met him, which still gave him the look of some nefarious cartoon character.

"That's fine," Lovie answered.

"Peyton," Christopher started as he turned to face me, and I prayed he wouldn't bring up the possession ritual. "Have you noticed any spiritual activity in the last few days that might hint to the entity still being here?"

I immediately shook my head. "It's actually been very quiet. Nothing has happened at all." And even though I was grateful that there hadn't been any activity, I was also suspicious.

Christopher nodded. "Very good. We may very well have cleansed the majority of the presence during our last visit—"

"So anyway," I interrupted him and grabbed Ryan's hand as I started to walk from the room but then thought better of it. "Do you need us for this exorcism? Or should we just find something else to do?"

Christopher eyed me pointedly but didn't say anything. Ryan, on the other hand, offered me a dubious expression and then freed his arm from my grasp, shaking his head. "I'd like to see what an exorcism entails," he said to me before bringing his attention to Christopher. "If that's okay with y'all?"

Christopher shrugged and looked nonplussed. I had to wonder if anything was ever "okay" with him. "You can watch as long as you do not get in the way."

Then without saying anything more, he bent over and opened one of the black cases he'd brought with him, producing a red candle that bore the image of some religious saint. Next were two small white porcelain bowls, a brass incense censer that hung from a fairly long chain, a small steel sword, and the same bell Lovie had used last time in the possession ritual. Christopher set both bowls on the floor and then filled one with what looked like kosher salt and the other with a bottle of water. Then he closed his eyes and started doing that REM sleep thing before opening them again. He spilled a palmful of the salt into his hand and then dropped it into the bowl of water.

"So what does that do, Christopher?" Ryan asked as I inwardly winced, knowing Christopher wouldn't react well to questions.

Christopher offered him a disgruntled expression and then sighed. "I'm blessing the water and the salt," he answered succinctly before he started drawing in the air above the bowl of salt and water. "Now I'm drawing the pentagram. It's important to start the drawing at the top point and then move to the left, ending at the top again." Then he raised his fingers up in front of him and brought them down again in a straight line. "Next I make the sign of the cross." Then he cleared his throat.

"I bless this salt by the power of Michael the Archangel and my own power that this salt rid this space of all malevolence and evil!" he said out loud and in a very strong voice. Then he drew a pentagram and the sign of the cross and said the same mantra over the bowl of water, the red candle, and the incense censer. I wasn't sure but I thought I recognized the pattern from our last ritual. This wasn't my first rodeo . . . or ritual, as the case may be.

"Are you ready, Lovie?" Christopher asked as he shifted his cloak dramatically over his shoulder and placed the steel sword in a little scabbard attached to his thigh. Then he started forward.

Lovie wasn't really given the option to respond and instead brought up the rear, but not before taking the candle and the incense censer from him. She was already holding the bell.

"Do you want us to hold anything?" I offered, but Lovie immediately shook her head although it was Christopher who answered.

"Don't touch anything!"

It wouldn't have surprised me to learn that Christopher didn't have many friends.

Holding the two small bowls of water and salt, he approached the far side of the foyer and sprinkled salt in the corner. Then he turned to his right, sprinkled a handful of salt in that corner and then proceeded forward, toward the hallway, repeating, "By the element of Earth, this salt and the power of my will and Michael the Archangel's, I banish all evil and malodorous spirits from this room!"

"*I am quite fortunate to be taking refuge in you, ma minette*," Drake piped up with a laugh. "*Otherwise I would wonder where I would be banished to!*"

That was an interesting thought. If Drake had never taken possession of my body and did still exist within the walls of the house would this exorcism drive him from it? "*It's only evil and malodorous spirits, and I wouldn't say you're either . . .*"

"*I believe the word he was looking for was malevolent or possibly malicious,*" he responded with a laugh. "*Malodorous implies that the spirits do not smell good!*"

I hid my own laugh beneath an impromptu clearing of my throat and was relieved when no one noticed.

I watched Lovie hold up the incense censer and swing it into each of the corners of the room and repeat the same phrase, only substituting the element of air for the element of earth. Next she lit the red candle, which by now I assumed featured a picture of Michael the Archangel, seeing as how he seemed to feature pretty prominently in this ritual. She held the candle up to all four corners of the room and repeated the same mantra again, this time substituting in the element of fire.

Christopher followed suit with the bowl of water and repeated the same quote, this time referencing the element of water. Lovie rang the bell three times as Christopher announced, "Let all things evil and impure hear this ringing bell and depart from this space at once! At my command, I banish all evil from this place!" Lovie then walked over to him and released the sword from the scabbard on his thigh, offering it to him as she took the bowl of water and played a precarious game of balance. Given everything else in her possession, it was a wonder she didn't drop anything.

I would have offered to help again but after Christopher's last discouraging comment, I zipped my lips.

Christopher accepted the sword and, similar to the possession ritual, he approached the windows and the door leading from the foyer outside and drew the sign of the cross in the air before each one. As soon as he was finished making the sign of the cross, it felt as if the temperature in the room plummeted at least ten degrees—like someone had opened a window during a snow storm and let in the freezing cold air. I glanced around myself, at Christopher and then Lovie, looking for an indication that either of them had felt the change in the atmosphere, but neither looked especially concerned.

I watched Lovie offer one of the bowls to Christopher, who reached inside it and produced a palmful of salt that he then sprinkled along the threshold in front of the windows and the doorway. He said, "By this salt and the power of my will, I consecrate this threshold that it shield against malevolence and evil and all creatures that would do us harm from now until forever!"

At that, the temperature in the room plummeted even more—so much so that I could see my breath as I exhaled. I glanced over at Ryan and noticed he was focused on his own breath, which billowed out of him like a white cloud. "It's freezing in here," I whispered.

Ryan just nodded as his attention fell to Christopher and Lovie, who just continued busying themselves with the ritual, acting like they were used to subzero temperatures. When Ryan glanced back at me, he smiled consolingly. "They don't appear to be concerned," he started.

"So I guess we shouldn't be either?" I interrupted.

He shrugged. "Guess not."

We followed Christopher and Lovie as they walked single file into the next room, the incense wafting behind them and reminding me of some sort of holy procession. 'Course I really couldn't say there was anything holy about Christopher.

The room into which they ventured happened to be a bathroom, but apparently evil spirits were not immune to restrooms because Christopher and Lovie repeated the entire ritual all over again. Approximately five minutes later, they retreated from the bathroom and started down the hallway again. I could have sworn the feeling of freezing air followed us; it seemed like it was nipping at my heels as we walked. As soon as we paused, it surrounded me in its icy embrace.

"Are they gonna do this to every room?" Ryan whispered down at me, an expression of concern spreading across his handsome face. Apparently neither of us had been prepared for how lengthy this process was. Or maybe it was that neither of us were prepared for the bitter cold.

I glanced up at him with a consoling smile. "I think so."

"We'll be here all day!" he whispered back with a laugh as he gripped my side and pulled me into him, whispering into my ear, "Good thing I've got you to distract me."

I playfully swatted him while I wondered if Drake would pipe up with one of his snide comments. I was surprised when he didn't.

Meanwhile, Christopher and Lovie finished their ministrations in the next bedroom, so Ryan and I followed them to the next room as Lovie continued to do her juggling act with the various artifacts involved in the exorcism.

"*Well, I would consider yourself lucky that neither of them have yet mentioned the possession,*" Drake said.

"*I'm still going to tell him,*" I responded resolutely.

"Je ne suis pas convaincu. *I am not convinced.*"

"*Why is it getting so cold in here?*" I asked him, deciding to change the subject.

"*I did not notice that it was,*" he responded, which I found odd since I figured he could experience the same outside influences that

I could. But apparently that wasn't the case because I was shivering; it was so cold in the room.

After what felt like an eternity, Christopher and Lovie had "cleansed" the entire upstairs as well as the majority of the downstairs with the exception of the kitchen, but we were merely a salt bowl and a steel sword from completion. Once the salt had been spread and drawings of pentagrams and crosses had been drawn, Christopher turned to face us with a sigh.

"No doubt you feel the presence?" Christopher asked, first spearing me with his expression, and then Ryan. At the mention of "the presence," I felt my heart drop down to my feet as a sense of foreboding and fear began working its way up my spine.

"All I feel is the bitter cold," I answered, my teeth chattering as I faced Lovie, who looked as if she were completely comfortable in her short sleeves. "Aren't you freezing?" I asked, shaking my head in wonder at the realization that she didn't appear to be. "Can't you feel that?"

Lovie shook her head and offered me an expression of consolation. "We have trained ourselves ta deflect the imprintin' o' the spirits. It is cold only if you allow yerself ta be influenced. Otherwise, it's all in yer head."

As soon as she finished speaking, and almost in response, there was a sudden howl of wind that started at one end of the hallway and blew through to the end, throwing itself against us full force. I felt my hair blow out behind me and had to right myself against the intensity of the blast so I wouldn't get knocked over. I wasn't sure if the sudden pounding in my ears was my own heartbeat or something else.

"What the hell?!" Ryan exclaimed at the same time I heard myself scream as another gust of wind slammed against us.

"Quiet!" Christopher wailed out over the growing gust, which continued to howl with an uncanny roar. "Do not grant it the strength of your beliefs!"

I figured that meant *if you don't believe it, you won't see it.* Well, one, if not all of us, had to be believing in something because before I could so much as blink, it felt like the ground beneath me was giving way. I grabbed Ryan's arm as I tried to right myself, but it felt as if the floor was shaking in a violent earthquake, the walls of the house looming impossibly low and close to me as it attempted to ride the rumbling earth.

"Ryan!" I screamed as I felt myself start to fall toward the floor. I felt his big arms suddenly encircling me around the waist as he thrust us both up against the wall. I was so scared, I couldn't even think, could barely even command myself to breathe.

"Do not grant it power over you!" Christopher's voice suddenly rose up over the cacophony of the wind and the rumbling of the earth. "I consecrate this threshold that it shield against malevolence and evil and all creatures that would do us harm from now until forever!" he yelled out as he gripped Lovie's hand, and the two of them continued to throw salt and holy water into each corner of the room, doing their best to move forward on their unsteady legs.

When Christopher held his sword up to draw the image of the pentagram, it seemed as if the entire house were twisting and turning around him. I could hear the sounds of creaking floorboards, slamming doors, and groaning as the house appeared to vacillate this way and that. The floor looked as if it were miles away as I glanced down at it, my vision suddenly going blurry only to become clear again. The walls seemed alive as they throbbed back and forth, as if in response to my throbbing heartbeat.

"*Drake!*" I yelled in my thoughts. "*What's happening? What's going on?*"

"*I feel and see nothing, ma minette,*" he answered coolly. "*I do not understand of what you speak.*

So somehow and for whatever reason, Drake couldn't see or hear any of this? Maybe all of this really was just a hallucination, then? Maybe it wasn't real? The floor seemed to buckle beneath me as soon as the thought left my mind, and I screamed out as Ryan wrapped his arms around me more tightly, pulling me toward him.

"Close your eyes, Pey," he crooned into my ears. "Close your eyes an' don't let it scare you."

I did as he instructed and felt the cold suddenly give way as the sounds of destruction settled into oblivion around me. I could still feel the floor moving beneath me, though, as if it were floating on an upset river.

"Deny the hallucinations!" Christopher wailed. "Deny the artifice!"

"I consecrate this threshold that it shield 'gainst malevolence an' evil an' all creatures that would do us harm from now 'til forever!" Lovie called out, her voice loud and strong.

The earthquake rumblings suddenly ceased and the house was completely quiet and still. It was as if nothing had ever happened, as if there hadn't been an arctic and vindictive wind blowing through the hallway at all. I opened my eyes and took a deep breath, turning my gaze to Christopher, who wore the expression of someone nervous . . . worried.

"I consecrate this threshold," Christopher started again, his voice barely a whisper. He lifted up the bowl of salt and flung it in each corner of the kitchen as he fought to catch his breath. "That it shield against malevolence and evil," he continued. As he spoke each word and then flicked holy water in each corner of the room, the silence in the house was almost more difficult to deal with than the wind and the earthquake had been. "And all creatures that would do us harm from now until forever," he finished and drew the sign of the pentagram in the air, followed by the sign of the cross.

Then it was eerily quiet for three seconds. As I was about to breach the silence by asking whether or not the entity had been cleared, there was a horrible, high-pitched cracking sound like ice breaking.

"The windows," Ryan said in awe, as I glanced over at the row of kitchen windows and noticed each one of them had cracked down the middle. I looked back at him and realized his breath was coming out of his mouth in cloudy wisps. I shivered in spite of myself, my heart pounding through my body. I couldn't remember ever having been so scared.

"Let all things evil an' impure hear this ringin' bell," Lovie spoke as she rang the bell that she'd been carrying in her hand. I couldn't understand why I hadn't heard the ringing of her bell in the gusts of wind that attacked us earlier, which just further spoke to the fact that it must have all been in my head.

"Depart from this space at once!" she finished, continuing to ring her bell.

"At my command," Christopher said suddenly, holding his silver sword up above his head as he made the sign of the cross in the air. "I banish all evil from this place!"

The sudden sound of exploding glass blasted through the air as Ryan shielded my body with his and I heard myself scream. And then there was nothing but silence again. I opened my eyes and noticed there was glass all over the floor. Glancing up at Ryan, I found his attention on me.

"Are you okay?" he asked, his eyes wide with worry.

"I'm fine," I answered in a mousy voice as I faced Christopher, who stood up stock straight, his mouth held firmly in a tight white line.

"It is complete," he said simply.

"The windows," I spoke as I glanced at the windows in the kitchen and noticed the glass from each one had been completely blown out.

"We forced the entity from the house," Christopher said in his usual tone of indifference. "It is only natural that it blew all the windows to escape."

"*Drake, are you able to detect any residual ghostly energy?*" I asked, wondering if maybe he would be able to tell if the house really had been cleansed.

He definitely hadn't been much of a help during the cleansing ritual itself, so I assumed I was just being hopeful.

"*I do not, ma minette,*" he answered. "*But, of course, that could be due to the fact that I now reside . . . inside you.*"

It was becoming more and more obvious that Drake was thrilled to find as many different nuances as he could regarding the subject of him residing inside me. In fact, he never seemed to get tired of it. As for me, I was still so completely floored, scared, and shocked by what we'd just undergone that I couldn't think of much else.

"I will leave some of this kosher salt here," Christopher continued while eyeing Ryan and then me. "You both should cleanse yourselves with a ritual bath of kosher salt, or you can also use it in the shower. It will cleanse you of any residual spiritual dirt."

"Are you able to tell if you forced the entity out?" I asked expectantly, because I was still scared to death that they hadn't.

Christopher eyed me with little interest. "I believe we forced the spirit out. Its energy is gone."

"How sure are you?" Ryan asked, the look of shock resident in his eyes, just as I was sure it was in mine.

"Sure," Christopher answered with a drawn eyebrow. He started for the door but then eyed me over his shoulder. "I shall send you a bill," he finished. "Of course, I will have to amend my customary prices given what we experienced."

I couldn't say I was at all concerned with money at the moment. Instead, I found myself speechless and just watched Christopher as he stopped short in front of his two bags, which sat on the floor in the foyer. He bent down and loaded all the paraphernalia he and Lovie had used in the ritual into the receptacles and then, standing up, started for the front door. Again.

"Thanks, Lovie," I said in a soft tone. She turned around and nodded, offering us both a smile.

"You keep yer eyes open fo' anythin' that feels wrong," she said and then eyed me in particular. "If you even get a hint that this thing hasn't cleared out, you'll call us?"

"I will," I answered with a nod as relief started to suffuse me once they were both standing at the mouth of the doorway.

Lovie smiled before she closed her eyes and held her hands out to her sides as if she were checking the air with her psychic abilities. She opened her eyes moments later. "The house feels clean ta me," she announced. "But one can neva be too careful."

Christopher opened the door as the wind picked up his cloak and blew it out behind him. He walked into the dark afternoon sky and unlocked an old black Lincoln Town Car, placing his two bags in the trunk. Then he approached the driver's door and, opening it, took a seat and closed the door without even saying good-bye. Lovie offered us a quick wave before she disappeared into the passenger seat, and the two of them drove off.

Ryan and I watched the car drive away from inside my house, neither of us saying anything. Finally I closed the front door as Ryan exhaled, throwing his arm around me. "Are you alright, Pey?" he asked.

I was beyond exhausted. It was as if the lack of sleep, the worry, and the anxiety that had been culminating for the last three days, and now the intensity of this exorcism, had finally come to a head.

"*Incroyable!*" Drake sounded inside my head, so I immediately thought the words that would shut him out. I couldn't deal with him at the moment.

"Peyton, I want you to promise me that you aren't gonna shut me out again," Ryan said as we started for the guest bedroom where I wanted nothing more than to relax against his chest and feel his large, powerful arms around me. "If I hadn't randomly shown up, you would've gone through all that yourself," he said, eyeing me warily. The thought was enough for my heart to suddenly ride into my throat.

"I'm so glad you decided to come over when you did," I answered honestly.

He tipped my chin up and smiled down at me. "We're supposed to be in this together from here on out, right?"

I nodded and then sighed. "I promise I won't shut you out again."

"Good," he said and hugged me tightly as he kissed the top of my head. Even though I still hadn't worked up the cojones to tell him I was possessed with Drake's spirit, I made myself the promise that I would do so tomorrow. For now, I just wanted to enjoy the fact that for the first time since I'd taken residence in my house, it was spirit-free.

Or so I hoped.

Author's Note

The story of the Axeman is based on a true crime spree that occurred in New Orleans at the beginning of the twentieth century. Accordingly, I've used many of the actual names of those involved in the original crime. As this is a work of fiction, some of the circumstances surrounding those involved are fictionalized.

Acknowledgments

To my husband and son: Thank you for all your support and patience.

To my mother: Thank you for always being the first set of eyes on all my books!

To my editors at Montlake, Kelli Martin and Maria Gomez: Thank you for your guidance and your constructive criticism.

To my agent, Jane Dystel: You're awesome!

To all my readers: Thank you all so very much for your continued support. I wouldn't be here without you!!

About the Author

A *New York Times* bestselling author, H.P. Mallory began her writing career as a self-published author. She's a huge fan of anything paranormal, and anything ghost or vampire related will always attract her attention. Her interests are varied but aside from writing, she's most excited about traveling. She's very fortunate to have lived in England and Scotland, both places really having a profound effect on her books. H.P. lives in Southern California, where she is busily working on her next book! Please find H.P. on the web at: www.hpmallory.com